Meeting Dr. Praigale *Marie-France Leger*

Publisher's Note: This is a work of fiction. Any resemblance to actual events, or persons, living or dead, is entirely coincidental. Names, characters, places and incidents are either the product of the author's imagination or are used for the purpose of this fiction tale.

Cover Design by: Marie-France Leger

ISBN Paperback: 9798850512668

For more information, updates, and/or teasers, follow @mariefranceleger on Instagram.com or @maariefraance on TikTok.

Copyright © 2024 by Marie-France Leger
All rights reserved. No part of this publication may be reproduced, distributed, or transmitted in any form or by any means, including photocopying, recording, or other electronic or mechanical methods, without the prior written permission of the publisher, except in the case of brief quotations embodied in critical reviews and certain other non-commercial uses permitted by copyright law.

Meeting Dr. Praigale Marie-France Leger

Also by Marie-France Leger

The Gates of Gabriel
2204 Hunter Lane
A Hue of Blu

Meeting Dr. Praigale *Marie-France Leger*

Astra's Playlist

To Build A Home – The Cinematic Orchestra

Apocalypse – Cigarettes After Sex

Dandelions – Ruth B.

Midnight Love – Girl In Red

You – James Arthur

Meant To Stay Hid – SYML

Someone To You – BANNERS

Cinnamon Girl – Lana Del Rey

The Night We Met – Lord Huron

If I Lose Myself – One Republic

Heather – Conan Gray

Transatlanticism – Death Cab For Cutie

Somewhere Only We Know - Keane

That's Us – Anson Seabra

Girl - SYML

Meeting Dr. Praigale *Marie-France Leger*

"We're all stars that think they're dying until we realize we're collapsing into supernovas – to become more beautiful than ever before."
- C. JoyBell C.

To Snowball.
I will miss you forever.

To my younger self.
I'm sorry for everything you went through.

To my readers.
You make up the stars that light up this world.

Author Note and TWs:
This is a character-driven love story. It includes heavy topics dealing with abusive relationships, sexual assault and domestic violence, toxic family dynamics, mentions of alcohol, o/w/m circumstances, mental health, loss of a partner and mentions of infidelity.

Meeting Dr. Praigale

Marie-France Leger

Meeting Dr. Praigale *Marie-France Leger*

THE PAST

Meeting Dr. Praigale *Marie-France Leger*

<u>Woodstock Press Freeholder</u>
05/13/21

BREAKING NEWS
DECEASED LOCAL FOUND IN "SHARP-EDGED" PEAK
Published by Casey Collings

Twenty-two-year-old Malcom Matheson, star athlete and hometown local to Woodstock, ON, was found deceased in the early morning of Monday May 12th, 2021. His body was located along the base hiking trail of Crimson Peak, commonly known as "Sharp-Edged Peak" for its steep cliffs and rocky terrain.

Two witnesses reported seeing Matheson enter the trail at around 8am, though he never returned. The police declare that no foul play was involved and suspect that Matheson slipped from the upper-level hiking trail, tumbled down the terrain, and collided with a jagged boulder.

Upon police arrival, Matheson was pronounced dead at 2:22pm. The coroner at the scene declared that his skull had been fractured, with a diamond cornerstone lodged into his head that led to a severe brain hemorrhage…

Astra
One Week Later

I should have felt something.

Malcom was gone, after all.

He was gone.

Dead.

Impossible to revive.

Never coming back.

Five years ago, things were different. Five years ago, I didn't know him. Five years ago, he was a stranger.

He should have stayed that way.

Bodies clad in black and charcoal grey passed by me like wraiths, heads low, shoulders slumped forward with deadweight.

I just watched.

I watched everyone who loved him. Everyone who cared about him.

Everyone who didn't know him.

Not like I did.

His mother stood at the front of the funeral hall, eyes rimmed in dark shades of purple and bruised reds. She began to speak, to cry.

I just watched.

"*He was a good boy.*" Her scratchy voice echoed between stone walls, amplified by the silence. "*He was... He was my good boy.*"

Meeting Dr. Praigale *Marie-France Leger*

The lies beneath her words ricocheted in my skull, piercing the vital nerves that made me think. Made me see. Made me feel.

It was a paralyzing feeling.

The emotion of nothing.

I couldn't feel a fucking thing if I tried.

A good boy.

A good boy.

A good boy, she kept repeating. Her entire sermon consisted of those three simple words.

Three words she knew nothing about.

Minutes stretched on by. People cried. People comforted. And it was over.

His lifeless body was shut away behind a wooden lid. Closed.

Forever.

Magdalene Grace Matheson, Malcom's mother, finally approached me. There was sadness radiating off of her like hot fire. I felt no shame in admitting that it meant very little to me.

"You lost him too, Astra," she sniffed, removing a used handkerchief from her clutch. "He was also your good boy."

I took the thick, white napkin away from her. Not because I needed it, but because it existed to be discarded. Perfectly good material wasted on slobber.

Disgusting mucus.

Crusted snot.

Wasteful, glass tears she shed for her *good boy*. The one she loved so fiercely and dearly.

Meeting Dr. Praigale *Marie-France Leger*

The one I claimed to love as well.

For many years, I suppose I had.

But watching his mother walk away from me, carrying the grief and sorrow of her son, felt like a stark blessing.

Because while she wept for her fallen child, I pulled my sleeve down to my knuckles, covering the bruises and gashes along my forearm that her *good boy* left me before he left this world.

Meeting Dr. Praigale *Marie-France Leger*

THE PRESENT

Chapter One
Astra

Last Edit - 6:14pm: No Title

They say you meet your soulmate by accident. You're never prepared. You never want to be prepared because that kind of love is terrifying – all consuming, even. She hadn't known that the love she always wanted was just around the corner, waiting for the right moment. ~~Not when there was a love before. One she could never shake.~~
(REVISE)

I felt the mug shatter before it collided with the ground.

My brain could work out the image well enough: the lukewarm coffee pooling between shards of blue and white porcelain, seeping through the cracked floorboards. Broken pieces rattling slightly, then stopping altogether.

I didn't look, not right away. It was a mess I had to clean up, something *I* caused. Even though it felt involuntary, I had to pick up the pieces.

Every single one.

This was Malcom's cup. The one part of him that still remained in my apartment.

A shadow of a smile appeared on my lips at the thought of it destroyed. That same smile was stamped onto my face throughout the entire clean-up process.

Not even a minute later, heavy steps sounded outside my door, followed by two knocks, a squeaky turn of the knob, and I was face-to-face with Ruby Hutchinson.

"What's the racket about? You hurt?" Her apron was tossed in flour, bits of dough still caught in her curly, silver hair.

I tilted my chin in the direction of the dustpan, remnants of Malcom's third anniversary present swept inside. "Broke a mug."

She placed a wrinkly hand over her heart, quickly finding a yeast ball to flick onto my floor.

I rolled my eyes, collecting the broom once again. "You're adding to the mess, Rubes."

She didn't respond and patted down her checkered dress, sending a plume of flour particles wafting through the air.

"Okay," I snorted, "that's enough."

"Sorry," she grumbled, wiping the back of her hands against her torn skirt. "Didn't hear ya."

"That so?"

"Nope," she made her way to the kitchen sink, "got shit hearing, remember?"

I followed her path with my broom. "You heard me perfectly fine when I asked for time off."

She ran her hands under the water, throwing that famous Ruby Hutchinson look my way. "That's because I need you workin' here with me, Starburst. Can't run this café without you."

"You've done it before."

"And I won't do it again, now sit down and tell me how that mug broke."

I swiped a protein bar from the counter. "Not much of a story" – the grainy texture covered my tongue as I spoke – "and you clearly have much better things to do."

Her prune eyes narrowed. "Tomorrow's batch of cookies are already cooling off. I got time to talk, and you got time to tell."

"It slipped off the table."

"Uh-huh." She grabbed the washcloth from the oven rack, her gaze never leaving mine. "You've been livin' here two years now. Two years above my café and I ain't ever heard a peep."

"I'm a quiet tenant." I shrugged, taking another stiff bite of my bar. "People break things."

"You aren't people, Starburst."

A laugh bubbled in my throat. "I'm not?"

For a moment, she kept silent, eyeing the washcloth like it was a newborn. Then, she crumpled it up into a disastrous ball of creases and crooks, shoving it in between the oven rack.

We stared at each other, her waiting for the move she knew I'd make within seconds. And when I broke, when I went to unfold the tangled washcloth, she slapped the counter in hysterics.

"See!"

"See what?" I defended. "I don't like mess."

"Bit more than that, don't ya think?" she nagged. "You're a –"

"I pushed the fucking mug, Ruby, okay? Is that what you want to hear? I pushed it."

Deep breaths.

One. Two. Three.

One. Two. Three.

"It was an accident, but regardless it was..." I paused, scraping the dirt underneath my fingernail. There was no dirt. I wasn't a dirty person.

I haven't been for a while.

A strained breath escaped my lips. "It was time to get rid of that thing anyway."

Her deep, blue eyes left my face, scanning the apartment behind me and landing on my computer. "Were you writing about him?"

From the gentleness of her tone, the soft press of her fingers against my shoulder, she shouldn't have even asked why I broke that mug.

Him.

The boy who died nearly two years ago, yet lived on in my psyche like a warden – guarding and circling my thoughts like a shark desperate for blood.

Since that day, that bittersweet, brutal day, when the mud swept Malcom's body into a pile of sharp rocks and impaled him like a scarecrow –

That day.

That was the day that I vowed to become someone different.

Meeting Dr. Praigale   *Marie-France Leger*

    Someone so completely and utterly separate from the girl that he made me. The girl that he touched and wounded, shattered into a shell of nothing and everything all at once.

    Every kiss was poisonous and rancid, every touch designed to hurt.

    To give him pleasure.

    To give me pain.

    No. No, he wouldn't control me in his death. Never would he control me again.

    I wrote the first page of my book that day. The second that evening. Two months later, I had finished the story of a girl who fell in love with a boy who actually wanted her.

    His name wasn't Malcom.

    And her name wasn't Astra.

    But it made me happy all the same.

    I lucked out finding agents on a freelance website. One of them I hated, but the other, Teresa, made me forget about the first one altogether.

    She loved my stories, she had connections to the publishing world, and she was ready to drag me with her.

    But most of all, she believed in me.

    One year later, I had two more books under my belt. *Playscape* and *Gloria Haynes*, both about healthy relationships, passionate sex, and fairytale endings.

    None of them included abuse.

    None of them included punishment.

Meeting Dr. Praigale *Marie-France Leger*

Just a happy girl, a happy boy, both in love. The end.

I never knew how to explain this to people. How I could possibly write such fluffy, light-hearted romances while my own heart was plastered in scars.

Luckily, I never had to. No one knew a thing about me since I wrote under the alias M.D. Pont.

I didn't even realize that was an option until Teresa informed me of it. So many well-loved authors remained inconspicuous, just to preserve their sanity.

I wanted that more than anything.

Then suddenly, the stars aligned.

Thousands upon thousands of copies sold worldwide, I signed with one of the three main publishing companies in the province, and I was invisible.

M.D. Pont could stand for anyone.

Medical Doctor Pont.

Marcella Draker Pont, perhaps.

Or Meredith DuPont, my middle and last name.

Either way, my success wasn't attached to Astra anymore. It was attached to a whole new person, given a whole new life, the chance to create new worlds, better worlds –

While I lived in this one.

As Astra Meredith DuPont.

The loveless writer.

The manager of Cloud Café.

Meeting Dr. Praigale *Marie-France Leger*

The only friend to seventy-three-year-old Ruby Hutchinson.

And the girl who broke that stupid mug, the mug she drank coffee from every single morning, because she couldn't detach herself from him even if she wanted to – even if she *hated* him with all her might – he haunted her.

Even if the mug was broken, *he* was not.

And even in death, he was determined to destroy her.

Chapter Two
Noah

"Dr. Praigale?"

Vern, my receptionist, rapped gently on the office door as I flipped through a file of invoices.

"Come on in," I called, stapling together an ointment receipt for Connie the retriever. "What can I do for you, Vern?"

She always regarded me with kindness, those tender eyes filled with warmth and sunshine. But at the sight of her slumped shoulders, the tension in her posture, I immediately questioned, "Is everything okay?"

Her lips pressed into a thin line. "Annika is on the phone hoping to speak with you."

My fingers froze for a moment, just a moment, before I placed the stapler down and let out a quiet sigh. "Did she say why?"

Vern shrugged. "I'm just the messenger."

I stacked the invoices and pulled the office phone towards me. "Transfer her to my line, please."

She nodded once, about to exit, when I tapped my desk. "Oh and Vern?"

Her hazel eyes met mine, a smidgen of that warmth returning. I smiled. "How many times have I asked you to call me Noah?"

A soft chuckle. "As many times as the –"

"– the setting suns," I finished for her.

Meeting Dr. Praigale — *Marie-France Leger*

At the click of the door, I sat up in my chair, dreading whatever conversation I was about to face.

Annika shouldn't have been calling me. Not at this hour, anyway. She had duties, *veterinarian* duties I knew and understood all too well.

After all, I *was* – "Dr. Praigale," I answered the line, clearing my throat.

"Noah, baby," she started. My body tensed. "Do you always have to start calls that way?"

"Just a habit," I responded, leaning into my chair. "What is it, Annika?"

I could hear the chatter of employees through the line, the clang of metal and the *whoosh* of a revolving door.

She didn't seem bothered by any of it; the fact that she had a job, patients, an actual obligation to save the lives of animals.

Instead, she just asked, "Can you pick up some Thai food for dinner? I have a dental surgery scheduled for five."

I couldn't even get a word out, couldn't even *think*, before she added, "So I won't be home until late. I can't cook."

Uncomfortable silence seemed to stretch on for minutes, but when my eyes finally glanced to the receiver, only eight seconds had passed.

Eight seconds that granted me some leeway to readjust my bearings.

I inhaled a breath. "We don't live together anymore, Ann."

Meeting Dr. Praigale — *Marie-France Leger*

Her voice climbed an octave. "I know, but we still had dinner plans."

"We'll reschedule."

"I don't want to reschedule," she insisted. "I want to see you after my shift."

A soft knock, unlike Vern's usual tap, drew my attention to the doorway.

"Dr. Praigale, your four o'clock is here," said Courtney, Vern's intern.

I shot her a thumbs up, mouthing a silent thank you for the interruption and said, "I have to go, Annika. Duty calls."

I knew she was pouting. She always pouted when she didn't get her way. There was a time when I caved in, when I wanted to flip her frown and give her the world.

There was a time.

And that time has passed.

"Okay, baby, I love you," she cooed, awaiting the reciprocation.

The hands of the clock ticked by, a mere few milliseconds separating me from the end of this phone call. I thought about the beginning of our relationship, when everything was good and raw and real. When we spent nights laughing over cheap wine and Monopoly, chatting about our similar dreams and ambitions.

Those thoughts pushed me to say the words, "You too," before ending the call.

Meeting Dr. Praigale   *Marie-France Leger*

    The dead line welcomed me, the flat buzz of static and no voice – absolutely no sound – but my breathing filling the space.

    I sank back into the soft cushion of my leather seat, allowing the quiet to bring me momentary relief.

    The biggest part of me hated that I hated us. Me and Annika, not exactly together, but not exactly apart.

    There were good moments, and maybe those moments were the reason I stayed. But the past was the past. I couldn't keep falling in love with old memories.

    Before Annika cheated on me with her vet tech, the world really was rosy. Whatever she wanted, I gave her. Whatever she needed, I provided. I was thrilled to receive her calls, her texts, her invitations.

    But that sole act, that "one-time-thing" she swore meant nothing, washed away all my sense of trust, of loyalty – of love.

    If I were a bystander, a friend, I'd say to hell with the relationship. Truthfully, a considerable amount of people in my life reiterated those exact words.

    But love wasn't a simple thing.

    If it were, we'd all have a much easier time moving forward, not tumbling back.

    Annika and I met in our last term of vet school. We'd known about each other, spoken a handful of times, but it was only during the last few

Meeting Dr. Praigale *Marie-France Leger*

weeks of clinical training that I decided to make a move.

"Animals aren't talked about enough," she'd told me over a bottle of Malbec. "If I had a mission, it would be finding good homes for those fluffballs."

She won me over that night.

She won my parents over two weeks later.

My father, who ran his own veterinary practice for over forty years, took her under his wing like a protégé.

"She's good for you, Noah," he pressed. "Keep her."

I'd said yes at the time and I meant it. *Yes*, I'd keep her. *Yes*, she was good for me. Of course if I had known then what our lives would turn into now, I wouldn't have said, "I promise."

Our entire relationship moved incredibly fast, built on a foundation of shared interests, similar career paths and heavy infatuation.

Six months in, we moved in together. One year later, I was looking at wedding rings.

If it weren't for Tav and McLean, I would've bought that emerald diamond from Aubrey Jewelers.

And that would have been the biggest mistake of my life.

Because two months after our one year, she came home a belligerent mess and slurred those spike-pointed words: "*Brennan won't be working with me anymore.*"

Meeting Dr. Praigale — Marie-France Leger

It didn't take me long to figure out the reason. Or why her lipstick was smudged, the face makeup around her chin crusted and erased.

I don't remember feeling anything in that moment but shame. Shame that I'd been so blind to who she was. Shame that I'd been charmed into thinking I could have the picture-perfect life my family envisioned for me.

The life I envisioned for myself.

All the fantasies I'd built in my head crumbled down and melted into a thick pool of lava beneath my anger.

There wasn't a word in the world to describe the feeling. So nothing came out.

Not as I stood up, walked straight into our bedroom and began packing my things.

Still, my voice was restrained.

"Keep the apartment," I'd choked out at last, before sealing my luggage, and our relationship away completely.

She reached out in desperation, the scent of alcohol wafting from her mouth. The lips she kissed Brennan with.

The destruction of our unity.

"No, please, *baby* -"

"Don't." I snatched my arm away, falling into that cold, callous calm.

Baby.

That word. God, out of all the words she could have said, it was that one. The universal term of endearment that I could now never give anyone else, because it was tainted by her.

Baby.

If only she understood the gravity of cheating – how it ripped away all trust and loyalty for meaningless, temporary desire.

For one useless night.

I suppose some people didn't view it that way, and sadly, I saw it first-hand, way before Annika came along.

Maybe that's why the promise of keeping her burned tenfold at her admission.

I always kept my promises.

But I couldn't keep this one.

For months I stayed with Tav, his rocker-themed apartment shielding me from the broken relationship I mourned.

Every day I would go into work as Dr. Noah Praigale, the soon-to-be inheritor of the great Dr. Mitchell Praigale's veterinary practice.

"He's as great as they come!"

"Always so cheery and helpful!"

Over one thousand stellar reviews. Not a bad comment in sight.

I'd go into work as Dr. Praigale.

I'd leave as Noah.

Just another tired man, who pretended to be anything but.

Meeting Dr. Praigale *Marie-France Leger*

Eventually, I found my footing after Tav's edge-lord music took a toll on my hearing, and moved into a one bed plus den near my clinic.

It was never about the money, what I could afford or could not afford after the breakup. Our apartment was always *hers* at the end of the day. Her furniture, her tea pots, *her way.*

Tav gave me the company I craved for a while. My oldest friend since kindergarten, taking a completely different path from vet school to open a grungy bar.

"Stay as long as you want, man," he'd told me.

And I did.

Until the pain eased, the memories fled, and I was that steady mix of Dr. Praigale and Noah again.

It worked for a while. My new life. My own space. But distractions couldn't heal the pain, just soothe the infection before it festered.

At the end of the day, my own space caved in on the loneliest parts of me. And I don't know how, or when, or why, but when Ann reached out a few months later, I answered her call.

It was a slow progression, unlike the start of our relationship.

"I'll work for your trust," she swore. "I promise you."

In a way, she had, otherwise we wouldn't be in this odd dynamic now – together, but not together – friends, *maybe*, but a little more.

Meeting Dr. Praigale *Marie-France Leger*

The biggest part of me couldn't love her, but a part of me still continued to try.

I promised, after all.

My father was thrilled about us reuniting. My mother, on the other hand, was not.

One thing to note about Dr. Mitchell Praigale, he was damn good at his job. An intelligent man, a business owner, a healer... but he was far from perfect.

His stellar reputation extended into the world of veterinary medicine, but behind closed doors, my father was a terrible husband.

To this day, I don't know how many affairs he's had, how many women have been in my mother's bed when she was on call at the hospital.

He was perhaps a good man in all the ways that appearances held, but he wasn't loyal. My mother knew that. But when you live in an abusive household and someone promises you a better life, you take it.

She took it.

She had me and my sister Bridget.

Even if she never really had Mitchell Praigale.

"Dr. Praigale?" Courtney seemingly appeared out of nowhere again, pulling me out of my thoughts.

I swiped my palms along my knees and stood up. "Yes, coming Courtney, thank you."

The illuminated hallway held much of my staff, rushing in and out of medicine coves in preparation for two later surgeries. Dr. William

Meeting Dr. Praigale *Marie-France Leger*

McLean, or just McLean to myself and Tav, was in charge of those appointments today.

"I'm handing you the bitch boy work," he said with a smirk, pushing a stack of papers and sticky notes into my hand.

My eyes clung to the cat bandana he wore. "I own this clinic, McLean."

He waved me off. "Until your ol' daddio kicks the fan, technically Dr. Mitch does."

I hated that he was right. That my name was attached to his. But it was that name that also put food on the table, a roof over my head, and the ability to save lives.

So here I was, ready to enter patient room number two, doing the so-called "bitch boy" work my colleague assigned his boss.

As Doctor Noah Praigale.

Chapter Three
Astra

One Hour Earlier
Last Edit – 2:59pm: No Title
Taylan Nichols lived in a dream-state of mind. Watching people pass her by, holding hands on the subway train and murmuring praises in their partners' ears. It was a dream-state of mind because it was a dream. Something unattainable. Something a dreamless girl could only imagine in subconscious thoughts. Not reality, never reality. That type of love only existed in your head.

I pressed the phone to my ear at the fourth ring. "Hello?"

"Take Snowball to the vet, will you? His appointment's at four and I can't make it."

Slowly, I held out the device in my palm, my eyes flipping between the manuscript on my laptop screen and the name **SUSAN** on the ongoing call display.

"Nice of you to ring, Mom," I started, gripping the edge of my cell a little too tightly. "Always good to hear your voice."

"I need a yes or no answer before I try your father." Soft jazz music played in the background, a tell-tale sign she was getting ready for a date.

"He's not going to answer."

Meeting Dr. Praigale   *Marie-France Leger*

Her snort followed. "I have ways of persuading."

Bile rose to the base of my throat, reminding me why I was glad to be rid of the toxicity running through the DuPont family bloodline.

Andre DuPont, my mess of a father, left my mother when I was six. My little sister Eva and I didn't really know him, didn't really try to, until we were older and curious.

"Waste of time," my mom had warned, "but try your luck all the same."

So we did.

Back then he worked at Walmart, changed his name to Beasley something and weighed one-fifty sopping wet. Mom told us that the drugs got to him, that at six-foot-three he should've weighed over two hundred.

"Crazy, skinny bastard." That's what we knew him by all our lives. Crazy. Skinny. Bastard.

I didn't have any expectations going into our meetup, just that I was to do all the talking and eleven-year-old Eva was to remain behind me in silence.

He really was thin. Uncomfortably thin. Pale, blue veins protruded from his pressure points – begging to be injected by something of the "Devil's work" (Mom said) – his eyes hollow and glazed over.

My fourteen-year-old legs were the size of his whole body, my steps weighing more than him as I approached with weak confidence. "H – Hello."

Meeting Dr. Praigale *Marie-France Leger*

"Needa buy meat? What kind?"

He wasn't looking at me or my pebble-sized sister, our eyes still full of hope for this hopeless man.

"I'm... *We're* actually your daughters." My voice was lower than I thought it'd be, soft like a baby bird. "We just wanted to say –"

"Speak up doll, I can't hear ya from up here." Then he looked at me. His eyes weren't actually black like I initially thought, but a dark brown. The colour of burnt cookies and soil.

For a second, I thought I saw recognition. I thought I saw a flash of *something* in his eyes. A memory, a moment, a connection but no – *no*, it was just a thought.

It was just hope.

"If you lot aren't buying anything, move aside," he said, and then muttered to some employee at the back counter, "*young kids. Where'd their parents go, eh?*"

The tears sizzled, but I didn't let them fall.

Not when Eva was cowering behind me with the hope I lost in seconds.

Not when I snagged two candy bars – Cookies'N'Creme for her and Kit Kat for me – off the snack rack and placed them in front of the cashier.

His name tag read Malcom.

I didn't know how important he'd be to me, then. Just that he had dimples and a nice smile and fluffy black hair that swept over olive green eyes.

Meeting Dr. Praigale — *Marie-France Leger*

But for once, Malcom's not the focus of this memory. Andre – or Beasley – is. And neither my sister nor I ever held hope for a connection with our dad ever again.

Never held hope for much after that day, really.

Mom however... well... Mom plowed through a plethora of men on Tinder. That's who she always was. A survivor, a bachelorette, a con-woman at heart.

"I'll change for the right man," she'd told me at my eighteenth birthday party, when I found her in the powder room getting fondled by the caterer.

She was dating "the right man" named Philip at the time, she told me so. But apparently she didn't. Apparently I misheard her when she broke up with him a day later to pursue the gardener, not the caterer, and sure as shit not Philip.

Of course, my sister and I could never question it. She gave us the space we lived in, she fed us, she bathed us and clothed us until we were able to do so on our own.

After Malcom died, my mom suggested that I take a little stay-cation at a neighbouring town for a little while. Probably the only good thing she'd ever done for me was fund the trip, feeling all sorts of bad that I lost my abusive ex-boyfriend in such a tragic way.

She didn't know the extent of what he'd done to me all those years. I don't know that she would've cared.

But someone did.

Someone I ran into just a few days after I checked into my spot at the B&B, and her name was Ruby Hutchinson. She was working the counter at Cloud, conveniently positioned next to the overpriced flat I was staying at in Stratford.

The first conversation we ever had set the tone for our whole relationship, when I was sitting in the corner of the shop, reading *The Great Gatsby* for the fourth time, and she asked, "How'd you afford it?"

Curious eyes met curious eyes. "Afford what? The book?"

"Not the book, sweetheart," she nudged her head towards the B&B, "that place. You livin' there?"

I remember thinking that it was such an intrusive question, that she was such a strange woman, but found myself answering honestly. "Mom's dime. Had to get away for a bit."

"How old are you?"

"Twenty-one."

Her eyes narrowed as if peering into my soul. "What're you running away from?"

The million dollar question.

Malcom.

My broken family.

Myself.

"Everything." That's what I settled on. "Just, everything."

She placed a hand over mine, her fingers covered in cheap rings, and smiled. "Got a name?"

This. This was the only thing clear to me at the time. This was the only thing I was sure of. Because despite the alias I planned to write under in the future, this part of my present was untouched by my past. For once, I could be me, without being *her*.

"Astra."

Deep, blue eyes twinkled like stars in the sky. "Like the painting."

"Painting?"

"We'll talk when you come back to work for me." She pulled out a business card, a cream-coloured rectangle with cartoonish flowers encircling Cloud's logo.

The corners pricked my fingertips. "Work for you?"

"Got a loft upstairs and everything. Cheaper by a mile than what you're paying for over at the B&B."

My mind couldn't process what I was being told. "Are you in the habit of offering sad strangers employment?"

She shrugged, playing on my words. "Stranger things have happened," she said, and walked away with a wave. "Call me if you're interested, Starburst."

There are moments in your life that change the trajectory of everything. Reuniting with my deadbeat-dad was one of them. Meeting Malcom was another.

But *losing* Malcom and finding Ruby, that set me off. It lit a fire underneath my ass. It was the fuel to my ignition. And when I decided to pursue a writer's associate degree through blended college classes, when I started writing books that actually did well, I realized that life really was a game and we were all players on the chessboard.

We decided our own fate.

Eventually I visited Mom a year after moving out, and found the man who I never thought I'd see again sitting on the grey couch he abandoned over a decade ago.

"Hey kiddo," my dad smiled, exposing yellow teeth. "Long time no see."

I didn't wave. I didn't acknowledge his presence. Not when my mother came up behind him and kissed his cheek. "Your father does favours for me sometimes," then ran her bony arms across his shoulders. "It's purely transactional."

I walked out of there and didn't go back for six months. But when Eva fell pregnant and her and her boyfriend moved in with my mom to help steady bills, I knew I couldn't avoid my family any longer.

The weekly visits restarted. The demands got passed down to Eva and Tyrell (her man), and whoever Susan DuPont was fucking at the time to help lower her debt.

And now, here we are.

Meeting Dr. Praigale — *Marie-France Leger*

"Eva and Ty can't take Snowball?" I asked, feeling the urge to write again after being uselessly interrupted.

"Nah, they're on a trip with Becks. She stood on her own the other day so they took her to Wonderland in celebration. Damn child fell over a second later but wahoo, right?"

Red hot anger pulsed through my veins. The fact I came from this woman was beyond my comprehension.

"*Bitch*," I muttered under my breath, quiet enough for her to ignore it. Or maybe she heard me and realized her words could topple mine in a heartbeat.

"Heigh-Ho butterscotch, yes or no?"

I had no choice, but it wasn't a burden. Of course I would go. Snowball was my childhood dog, and the only life that my mother seemed to show any amount of care for since she got him. "Yeah, I'll swing by and grab him. Why does he need to go to the vet?"

"He's got a breathing problem. Getting old and all. Don't want it to get worse."

There was concern in her voice. It almost startled me. But then she had to go and open her mouth again. "Aren't you going to ask what I'm doing? Why *I* can't bring him?"

At this point, I already had the Volvo keys in my hand and my sneakers on. "Nope."

"Have you heard of Tav's Tavern, Astra?"

Meeting Dr. Praigale *Marie-France Leger*

Objections of any kind didn't apply to Susan DuPont. It was yes or yes. Yes, I would like to hear the story, Mom. Yes, even if I don't want to listen, I will Mom. She loved to hear herself speak. She thought everyone did too.

Met with my silence, she continued. "I'm going on a date with Rourke Flance, a bartender there. Real hunk. Tattoos, tongue-piercing, and you know what that means –"

"Be there in thirty," I cut her off, ending the call immediately.

As I strapped myself into the driver's seat and began the trek back into Woodstock, I tried to shake the vile description of my mother's escapades from my head.

An alert rang through my Bluetooth, my mother's text reading: M & N's Vet Clinic on Colborne Road. Ask for Dr. Praigale.

"Dr. Praigale," I huffed. *Sounds like Pringle.*

When I finally reached my childhood home, my mom was already on her way out with Snowball in his carrying cage.

"Here," she practically shoved him in my arms, "you can baby talk him when he's in your car."

My eyes trailed the mahogany brooch pinned to her red blazer, dark waves pinned into a bun atop her head.

"Fancy." I couldn't hide the bitterness in my tone. "What look are you going for today, Mom? Lawyer? Realtor?"

Meeting Dr. Praigale

"No comments, Astra," she zipped her lips in mockery, her black stilettos clicking against asphalt. "If I'm not back by nine, keep him overnight."

There was no room to argue, no room to dispute her demands.

Yes. Yes. Yes. That's all that mattered. That's all she needed to hear.

But as she drove away and I followed suit, Snowball's excited whine cooed from the small blue cage in the passenger seat. A sense of relief flooded over me at the thought of my childhood companion seeing my place for the first time.

I stuck my finger in the square space between tiny metal bars, allowing him to lick my pointer. "Let's hope she has fun tonight, B," I whispered, reminiscing on the happy moments of childhood chase and go-fetch. "I have a jar of cookies at home with your name on it."

Chapter Four
Astra

"Susan, lovely to see you again."

Dr. Praigale, or *Mr. Pringle* as I liked to call him, didn't glance up from his clipboard as he entered the room. Snowball was perched in my arms, burying his snout in the crook of my armpit. I pet the spot between both his eyes, soothing his nerves.

"Hi," I let out, eyeing the dancing dog bandana that pushed back the doctor's hair. "Cute design."

"Hm?" He finally looked up at me with rich brown eyes, and blinked. "You're not Susan."

I couldn't help but stare as he flipped through a stack of papers on his clipboard, scanning words with haste and confusion, then finally set it aside.

"This *is* Snowball," he pointed at the Pom in my arms, then lifted his finger at me. "You... I don't know."

"Susan's my mom." I leaned down as Snow's whines began to start up again. "Shh, it's okay boy."

Again, Mr. Pringle looked at me as if analyzing a lab chart. "Susan's daughter," he nodded, then moved forward, extending his hand. "I'm Dr. Praigale, but call me Noah."

I snorted at my inner monologue – Praigale, *Pringle* – and lifted my hand. "Astra."

Meeting Dr. Praigale   *Marie-France Leger*

Just as I was about to accept the greeting, I thought better of it and retracted my fingers. "I probably shouldn't. My hands are covered in dog hair."

"No, no," he took a step closer, "give it here. My hands have seen all kinds of places."

The comment made me chuckle, most likely his intention, but it was still a bewildering feeling. It felt like forever since I've truly laughed.

He shook my hand firmly, his grip intentional. "Unique name, that. Astra."

I shrugged. "People seem to think so."

He cocked a brow. "You don't?"

"Well it gets the heads turning, clearly."

A full laugh escaped his lips. "I'm almost jealous now, being that mine is the most generic name to exist."

"Noah?" Saying this felt like a breach of professionalism, and yet I couldn't help but repeat it soundly in my brain.

Noah, I thought. *It fits.*

"Simple, right?" He folded toned, tanned arms across his torso. "Not much of a conversation starter."

"It started this conversation."

"Yours did, Astra," he released smoothly. "Yours did."

I took a moment to answer, fully enraptured by his presence. I just wanted to look at him.

"Call me blessed," I settled on.

He moved to collect a treat from a clear jar. "So, you like my bandana?" he asked, holding out the bone-shaped cookie to Snowball.

The Pom reached out and took it between his teeth, chewing in smacks. "It's certainly a choice."

A smile stretched across his face, exposing two sunken dimples indenting both cheeks. "We all wear them here."

"Quite the fashion statement."

He shrugged. "I try my best to modernize."

My grin formed naturally, the easy flow of this conversation feeling oddly refreshing.

I mingled with a few regulars at the café, but after Malcom died, I shrivelled up into a bubble of isolation. Even still, it felt impossible to claw my way out of the hole; friends became fewer, my social life practically non-existent. Everything revolved around writing. It was the one thing that continuously saved me when nothing (and no one) else could.

My eyes caught sight of a loose thread that poked from beneath the vet's bandana, then shifted to a crooked fold of the dancing dogs. I fought the urge to readjust the material.

"I didn't think it was that bad."

My gaze flicked to his. "What?"

He pointed to his head. "The bandana," he pointed, "you keep staring at it. I'm starting to wonder if my eyes are up in my hairline."

My cheeks heated. "You just have a few loose threads hanging back there."

"In that case" – he untied the knot that held the fabric together – "I'll sort that out later."

Once he set the headwear aside, his dark brown hair fell into view. It was a cleaner cut, with short waves that curled around his ears in a way that accentuated the stubble across his jawline.

It was... it was nice.

"Can I have Snowball up on the table please?" he asked, tapping the metal slab that stemmed from the beige wall.

I got to my feet and positioned Snow in between us, making sure to pet his mane while Mr. Pringle took out a stethoscope.

"You really didn't have to remove it," I let out, knowing I probably shouldn't have been speaking throughout this process. "I don't want your hair obscuring your view."

He kept silent for a few moments, adjusting the chest-piece to position before diverting his attention to me. We were closer now, his body just a few feet away, leaning towards my dog. Even bending, he was so much taller than my five-foot-four self. I'd give him six, six-one at least.

The room was placid, my dog's whines turning to soft pants as the doctor kept his eyes on me. "I can see perfectly fine," he released.

I swallowed as the doctor briskly looked away, his head angled towards Snowball's chest, then straightened out altogether. "Heart sounds good, now let's hear that cough."

Meeting Dr. Praigale *Marie-France Leger*

"Cough?"

"Your mother mentioned that he's having some breathing issues." The clipboard was back in his hands as he read through a sheet of paper. "Small dogs like him are prone to tracheal collapse."

"Is that life threatening?"

"It can be," he scratched his jaw, "but this won't be one of those cases."

Some tension subsided. "How do you treat it?"

"Exercise and avoiding air pollutants, I mean as best as you can, is number one. You don't smoke, do you?"

I shook my head. "No, never."

"And your mom?" He uncoiled the stethoscope around his neck and placed it atop the clipboard.

I rubbed my palms together nervously. "I don't think so. She never used to, but I um, I can't speak for now."

His eyes softened. "Do you know if she walks him often?"

God, I wish I could say. I wish I knew. I felt like an idiot, standing clueless with zero knowledge of her life, or my damn dog's conditions. It's been over two years since I've lived with my mother and Snowball, two years where she could've neglected him beyond my understanding.

Before I left for Stratford, she treated the dog like a newborn baby. As many guys as she went through, they all seemed to have a soft spot for animals so I assumed he'd be in good hands when I chose to get away.

But a lot can happen in two years.

A lot can happen in one single day.

I felt the cells underneath my flesh congregate to where Malcom grabbed me so hard that his nails pierced my skin. The bruises he left on my legs and thighs when I refused to...

When I refused to give him what he wanted.

I just want one night to myself, I'd told him. *I don't want to do this right now.*

My wants never mattered much. They were just empty words that dissipated with his needs.

"Astra?"

I didn't realize how lost in thought I was until Dr. Praigale addressed me by name. My grip was tight on the back of Snowball's fur, his small black orbs peering at me with concern.

"It's okay boy," I murmured low, then stood up tall. "I'm sorry, you were saying –"

I cut myself off, acutely aware of the impression I was surely giving off. A nut case, probably, commenting on his bandana strings, coaxing him to remove it and now – now, just, unable to answer a damn question because of that piece of shit relationship that's dead and gone.

He's dead and gone.

And still ruining me.

Meeting Dr. Praigale *Marie-France Leger*

At risk of going off the deep end, I tried to salvage and explain. "I have a deadline coming up so I'm a bit scatterbrained –" *Not that you care*, I wanted to say. "You're not boring me –" *Oh my God. Shut up.* "I don't know if my mom walks him a lot, to answer your question. We aren't really that close. I was just doing her a favour."

The urge to curl up into a ball and die was strong. Very fucking strong. As decent of a writer as I was, I couldn't articulate words for shit. I either overshared, or kept everything bottled up. Which one was worse, I really couldn't tell. I never learned how to.

It seemed like everyone else held some foreign power over me when it came to speaking. I'd never mastered the art of it. Never tried to.

No one could judge you in silence. No one could know you.

"What sort of deadline?" he asked, seemingly curious.

My cheeks reddened. "A book. I'm uh, I'm an author."

I avoided eye contact, petting Snowball's soft fur. I didn't want to look at him, didn't want to witness his reaction. But after a few seconds, Dr. Praigale spoke. "You're an author?"

There was sincerity to his voice, a fondness that I could only describe in books. When I chanced a look at him, his eyes held a sparkle of interest. Not in who I was, never, but in my craft. *The only thing noteworthy about me since the incident.*

M.D. Pont was a star, and Astra was behind the scenes, allowing her golden glow to glimmer.

"What genre do you specialize in?" he questioned.

Specialize in. Of course that's the wording he would choose.

"Why do you ask?"

"Just intrigued," he shrugged. "It's not every day you meet a writer."

I kept my gaze down as I continued to pet Snow. "I don't think you'd be very interested in my genre."

"Try me," he raised an arm. "Enlighten me."

"Really?"

"I wouldn't ask if I didn't care, Astra." At the way he said my name, I was tempted to look up, to bathe in the sparkle of his curiosity; curiosity that seemed to hold honest interest.

I cleared my throat. "Romance mostly, but I'd love to write a thriller novel one day. Something to challenge me."

"Challenge you?" he asked, lips curled. "And romance doesn't challenge you?"

"In real life, I suppose it challenges us all." I cleared my throat.

He held my gaze. "But not in books."

"Not in books," I said. "It's easier to create romance than it is to live it."

"But then you don't experience it for yourself" - he folded his arms - "imaginary people do it for you."

I blushed, swallowing hard. "I'm okay with that."

"Huh." He leaned back against the counter, tilting his head. "How old are you, Astra?"

"Twenty-three."

"A twenty-three-year-old author," he whistled lowly. "That's pretty incredible."

"Anyone can write a book," I shrugged. "If they have the patience."

"And the talent," he supplied.

I turned away, unable to help the surge of pride that ran through me. On paper, releasing four books in your early twenties should be something to gloat about. But when you're good at something, that "talent" becomes second nature. You rarely see that you've been given it at all.

"You're a doctor," I pushed, diverting the attention. "That's pretty amazing, too."

Before he could open his mouth, I found myself adding, "What is that? Ten years of school? Hats off to you, really."

He laughed. "Eight, but I got lucky."

"How does one get lucky in school? It's about intelligence."

"It's about how bad you want it." His smile thinned as he added, "And I wanted it very much."

Meeting Dr. Praigale *Marie-France Leger*

Snowball barked suddenly, startling me enough to jump. Dr. Praigale twitched as well, as if that one interruption disrupted the flow of discourse. And maybe... maybe it was exactly that. Two strangers bouncing balls at the unknown. Two strangers who knew nothing about each other, and could unwind the thread of mystery.

Or maybe it was just me, living in the mural of my mind, romanticizing the possibilities.

"I hear you little guy, I see you." *Mr. Pringle* sauntered over to him with one stride, switching back to professionalism. "Now this is going to be uncomfortable, but bear with me."

He cupped the base of Snowball's neck, lifting his chin high, then gently pressed on his throat. Naturally, the poor thing thrashed and growled, which resulted in a coughing fit that lasted roughly ten seconds.

There were no "getting-to-know-you" moments after that. It was strictly client/doctor discussion which I didn't mind. He informed me about the different issues within dog breeds, and how Pomeranians like Snowball were prone to something called patella luxation and reverse sneezing.

Now in the corner of the room, Dr. Praigale was writing notes while I held Snow in my arms. "I'm going to print out an article on preventing tracheal collapse for you, along with some instructions."

I nodded, withdrawing back into my cage. "Much appreciated, Doctor. Thank you."

Meeting Dr. Praigale — *Marie-France Leger*

His pen stopped. He looked up at me with a gaze that stunted my entire body. "Just Noah. Unless you'd rather I call you Miss DuPont?"

"Please don't." I stifled a laugh. "I just assumed that doctors enjoyed flashing their credentials, you know, given all the hard work they put into obtaining the title."

He shook his head, "Not this one," and ripped a sticky note off a piece of paper. "Vern will check you out at the front desk."

With that, he was opening the door, looping his stethoscope around his neck and pocketing the folded bandana. "Next time I see you, I'll make sure to wear a hairnet."

I chuckled warmly. "I'll hold you to that."

In that moment, the force of a feeling hit me like a train. A string of words edged the tip of my tongue, a ballad of ideas bounced in and around my brain, begging to come out.

Inspiration. Interest.

Passion.

This one little conversation did something to me, something every author looked for without knowing what to find. I always did write best with muses in mind, and this encounter, I knew, pointed me to the trajectory of success.

Dr. Noah Praigale had become my muse.

Something to focus on.

Something to fixate on.

Something that wasn't Malcom.

Meeting Dr. Praigale   *Marie-France Leger*

With the rap of his knuckles against the mahogany wooden door, he smiled back at me, unaware of the shift in time that just took place. "It was nice to meet you, Astra."

And just like that, his presence, along with the spark of *something*, was gone.

***

"You're good to go," the receptionist with deep-creased wrinkles said. "Such a cutie."

I was keenly aware of the motion behind the staff door, my eyes searching for the tall veterinarian I was with only a few moments ago.

"Thank you," I responded, half a second later realizing she meant Snowball. "Oh, I mean, thank you on his behalf." I shook one of his paws to wave at her.

He hated that.

I stood in front of the counter, credit card in hand, staring at the check-up fee of eighty dollars.

"Is there anything else I can do for you?" the lady asked. Vern. That was her name.

"Oh, yeah, I'm just waiting to pay."

She flapped her hand. "No need. Dr. Praigale waived the fee."

Huh?

I was about to respond when she scribbled something on a pink note and slid it in front of me. "His next appointment is two weeks from now. Dr. Praigale would like to do another check-up."

Meeting Dr. Praigale *Marie-France Leger*

Next appointment? "Oh, right, okay." Then, "I really don't mind paying for the appointment – for his time."

She let out a hoarse laugh. "Hon, it's been taken care of."

"But why?" I stopped myself before I could babble further. "I mean, that's really... that's nice of him."

Her aged grin was prominent as she called over a woman named Grendel who held a yapping poodle.

Snowball began to stir in my arms, a cue to get the hell out of M & N's Vet Clinic and escape to my car. *I need to think.*

Once he was nestled comfortably in the shade of his carrying crate, I swiped out my phone to check if Mom had texted me.

Of course, she hadn't.

But that wasn't a bad thing. That meant I'd have a companion tonight. Something to do while I pondered the events of this interaction.

A once in a million encounter, unpredictable and unplanned, meeting the doctor who was polite enough to show interest in my craft.

The veterinarian who cared to know me, when all I could give were my words in return.

He was just being hospitable, I told myself. But at the stoplight, I raked my eyes over the notes he'd written down, and at the very top was chicken-scratch script that read:

I expect Snowball to be two pounds lighter by his next visit. No pressure. (:

P.S: I'm not much of a reader but maybe your books will change that.

All the best,
Noah Praigale

Chapter Five
Noah

It took a second for my eyes to adjust to the dim hue of my apartment.

I'd installed a sunset lamp next to my couch that ran on a timed clock – five to ten p.m. – which assured me that if someone somehow snuck into my place, I'd be ready.

Call me paranoid, but you never know these days.

The first time Tav and McLean came over, they wouldn't stop hounding me about the darkness.

"How do your eyes even function, man?" McLean griped, pushing two fingers against his temple. "I can't even think."

Tav had just surveyed my bookshelf, unimpressed. "No need for all these books if you can't read half the fuckin' sentences."

Now I was staring at that same bookshelf, contemplating wiping away the collected dust between the pages of unread novels.

My mom was a huge reader. She always said to make space for literature, since it was writing that moved the world. I suppose her advice stuck with me throughout the years since I'd adopted a bad habit of buying books, whether it be at charity shops or flea markets on my downtime. In reality, I hadn't read a non-textbook in months. Still, it was nice to keep a shelf.

Occasionally, I'd try a few chapters of a historical fiction, poetry too, but the pressure of the clinic took a primary focus in my brain, forcing me away from a good story.

An odd thought, but a real shame it was. Among other things.

My phone vibrated in my pocket, the caller ID reading: **VERN.**

"Everything okay?" I asked, hanging my corduroy jacket onto the metal hook. "Do I need to come back?"

"Ah, Noah," she started, letting out a snort, "always so cautious."

The tension eased from my shoulders. "Someone has to be. The five-star reviews aren't because of laziness, I'll tell you that much."

"You should let William take on some of your load."

I walked over to my coffee machine, swapping out the old Keurig cup for a new one and pressed brew. "He handled the surgeries today, he did plenty."

A second voice, deep and rough, was muffled in the background. Her husband, Arnold, most likely. She mumbled a few words to him, then addressed me. "Oh, come now, honey, he had to pry those surgeries from your hands."

"They weren't in *my* hands," I contested, watching the trickle of brown liquid drip into my mug. "They were in McLean's."

I could feel her protest bubbling before she asked, "Why did you cover that check-up fee?"

At first, I drew a blank. Check-up fees ranged from eighty to a hundred-twenty dollars, sometimes more with veterinary clinics. My father, with all his faults, was not someone who took advantage of the clientele that brought him business.

He may not have been a loyal husband, but he was devoted to his service.

Since taking over my father's practice a little over four years ago, I'd gotten to know many of the regulars. Their pets were my pets, which is why I never really bothered to have one of my own.

You take care of the things that bring you happiness, the things you grow to love.

My clients confided in me, so it wasn't all that surprising when I waived a few check-up fees here and there. If I remembered properly, I think I covered two today alone.

My brain began filtering through previous appointments when Vern clarified, "Astra DuPont, *Meredith* DuPont. She came in with –"

"Snowball." I knew exactly who she was talking about. The sole reason my subconscious guided me to the dusty bookshelf in the first place.

Astra, the girl with chocolate brown hair and eyes to match. The author who despised my bandana

Meeting Dr. Praigale — Marie-France Leger

so much I rethought our entire dress code because of it. But most of all, the pleasant distraction after my conversation with Annika.

That was why I waived her fee. Even if she had zero knowledge of what transpired before her appointment, I felt the need to thank her in some way.

I snagged my coffee and carried it over to the sofa. "She's never been to the clinic before" – the taste of burnt beans stung my lip – "I'm all about making good first impressions, Vern, you know this."

It was sort of a half-lie. Naturally, I did what I could to provide the best service possible for my clients and their pets. Owning an animal came with a cost, one I was trying my best to limit if possible.

But Astra... I couldn't pinpoint the feeling. She was endearing, for a lack of better words. There was something about her, something of rare substance, and yet I was left clueless.

I was not in the habit of psychoanalyzing *anyone*, believe me. But as a veterinarian, you had to know your clients, *read* your clients, in order to be the most suitable caretaker for their pets.

My radar went ablaze upon meeting Astra. And between the jaunty remarks and quiet hesitation, a seed was planted that fed my curiosity.

She'd dropped subtle hints throughout the short conversation – a tumultuous relationship with her mother perhaps – a poor parental dynamic I understood all too well.

Meeting Dr. Praigale *Marie-France Leger*

"*We aren't really that close,*" Astra had said, completely unaware of the dog's living conditions or health risks. "*I was just doing her a favour.*"

Since I was little, my mind conjured up a million paths and scenarios that led me through endless routes and spirals - usually resulting in dead ends.

"You've got a doctor's brain, son," Dad had told me. "Use it."

At the time, I assumed he just wanted me to follow in his footsteps; to take over the clinic when he was ready to hand it over. But pursuing the degree in veterinary medicine taught me that having a hundred different avenues was better than one. Every patient was different - different eyes, different minds, different hearts.

People were never the same. And I refused to believe that one person only ever felt one thing.

Behind someone's eyes, there was always a story to tell.

Astra had one. I was sure of it.

"She's aware of Snowball's appointment in two weeks?" Vern agreed and I added, "Four o'clock?"

"Yes, I wrote it down and pencilled it in. I also left a message on Susan DuPont's phone as a reminder."

For a split second, the thought of seeing Susan instead of Astra disappointed me. She wasn't a bad woman, Astra's mother, but she always held my

Meeting Dr. Praigale *Marie-France Leger*

hand a little too long in thanks – always flirted with me in sour ways that made me uneasy.

"The DuPont girl insisted on paying," Vern chuckled. "Had her card out and ready looking all sorts of confused that she didn't need to use it."

I sucked in a breath, taking in her words. I'd lowered Susan's fees many times in the last few years, a plead request out of courtesy to her financial situation. But Astra pushing payment... *This*, I wondered. *She's Susan's daughter?*

With my laptop open, I did a quick search of her name, waiting to find a list of books she published.

When she told me she was an author, it took me by surprise. And at the age of twenty-three no less, well, that was downright inspiring.

As a twenty-nine year old, I'd gone through the partying stages in my early twenties. My primary focus was having fun. For her to be an author, at such a young age... that took hard work and dedication, not to mention the time constraints of publication. I couldn't imagine the balance she had to find to make it work.

Maybe that's why she fascinated me.

Practicing medicine leaned on an analytically science-based perspective of life. Doctors could only take their creativity so far before they pierced a blood vessel or severed a vein.

Authors, painters, musicians – artists, in general, possessed such a colourful mind.

Meeting Dr. Praigale *Marie-France Leger*

Glancing at my shelf, those untouched novels seemed to jump out at me, screaming to pick up one of the old classics instead of my animal anatomy handbooks.

I cleared my throat. "Vern, I've got to go. I have to print out some sheets on brachycephalic syndrome for that pug, Libby."

Her strained, gruffy laugh made me beam. "Always working."

The line cut out and I threw my phone to the left, pulling my laptop back on my knees to scroll through articles.

I did in fact get more work done for Libby. Most of the suggestions included a relatively simple surgery, but I always tried different paths if I could. Surgeries were expensive and not everyone could afford it. I'd attempt every safe route known to man before reaching the last resort.

Forty-five minutes later, I found myself opening the tab of Astra's name again, puzzled as to why nothing of significance came up.

"*Astra McKinsey, head of legal at Jawbone Law...*" I scrolled and scrolled, reciting names aloud. "*Astra Bane, primary school teacher at Fort Hill High...*"

No Astra Meredith DuPont.

Not a trace.

I blew out a breath, lacing my fingers behind my head.

Well this was... unexpected, to say the least.

Meeting Dr. Praigale — Marie-France Leger

Was she even an author? Did she lie to me? "Why would she do that?" The question came out of my mouth, addressing nobody but my gullible self.

If that truly was the case, then maybe Susan bringing Snowball was the better option. I shouldn't have been thinking about her regardless, and questioning myself and her was a pointless waste of time.

Sure, Annika and I were still tangled up in an odd situation. Technically, she should be the only woman in my head. But she wasn't, and she hadn't been for a while now. I would never act on anything with anyone.

I was *not* my father.

And engaging in conversation with someone you found interesting wasn't a crime.

But a part of me felt guilty; guilty for even finding curiosity in the unfamiliar.

Well, that didn't matter anyway. There were no mentions of the Astra she told me she was, so maybe that Astra didn't exist at all.

Even though she did. She very much did.

And I had the pleasure of speaking to her.

My eyes caught on an article that detailed the origins and history of her name, prompting me to investigate.

It fascinated me from the start, and I was never one to hide my intrigue. Astra.

Astra, Astra, Astra.

Meeting Dr. Praigale *Marie-France Leger*

Despite the few people that showed up on my search, I'd never met someone with that name before. It had nothing to do with *her*, I told myself, just a simple history lesson.

What can I say? *I love to learn.*

There were paragraphs detailing the meaning in several different languages, accompanied by photos and captions. All in all, the name held universal significance:

Stars.

From the stars.

To the stars.

The corner of my lips lifted at those words. A true rarity to find such a beautiful name. Noah was so mainstream, so mundane. And Astra... well, that was anything but.

I paused on a photo of a painting, one done by a Finnish artist, that depicted a visionary woman with outstretched arms extended to the moon and beyond. It was called: ***Ad Astra.***

Closing my laptop, I leaned my head against the back of the sofa and eyed the hanging beams on my ceiling.

A title for the stars, I thought.

And for some reason, the notion made me smile. *A name has never suited anyone better.*

What do you know?

A story indeed.

Chapter Six
Noah

"Aren't you going to eat the shrimp?"

Annika and I were at her apartment, sharing Thai food from a hole in the wall place around the corner.

"You haven't touched the shrimp. It's good," she egged on, pinching the tail with her chopsticks and waving it in my face. "Try it."

Irritation bubbled inside me. *Has she always been this way?* "I'm okay. It's yours."

She raised her shoulders, taking not one, but two shrimp, and shoving them in her mouth, tail and all. "Mm."

I forced a smile, but that's all I could really do – all I've been doing the last few months but especially these last couple of days.

Sitting with McLean over lunch yesterday, I decided to confide in him before my brain exploded and guilt overtook me. "I just can't do it anymore," I'd admitted. "It's not... *She's* not supposed to be in my life. I feel it in my bones, Will."

He swirled some lentils around his bowl and spooned them into his mouth. "Took you long enough to realize."

"I feel like I always knew." And it's true. Since she cheated and I hesitantly let her back in, it was a mistake. All of it was a mistake. I was stupid

Meeting Dr. Praigale *Marie-France Leger*

and lonely and missed something – someone, who could fill the spaces on my couch, the extra seat at the dining nook and the left side of my bed.

    I thought it could be her.

    I *promised* it would be her.

    I was wrong.

    "End it," he pushed my cell towards me. "End it and spare yourself the trouble before you change your mind."

    "I'm not sending her a text. I owe her more than that."

    He scoffed, scarfing down the last of his food. "I'm sure she thought the same when she was slumming it up with –"

    Resurfacing that memory was all it took to bring me to this moment now, sitting across Annika eating shrimp, while I stared aimlessly at the floor to avoid what I knew would be the end.

    The guilt of losing her was nothing compared to the shame of breaking something I worked so hard to fix. My father's loyalty was never a quality of character for him, but for me... it was everything.

    Long ago I believed a relationship could work if you put in the effort to see it through. Now, for the first time ever, I drew the conclusion that just because you could make something work, doesn't mean you should – doesn't mean it's right for you.

    Before I could stop myself, I cleared my throat. "Ann, we need to talk."

    "You're ending it."

Meeting Dr. Praigale — *Marie-France Leger*

At first, I thought I heard her incorrectly. But upon realizing I hadn't, I froze, staring at the hem of my pants, before meeting her gaze. She was wide eyed, almost ready to receive the news I didn't realize she was expecting.

"What?" Was all I could muster out. She was right. I just didn't know how she pieced it together.

"I mean, it's pretty obvious Noah. You've been dodging me like the plague."

"Are you..." I cleared my throat, shaking my head. "Yes. Yes, I am, and I'm sorry Annika, but I really do think that –"

"– that I'm an amazing person and a great girl and an incredible vet? Yeah, I got that."

"I don't want to be on bad terms," I pressed. "We both have connections to each other's clinics, we can be civil."

Her eyes rolled as she swiped the box of cashew chicken from beside the noodles. "No hard feelings here. I was seeing Chris on the side anyway."

My mind worked against me, tracing back to Chris' of the past, of the future, and anyone in between. A *Chris* was entangled with Annika while I was, but no one came to mind. No one I knew, then.

And yet, it still felt like a punch to the gut.

"Don't look so shocked, Noah. This thing between us," she darted a finger back and forth, "it wasn't exclusive. You could've fucked the intern and I wouldn't have cared."

Meeting Dr. Praigale *Marie-France Leger*

My jaw worked hard to keep my mouth intact. The bite to her tone suggested she *did* care, at least somewhat. But not enough to be honest with me. Not enough to speak like adults and tell me she was with another man at the same time.

"You could've at least told me." It was straining to speak. "I wouldn't have hid anything like that from you."

"We were using protection," she didn't look at me as she plated her food, "it's not like I gave you syphilis."

I pushed away from the table, feeling the urge to empty my stomach. "Okay, we're done here."

It wasn't jealousy that left a bitter taste in my mouth, no. She had another relationship alongside whatever we were? Fine. But inform me of it. Tell me that it's not just me you're sleeping with because secrets make for reckless endings and in truth, I wasn't keen on the idea of multiple partners. Up until this point, I didn't know she was either.

For the final time, I was wrong.

And that's the part that stung. The fact that thinking about someone else, about *Astra*, even for a second made me ruminate in my own values.

While Annika was with someone else.

She was with someone else when she told me she loved me.

That's... That's exactly what my father had done to my mother.

Meeting Dr. Praigale *Marie-France Leger*

"Don't overstay your welcome," she jabbed, pointing at the door.

The muscles in my body fused together, forcing my feet and legs to carry me to the exit of my relationship for the second time around, and into the dimly lit hallway that reminded me so much of last time.

Dragging myself away from something I wanted for myself, something my family wanted for me.

And ended up right back where I was all those months ago.

Alone.

***

My breath fogged the air as I walked the tired street of Avondale Avenue, hands in my pockets to keep warm.

Annika's apartment didn't have parking, so I usually just paid the dollar an hour fee at the town pharmacy to keep my car spot.

The late Spring was unusually cold this year, especially at night, when the wind could dance in the darkness and freeze your face.

Annika lived in Stratford, a small town outside Woodstock where she worked at the only vet clinic in the area. From what I gathered over the course of our two years together, it was sort of a retirement town, quiet for all the right reasons and especially safe. There were a few bars scattered around the main core, but the livelier spots primarily

Meeting Dr. Praigale *Marie-France Leger*

consisted of old folks playing buy-a-beer-bingo on the weekends.

I grew up in Guelph, a city not too far from here, and completed my education before moving away. Dad had two clinics, one back home and one in Woodstock, but even during his retirement he didn't want to give them up.

"It's a fair compromise, son," he'd told me before I relocated. "You got a job handed to you on a silver platter. All you have to do is move."

Handed to me, were his words. As if taking over a vet clinic was mindless work, and moving into an unfamiliar city aided in my sanity. His ideals have always been questionable, so I clung to the one thing we had in common – being a veterinarian.

Distant chatter and music sounded from a coffee shop a block away. I squinted to read the pale neon sign: Cloud Café.

A group of kids walked out with pastry bags in their hands, the dinging bell of the door ringing through the quiet night. I'd never heard of Cloud Café before, not that I was a coffee connoisseur or even a local in this area. Krispy Kreme K-cups kept me up just fine.

Tea-time hopping was Annika's thing. She was always on the lookout for new tea houses to try. I remember some of the trendier places we used to go to that carried peppermint and lemon, cherry and lavender… the strangest of combinations, yet she adored them all.

Meeting Dr. Praigale *Marie-France Leger*

Internally, I beat myself up at the thought of her, but quickly forgave the parts of me that attempted to heal. Again.

Just because you fall out of love with someone, doesn't mean you didn't love them in the first place.

People tend to forget the hours, days, months spent with that person – in my case, years. That's not an easy feeling to shake, even if the very thing you struggled to keep together fell apart.

I let out a long exhale as I crossed the sidewalk, my eyes flitting to Cloud Café once more. Despite the events of tonight, I still had research to do this weekend. A client of mine brought in a two-month-old chihuahua that fractured its right arm. The owner, Miss Meryl, was a retiree who barely had enough pension to cover her daily expenses. I promised her I'd find another way to help mend his bones. I always kept my promises.

But some promises couldn't be kept.

Another painful thought pushed to the backburner of my brain forced my attention elsewhere. Somewhere. *Anywhere.*

The whistle of teenagers.

Leaves slapping the pavement.

And that damn neon sign that kept flashing in my face: Cloud Café.

I exhaled, taking a step onto the stone stairs. *One cup of coffee won't hurt.*

Meeting Dr. Praigale *Marie-France Leger*

    That same bell jingled above me as I strode inside, remarking the vintage interior with bistro sets lining the walls and a very... *very* familiar barista behind the cash, swaying her hips to house music. With cocoa-coloured hair and a striking gaze, the semblance was uncanny. She looked almost like –

Chapter Seven
Astra

Last Edit - 4:19pm: No Title
*Taylan met someone today. Tall, brown hair the colour of a blonde roast and pinecones. He reminded the dreamless girl of someone. A person, perhaps, she had yet to meet in this life, but maybe a soul in another one. He smiled, and it began to melt the hard ice that typically lodged around the cell of her heart, the prison that kept hold of all of the painful memories – the memories that kept her buried alongside **him** in the past.*

"D*r. Praigale?*" I gasped, dropping the broomstick in my hands.

My best attempt at withholding shock was pointless. Not when my vocal cords hit an impossibly high octave, sounding like a bunny that got run over by a train.

Safe to say, I was mortified.

No one could've predicted this coincidence, let alone me – *me*, who was just writing about the memory of *Mr. Pringle* six fucking hours ago.

I... I genuinely never thought I'd see him again. Not that I didn't want to, or couldn't, just – writing about the *idea* of someone versus who they truly were often spared a heart from hurt.

But this? This could not be happening. This was pure *fiction.*

I couldn't help but laugh at the absurdity as he approached the counter, those matching sunken dimples stamping his cheeks as he tipped an invisible hat my way. "You're a very good dancer."

"What are you doing here?" The words tumbled out of me as rational thought slowly seeped back into mind. Cloud Café was public domain and literally anyone could walk in if they chose to. I just didn't expect that *anyone* would be *him.* "I mean, do you live in this area?"

"I don't, no, just needed some caffeine." He dipped his head towards the assortment of bakery treats and asked, "What's good here?"

My mouth was still partially open as I watched him in disbelief. I tried to speak but failed. Miserably.

The Cloud Muffins, Ruby's specialty, were all sold out (as always), but I felt the sudden urge to go to the back and make a sub-par version myself. The cat clock on the wall read: 10:21 p.m., meaning my shift was just about done and the pastries were most likely stale.

I latched on to a single thread of sanity and released a breath. "I'd recommend it all, but the owner makes everything fresh so they're probably –"

"*Astra!*" Pots banging near the staircase alerted me to the storage room, the one and only Ruby Hutchinson stalking out with withered eyes.

Meeting Dr. Praigale   *Marie-France Leger*

"This man wants somethin' to eat, you get him somethin' to eat."

My hands flew up innocently. "I never said I wouldn't sell him anything."

She ignored me and placed a solid, flour-tossed palm on Dr. Praigale's shoulder. When she removed it, his brown jacket was stained. "What'd you want? Pumpkin pie? Strawberry streusel? I've got it all."

He looked amused as he dusted the flour residue off his sleeve. "This might just be the best service I've ever had."

Ruby grumbled. "Write that on my reviews, boy."

"I won't forget." Then, "Astra," he turned to me, "your recommendation?"

Astra.

The way he said my name churned butterflies in my stomach, the ones that had been dead for years now, refusing to surface.

With both Ruby and the vet staring my way, one with pointed blue eyes and another with soft brown spheres, I suggested, "Cloud muffins."

"That'll take me some time to make." Ruby responded.

I shrugged. "That's what I recommend. Are you really going to deny a paying customer, Rubes?"

She mumbled quietly and made her way to the back, snagging a translucent bag of almonds and

Meeting Dr. Praigale *Marie-France Leger*

chocolate chips before closing the door to begin preparation.

"She's not actually making muffins from scratch, is she?" Dr. Praigale asked.

"Oh, she is."

He blew out a breath. "Tell her not to worry, I have a granola bar –"

I shook my head. "There's no talking her out of it, trust me. Plus, she has to make a new batch for tomorrow and if anything, she'll thank you for sparing her the extra work in the morning."

"Well, I guess that settles it." His posture sagged as he pulled out a chair near the window and sat down. "Looks like I'll be staying a while, then."

I forced a smile, fighting the tension. "Make yourself at home."

"Won't be hard," he supplied, settling into his seat.

Christ. This was odd.

This was very fucking odd.

An oddity among all oddities.

And yet, a small part of me couldn't help but thank the gods above that I had more material to work with. More *him* to write about.

I suppose that sometimes, fate did favour the faithless.

He glanced around the shop, taking in all the antique decorations Ruby hand-picked from garage sales. I cleared my throat. "A bit kooky, huh?"

"What is?"

Meeting Dr. Praigale   *Marie-France Leger*

"All this." I pointed to the hideous cat-clock wagging its tail to count each tick, the torn painting of a seascape that Ruby insisted would be worth millions one day, and the neon yellow OPEN sign that flickered in beats.

His head followed the direction of my hand as I pointed each item out.

"It's certainly a choice," he smiled, reiterating my words from our first encounter. "Where's Snowball? Is he with your mom?"

Sadly, I wanted to say. Having the little guy over just for a night made me reminisce in the moments of my childhood – the moments well spent with him – that made me nostalgic. It pained me to give him back, but I told Mom I'd take him off her hands once a week. Her agreement made my whole year.

"He is, yeah. I told her about his next appointment... I wasn't sure if you called about it but –"

"My receptionist did." A curt response. "How is he doing?"

I brushed off the sharpness. "Well, he didn't cough much in my presence. I'll take that as a good sign."

"I'm glad to hear," he nodded. I didn't have the chance to retort before he spoke again. "Your books... I couldn't find them anywhere."

I swallowed hard. A swell of emotion formed in my chest, threatening to penetrate the fortress I'd

Meeting Dr. Praigale *Marie-France Leger*

built around my heart. *So that note really did mean something.*

"I'm not doubting your credibility, I was just a little confused when I googled –"

"I write under an alias," I rushed to explain. "M.D. Pont."

"Really?" He adjusted his position in the wooden chair. "How come not your real name?"

The question of the hour.

When I told Beth, my best friend from college, that I'd started writing under a pseudonym, she asked the same thing. So did Mom, Ruby, Eva, and just about anyone who came into my inner circle and found out that I was an author.

No one knew the real reason why I wanted to be immortalized in a different form: that I wanted a completely separate identity from the one I possessed, much like my characters.

Astra didn't exist, not when I wrote my books or submitted my interview articles. My publication house understood my preference for privacy, so they pushed out my books without pushing *me*.

I still existed, naturally, but there were no photos lurking around that tied me to the death of Malcom or who I used to be back in high school. And thank God for that, because I could hear them all now:

"Astra... Wasn't she the girl who dated football captain Malcom Matheson?"

Meeting Dr. Praigale *Marie-France Leger*

"I heard she gave him head under the bleachers after game six!"

"Her mom slept with my dad last summer."

"She's kind of hot, in a weird, loner way."

Yeah, that's me.

Astra Meredith DuPont, the girl who was *lucky* enough to bag a varsity athlete, the "loser" who no one understood could be manipulated by an abuser who grabbed her by the throat when he lost a match.

Because when "Macho-Man-Matheson" came to school, he was an icon. A legend. The vital artery to his league.

And I was his punching bag.

He wasn't always that way, not at first. Just like most men, he wooed and cooed his way in.

Then, you never escaped.

I tried, so many times I tried. But abusers and manipulators go hand in hand, and Malcom was an expert in his field.

Back then, the only friends I had were the outcasts in my Writer's Club, the school newspaper's journalistic "freaks," and my sister. So believe me when I say I was shocked to see Malcom Matheson approach me after school, smoking a joint with his left hand, carrying a bag of sour gummies in his right.

"Want one?" he'd asked.

I didn't answer. I didn't think he was talking to me.

Meeting Dr. Praigale *Marie-France Leger*

"Astra, right?" When he said my name, my head zipped to him in shock.

We only spoke once, when he cashed me out for the chocolate bars at the check-out line years prior. *How did he know my name?*

Malcom just laughed, that hoarse throaty laugh that matched his entire persona, and pulled out a pink and blue candy worm. "Eat up."

I took it and bit clean through the head, chewing as I admired his stature. My confidence was a blank canvas. It existed, but nothing shaped me to be extraordinary. So I blended in.

"I remember you, y'know. You bought..." he narrowed his eyes, squinting at the sky, "Kit Kats or something." His mouth continued to work on his worm. I kept quiet.

"I see you floating around the halls sometimes." He extended his hand, offering me that skunk-smelling stick. "Puff?"

I shook my head. Again, saying nothing.

"Suit yourself." His lips pursed to fit the joint, inhaling a plume of smoke. "You don't talk much. Not a talker?"

"No," I finally responded. So quietly. So docilely. "Not really."

"How about I make you talk over lunch tomorrow?"

It was that one line that flattered me. The vulnerable, sixteen-year-old girl who never talked to

Meeting Dr. Praigale *Marie-France Leger*

boys besides the man-children her mother brought over, and Owen Coxley from Writer's Club.

To this day, I never understood why he approached me. When he got angry, he told me it was a dare. In a lighter argument, he said he felt sorry for me. But when I was truly afraid, he stepped on my foot to keep me from moving and whispered, "*Players prefer their prey sweet and willing.*"

I shuddered back to existence, pushing away the sociopath and his death to the fucking great beyond.

"Sorry, your question..." I apologized, taking in the atmosphere around me and its safety. "What was it again?"

"Always zoning out, Stargirl."

"Hm?" I furrowed my brows. "Stargirl?"

His expression was playful, brown eyes gleaming with kindness. "The nickname stays." Then, "Why do you write under an alias?"

Stargirl.

I shelved the thought and answered his question. "I just thought it could be fun, I don't know. To play a different character in real life."

"But this is your job. Wouldn't you want to be recognized for your success?"

"I don't care about the spotlight," I admitted, falling back into young Astra's mindset. "I'd rather not have that kind of attention."

He pulled out his phone again. "M.D. Pont, right?"

I nodded as he began typing once more, his eyes growing wide as he scrolled through what I knew were the list of achievements plastered all over the web.

"*Wow*," he muttered. "*What in the...*" His fingers stopped as he pinched to zoom in, and glanced up at me with wide eyes. "New York Times – You've made the New York Times bestsellers list?"

Hardly. Just an impressive label that meant nothing in the end. Status didn't measure levels of creativity, I always believed that. "M.D. Pont did, yeah."

"Oh come on, don't say that." He pointed at me. "*You* are a bestseller. Just because you choose to play a character, doesn't mean that character isn't you."

I felt my heart pulse, the slow and steady thump of my blood thick with emotion. My eyes willfully searched for something to pick out – a flaw, a loose thread – but there was nothing. Just a man who looked at me, *really* looked at me, like I was something worth looking at.

It made me uncomfortable.

"Why'd you decide to become a vet?" I asked hastily, changing the subject.

"Unbelievable," he uttered, barely a whisper. "You want to talk about me? After what I just found out about you?"

I leaned back against the counter, steadying my heartbeat. "Don't dim your success on my account."

"You're an author, Astra. Not some unknown wannabe. You're the real deal." He raked long fingers through his hair. "Your name is world renowned, and you want to talk about *my* accomplishments?"

Not my name, I wanted to say. But instead I responded, "I do."

"Can I at least ask why you work in a coffee shop?" Those soft eyes slackened. "Just answer that and you can pick my brain as much as you'd like."

Hm. Fair trade. "The owner, Ruby," I pointed to the back, "she picked me up off the ground when I was in a tough spot. Gave me a safe haven, so to speak. I don't need the money, but she needs the help. I'd never deny her that when she's done so much for me."

His mouth opened but Ruby banged the wall behind me and yelled, "Aren't you just a soft bag of sugar!"

I resisted the urge to throw a nasty comeback, only knocking on the door in response. That meant a tender 'fuck you' in pleasantries.

Dr. Praigale was right in saying, "So you two are close."

I nodded in agreement. "It's my turn to ask the questions."

Meeting Dr. Praigale *Marie-France Leger*

He leaned back, aligning his ankle with the edge of his knee, and lifted a hand. "Go ahead."

"You said you don't live in this area," I began, fiddling with the string of my waist apron. "How'd you end up here?"

"Ah." He exhaled, his body tensing.

I knew all too well what that meant. Hell, if I had a dime for each time I avoided that motion when asked about Malcom I'd be a trillionaire.

"Don't answer if it's something personal –"

"No, it's fine. My –" he paused. "My ex-girlfriend lives just up the road. We split up, so, I was walking back from uh, *that*."

Oh.

"Right, that's..." My lips were tight attempting to form the words.

"Personal?" he quipped, wearing a tired smile.

"Sad," I managed. "Really, sad, I'm sorry."

His shoulders sunk. "What's worse is that I'm at a coffee shop near midnight talking to a girl I barely know about my failed relationship." He let out a strained laugh. "Pathetic, if I'm being honest."

I willed my feet to move past the counter, and pulled up a chair across him under the neon OPEN sign. I unplugged it. "Well, they don't teach you how to cope with breakups in vet school, do they?"

He snorted at my piss poor attempt at a joke. It lifted my spirits. I hoped it did the same for him.

"No, they do not," he chuckled, shaking his head. "I'd be a lot wiser if they had."

"Do dogs often get broken up with? Or cats?"

"You'd be surprised how many lowly singles exist in the animal kingdom."

"Poor things," I teased, looking out the window to a barren street.

"You know," he started, "I've been around this area for two years and we never crossed paths. It's strange, seeing you now after just seeing you."

"Must be fate," I supplied, acting as unbothered as I *wanted* to feel.

"Must be," he added softly.

My eyes caught on a night walker strolling underneath the shop awnings with his dog. "What breed is that?"

He narrowed his eyes, following the direction of my finger. "A Border Collie, I think. Why do you ask?"

"Just wanted to test your knowledge."

He let out a laugh. "That's one way to do it."

"It's just an admirable thing," I turned to him, lacing my fingers together. "Being a vet and all, saving animals."

"You do too, you know." He worked a hand against his jaw, rubbing the stubble that lined his cheeks. "Save lives."

"Yeah, okay. How do you figure?"

"Words are powerful."

Meeting Dr. Praigale *Marie-France Leger*

I opened my mouth to argue but he held up a hand, halting my intrusion. "Have you ever read *The Book Thief*? It's by –"

"Markus Zusak, I've read it." I tilted my head, mildly shocked yet fully invested.

"Don't look at me like that," he grinned.

"Like what?"

"Like you're surprised I can read a book."

"Whoa, I'm not being accusatory," I countered, "just didn't realize reading was a hobby of yours."

"I try to find the time." He adjusted the silver watch on his wrist. "But like I was saying, they burned books because it contained knowledge of the outside world, alternative views and all that." His knuckles tapped the table as he said, "Words are power, Astra. You do more than you think you do."

I kept silent, pondering the 'what ifs' had I chosen not to write under a pseudonym. Would I have received letters from my readers? Direct messages detailing how I changed their lives through my words? If I'd just published under my name... if I hadn't deleted my socials after the accident, there was a good chance that I could interact with the people who silently supported me, the ones who killed to know M.D. Pont, not just by title, but by person, too.

"Maybe you're right." I whispered.

A tingle rushed through my body, the sense of someone looking at you when you're looking away. A feeling I often described in my books, yet never

Meeting Dr. Praigale — *Marie-France Leger*

truly experienced. Not until now, when my eyes met his, *his*, that were on mine, teeming with awe.

"Are you happy it's over? The relationship?" I asked, aligning all the jams neatly in their holding tray. I don't know what came over me, the urge to ask something so private, but in that moment... all I wanted was the truth. "It's not my business, I'm just – "

"Yes."

That was it.

One word – sure and serious – that told me everything, summarized all of it, without having to ask why.

"Muffins are ready!" Ruby announced, crashing through the door holding a tray of Cloud's special delicacy. "Hot and pipin' for you, sir."

No matter how hard I willed my body to move, something kept me planted in place. From the corner of my eye, I could see that Dr. Praig – *Noah* – hadn't made an effort to rise either.

After what felt like eternity, I decided to get up, snagged the wrapped muffin in Ruby's hand, and clicked open the register. "That'll be four-fifty, please."

His movements were languid, slow, or maybe that was my imagination when he reached the counter and slid a twenty-dollar bill my way. "Keep the change, Astra."

Meeting Dr. Praigale *Marie-France Leger*

The sound of my name on his lips paralyzed me. For some inexplicable reason... it felt different now.

When I finally glanced up, he was already walking away, sliding his chair back into place before exiting the shop.

"What about the caffeine?" I called out, eager to hear his voice once more. I couldn't say why... I just...

Just once more.

With that he turned around, pushing his weight against the open glass door, and smiled. "I got my fix."

Chapter Eight
Astra

Last Edit - 2:02am: No Title
Wherever Taylan went, the thought of their past followed her. He wasn't around anymore, but ~~his hands still lingered on her skin; the breath of his poisonous whispers like smoke to a fire.~~ Nothing could extinguish it – the haunting, the hurt. She locked herself up. Closed herself in. No one could penetrate it. No one but him. **[REVISE REVISE REVISE]**

I slammed my laptop shut, fully aware that taking my aggression out on an inanimate object did nothing for me or Taylan's happiness.

My eyelids felt heavy, but there was no remedy in the world that could put me to bed. Too many thoughts, too many dreams... all vivid, pained memories that wouldn't shut up. *They never shut up.*

The shittiest part was I thought real progress was being made. It'd been almost two weeks since I last saw Dr. Praigale at Cloud, and between those days and nights of creating fake scenarios, I referenced our very real one. The conversation that felt deeper than it was, because I wanted it to be.

That's the thing about imagination. You fall in love with what makes your heart swell, and ignore the fact that swelling almost always starts with a sting.

Meeting Dr. Praigale *Marie-France Leger*

We didn't know each other. There was no real connection between us, there couldn't be. I was being realistic about it all. Speaking to someone twice didn't mean anything. Which is why even though there may have been a moment of vulnerability, mostly on his end, there would never be on mine.

It was that mentality that kept me protected from pain since Malcom died. If no one could know you, no one could hurt you.

There was only one other time, five months after Malcom's accident, that I tried my luck with another man. Beth and I had gone out to a bar in Montreal, a girls' trip to celebrate the release of my first book, when I met Liam Drudard.

Tall and lean, a hockey player with that typical boyish charm and light blue eyes to match... I couldn't help but romanticize him on the spot. Really, sad little me thought this could be my ticket out of depression. Because where I had written a stellar debut novel, every single part of me was crumbling.

One thing life taught me was that presenting success as happiness was a recipe for disaster. Those who swim in a tub full of fame often forget the murky waters they tread to get there.

I never forgot.

I knew how much agony I felt writing that first book, bleeding between those pages and pouring my everything to escape the city of Woodstock. Even

Meeting Dr. Praigale *Marie-France Leger*

if I did only move thirty minutes away, a patch of distance still separated me from *him.*

Charming Liam Drudard was a good distraction for that weekend getaway. He kissed me in back alleys, tore through a rave crowd just to hold my hand, and treated me to a fancy dinner before my final night.

That fucking final night.

I closed my eyes, allowing my nails to stab the crevices of my palm.

Everything about that night hurt.

The way he poured shot after shot of tequila down my throat. Fuck, it burned. It burned so badly and I couldn't stop him from doing it because my awareness was all fucked and then he was naked – and I was naked – and he was inside me, pulling my hair and biting my breasts – BITING – my skin over and over and over.

And over.

I wanted it to be over.

I wanted it to end.

I told him to stop and he wouldn't stop. *Why wouldn't he fucking stop?*

I felt the tears but I wanted to feel everything again. Slowly, I lifted the head of my laptop screen and began to type.

This is good, I told myself. *Let it out, Astra. This is what you do.*

The next day I woke up to his dick pushing me open. He didn't ask. He didn't care. He just shoved it inside me like I was a ragdoll, like I was a plaything, like I was -

Malcom's punching bag.

At that point, I let him. I let him do it to me because I knew after him, well...

There was no after him.

There'd be no anyone.

Beth was staying at his friend's house. She didn't know what was going on.

I tried to assign blame to anyone but me, but it was no use. I'd willingly went with him. I'd willingly kissed him. Was I not complacent in this abuse? Or Malcom's?

I couldn't see that *I* was the victim. That *they* were at fault. Apparently his friend was a good guy. But like always, I never attracted the ones who'd treat me best.

I attracted the ones who wanted to control me.

When Liam was done, he slapped my ass and walked naked to the hotel bathroom. Everything was spinning. Not because I was hungover, I never got those. It was him.

His violation.

My silent cries for help.

I don't think it went unnoticed.

He just didn't care.

The double bed was pushed against the wall closest to the toilet.

I heard him shit. Burp. Then vomit in the same fucking toilet he just defecated in.

That was the same charismatic boy who held my hand over pasta and wine, who asked for permission before kissing me two nights prior.

He didn't ask for anything when he fucked me raw.

Or when he left puck-sized hickeys all over my chest that couldn't be concealed with makeup. He made sure of that.

When he emerged from that bathroom I was huddled in the corner, a sheet draped over my body to hide his work. I'm sure he was pleased with it. I didn't want to give him the satisfaction of seeing his art.

Because that wasn't art. That was sadism.

"Don't I at least get a hug?" he smirked, extending a hand.

I threw my best daggered stare under weak lids, and pointed to the door. "Go."

And he did, leaving without a scratch on his skin.

Me, I was scarred from heart to heart; the one Malcom had, and the one I just gave away.

I heard once that your heart only has three lives.

I was down to one.

And I needed that final life to breathe.

No one would be stealing that from me again.

Meeting Dr. Praigale *Marie-France Leger*

Last Edit – 2:47am: No Title
"My last heart belonged to me."

***

"Any pages?" Teresa asked, slurping her coffee over the FaceTime call.

"They should be in your inbox already," I yawned, finishing off the Red Bull from last night. It was warm, but still did the job to keep me awake. *As did the other two.*

"Shoot, must've missed it. Let me see here." She clicked her tongue as she leaned towards the phone, looking at what I could only assume was her email. "Got it!"

My eyes threatened to close, the sleep battling its way through my sanity, through Teresa's gasps as she praised, "Forty-three pages, Astra? In one night, you wrote forty-three pages?"

I nodded, blocking the tiredness before it came out. "Couldn't sleep."

"This is phenomenal work. I can't wait to sink my teeth into this story." She turned her attention to me. "So, you're back on track for writing?"

"It would seem so," I rubbed my eyes, "but I'm having a hard time finding ways out of the rut."

"What's been helping?"

Dr. Praigale.

The words almost came out. Almost.

Meeting Dr. Praigale — *Marie-France Leger*

I didn't want Teresa to know the ins and outs of my creative process. Where we were close – as close as an agent/writer relationship could be – it was still my personal life. My privacy. I wanted to keep this particular muse locked in my brain, and have him stored away from the contamination of this life.

Even though he was real, the story I'd been crafting around him was not. I wouldn't forget that. *Couldn't* forget that.

"These," I held up the energy drink, "and tons of coffee."

"Well, it's a good thing you live above a café. Keep doing what you're doing." She poked the screen, an indication that she was about to hang up, and after her swift goodbye I practically skipped to my bed in joy.

"Astra!" Ruby banged at my door, halting me mid-step.

With a groan, I called out, "Can this wait?"

"Not a chance, Starburst!"

I rolled my eyes, yawning as I let her in. She stood with a smile, holding out a package to me. "Delivery."

"I didn't order anything."

"Don't matter." She was already walking away with a wave, leaving me to my isolation, holding this crumpled, brown mailer.

I kicked the door shut with my foot, staring at the package. The only print it held was my name in bold, black letters: **ASTRA.**

Meeting Dr. Praigale *Marie-France Leger*

"Weird." I stared, then ripped it open.

A small card fell out before I could catch it, and floated to the floor. I ignored it though, because my fingers found the edges of a worn book, a familiar book, one that I'd just spoken about recently with –

"*Dr. Praigale...*" I whispered, running my hand over a copy of *The Book Thief*.

My heart hammered in my chest as I bent down to retrieve the note. It was one of Cloud Café's business cards, and on the back it read:

In case you forget that words are power.
- Noah Praigale

***

My phone rang, jolting me out of sleep. The clock read: 11:09 a.m., while my screen flashed the name: **BETH**.

"Hello?" I released, groggy and disoriented.

"You aren't working?" Her voice was chipper as always.

"It's my day off."

"That's great news because... We're going to a comedy show tonight!"

I threw the blankets over my head and retreated further into the fluffy darkness. "And that's great news for who?"

She scoffed. "For us, Grumps. I'll pick you up at eight?"

The 'no' was right there, right on the tip of my tongue. I had deadlines. This book wasn't going to write itself and I sure as shit didn't have the motivation to laugh.

"Stand-up comedy is never funny, Beth," I grumbled, suppressing another yawn. *Jesus Christ.* "Why don't you take Alan?"

"He's away on business."

I snickered. "Very mature of him."

"Easy," she warned. "He's really excited about this new marketing job."

"I would be too if I was flying out of Woodstock every other week to California."

"Right? Now," she barked, "you, me, Casamigos, and Durk Dillon at Tav's Tavern tonight."

"Tav's Tavern?" I flung the covers over my face. "Why there?"

"That's where Durk's performing," she slowed her next words. "Why? Is something wrong?"

I nodded a 'yes', even though I replied, "No."

Mom's recent date was at Tav's Tavern, or the guy she went out with was a bartender there or something. I couldn't remember, but I never usually recounted the men she kept on rotation.

She asked me if I'd ever heard about that place, and until today I never had, but as my mother mentioned, she and this Rourke man really hit it off. They were still going strong, even after two weeks.

Meeting Dr. Praigale *Marie-France Leger*

There was something to be said about Susan DuPont keeping a man around longer than her spinach containers took to rot.

Maybe it was morbid curiosity that got the best of me, or just my neglected inner child trying to weasel my way into Mom's business that made me say, "Eight is great. See you then."

I hung up and curled to my left, eyes adjusting to the chaos of my room. At the edge of my nightstand was Dr. Praigale's copy of *The Book Thief*, staring at me in the face.

I half imagined it to be a dream, one I didn't have to address if it was a figment of my imagination. But as I reached out to touch it, to hold it, the reality crashed onto me like a tsunami.

He thought of me.

He handed this package to Ruby.

He thought of me.

He gave me this book.

He thought of me.

And as I switched on my lamp and began to re-read the start of the story, eyes flitting over words and words and words... they seemed to scream out at me.

They seemed to say: "Power."

Chapter Nine
Noah

"Beanie dropped the ball," McLean said, tossing a shredded paper in the trash bin.

"The adoption assistant?" I asked, halting my signature. "Didn't she just start work a week ago?"

He took a bite of his apple. "Yep. Turns out she's allergic to cats. Go figure."

"Allergic to cats? She applied to be a part-time playmate for animals..." I shook my head, "and she's allergic to cats?"

"Uh-huh."

I dropped my pen. "She just found this out now? Why did she even apply? We could have found someone else. Tina's swamped, she doesn't have the time to -"

"I know, Big Bone, trust me."

I exhaled, pinching the bridge of my nose. Would I consider myself a high-stress man? Absolutely not. But when it came to my clinic, to running the business my father passed down to me, nothing could go wrong.

I wouldn't allow it.

"People are itching to work at this place. We'll find a hire." McLean tapped my shoulder and set off to exam room one, closing the door behind him.

Meeting Dr. Praigale *Marie-France Leger*

I checked my watch to see how much time I had left of lunch. Twelve minutes. Vern walked past the break room and I waved her in. "Do you have a second?"

She waddled in, tucking a clipboard under her arm. "I do, how can I help?"

"Corrigan Beanie, the playmate we hired for the adoption agency, she quit this morning." I dabbed the side of my mouth with a napkin and closed my Tupperware container. "Can you comb through the application forms again and see if we can get some interviews going?"

"On it, Noah."

As she took her leave, I called out, "No more 'Dr. Praigale'?"

"I learn from my mistakes!" she laughed, turning down the hall.

"Okay. We're okay." I muttered to myself, collecting my items.

There was no room for error at M & N's Vet Clinic. Not when the M was plastered in shiny bold letters, reminding me that this establishment still belonged to my father, and I was second in command.

***

I thought about her.

I really did.

I was naïve to think those thoughts would magically go away, but when my wandering eyes kept

Meeting Dr. Praigale *Marie-France Leger*

trailing towards my bookshelf, hovering over my dated copy of *The Book Thief*, I bit the bullet and wrapped it up.

The owner of Cloud Café, Ruby Hutchinson, was more than welcoming when I asked her to give it to Astra. In fact, she directed me to her loft just up the stairs.

At the time I thought it to be too forward, so I settled for the next best thing. But there were moments in the day, pockets of time at night, where I replayed the conversation we had at that coffee shop.

I'd never believed in coincidences. From a young age, my father taught me that plotting my own path was the gateway to a successful future. If I grabbed life by its reins, I would reap the rewards.

"Everything happens for a reason, son. Make no mistake of that." Dad's words left a wound at my side, as he recited that mantra the day he cheated on my mother.

I didn't know his reasons then, nor do I know them now. But this - running into Astra DuPont - left me questioning.

I didn't even have time to process what happened with Annika, to engage in *anything* with *anybody* after we parted ways. And yet I found myself wanting to stay, even after that fresh muffin was in my hand, and I had one foot out the door...

I wanted to stay.

A few times I drove home, my eyes drifting towards the two-lane highway that would lead to

Meeting Dr. Praigale *Marie-France Leger*

Stratford. I imagined walking up to Cloud Café, seeing her gentle smile behind the counter, and eventually saying hello. There was no point in holding out hope that she'd come to the clinic again. Susan already confirmed she'd be bringing in Snowball herself.

And Astra didn't seem to mind.

I was ashamed to admit that disappointed me. It was no one's fault but my own, to have assumed Snowball was more Astra's dog than Susan's when her mother had been a client of mine for years.

And yet, I'd never met Astra. Not once.

Never did she bring Snowball in with her mother.

Never did I see her walking about Stratford when I was in the area with Annika.

Not. One. Time.

And now, just as the saying goes, once you see a yellow car, it's all you see.

A growing awareness told me she was my yellow car.

She had to be.

A chance encounter, it might have been, but it was still rather disorienting.

Shaking *her* from my thoughts, I shuffled through my keys, selecting the one for my apartment door. There, I found Tav leaning against it.

"Hello, hello," he smirked, pulling me in for a rough hug. "Been some time, man."

"A month isn't that long, excuse me." I nudged him away from the lock. "Come in."

"You're always working, partner. I never see you, you never see me, it hurts," he covered his heart, "it really hurts."

I closed the door with my shoulder. "What's with the surprise visit?"

"Besides the fact I wanted to see you?" he asked, collapsing on the sofa.

"Besides that."

"Must I need a reason?"

I crossed my arms. "Do you have one?"

He stared at me for a moment before swiping one of my textbooks from the coffee table. "How d'you read this shit, man?"

"It's my job."

"It's a snooze-fest."

My cell vibrated in my pocket but I refused to check the caller. I could've guessed who it was, and that conversation could wait. "Out with it Tav, what's the deal?"

With a flick of his wrist, he tossed the book aside and stood up, smoothing out his faded Metallica tee. "There's a show at the Tavern tonight. McLean said he's down to come, and I'd be *overjoyed* if you could make it."

"I'm not a fan of rock music, I told you that —"

"It's just an opener, Big Bone, not the whole act. It's a comedy show. Durk's huge in the States and

Meeting Dr. Praigale *Marie-France Leger*

he was passing through, so I hit him up and paid some good money for this appearance."

He didn't give me time to respond before he insisted, "Please, man. It's being televised, put on his special and everything. This could be a big break for me and big breaks, Big Bone, are what you're here for." The floorboard creaked as he took a step closer. "You support me. I support you. That's who we are."

Tav Miller was impossible to say no to. It physically hurt him to get rejected, and where that posed an issue in many avenues, he never quit. He never stopped. He worked his way to the top from nothing. That was admirable, and through thick and thin, he was a brother to me. And sometimes, a *bother*.

"Just say yes, you're killing me. I see those questioning eyes movin' back and forth." He pointed at my face. "I know that look."

I hardened my features. "And what about this look?"

He snapped his fingers. "That's the look that tells me I better get going before you change your mind?"

I gave him a sharp nod and he scrambled for the exit. "Eight sharp! Be there!"

When the door shut, I turned the lock, fortifying myself in the confines of my space. My phone felt heavy in my back pocket, the weight of a looming confrontation awaiting my response.

Meeting Dr. Praigale — *Marie-France Leger*

It was my father. I knew it was. Nothing could get swept under the rug when it came to his clinics, even with my best attempts at trying to fix the problems alone.

Not one hour or one minute. He'd know.

Checking my lock screen confirmed what I already inferred as I clicked the 'Call Back' option and heard his brusque greeting at the second ring. "Son?"

I released a breath. "Dad, you called."

"What's the update on the adoption assistant position?"

There it is. "I have Vern checking all the applications again. I'm certain we'll find someone by –"

"And why aren't you helping her?"

I took in a sharp breath, switching my phone from left ear to right. "We're all helping her."

"You left that part out. What did I say about withholding information?" A heavy silence followed.

"Missing information is a missing limb." I repeated the line that my father had drilled into me ever since I started vet school.

He scoffed. "It seems you've forgotten that."

I kept quiet.

"Fill the position by yesterday." And the line cut.

There were no goodbyes with Mitchell Praigale, just like there were no hellos. Affection wasn't a trait he possessed nor was it something I was accustomed to. If one day he ever decided to ask about my well-being, I'd get him drug tested.

    No one expected his kindness.

    Just his respect.

    My thumb clicked Vern's name, shelving the greeting upon immediate response. "We need candidates. Do we have any updates?"

    I felt my father's voice in my head, heard it in my diction, but I didn't excuse myself. If this was going to be my clinic, solutions needed to be found without his help.

    So while my third cup of coffee brewed, I placed my receptionist on speaker, and set the timer for seven-thirty sharp.

    That gave me roughly two hours to get some work done, to prove my value to the clinic, before I could *hopefully* have a laugh.

    And maybe something stronger.

Chapter Ten
Astra

Last Edit – 7:31pm: No Title

*There was something to be said about dreams. What did they mean? Were they trying to tell her something? If someone kept reappearing, did that imply they were meant to be in her life? Lately, Taylan's dreams were happy, solid. She wasn't afraid of her past, but afraid that it would mess up her future. That the dreamless girl's chance of happiness was tethered to someone <u>dead</u> and **gone**, and only one person held the key to her salvation.*

"Are you seriously writing ten minutes before we have to leave?" Beth demanded, pulling a shoestring through her belt loops.

I cocked a brow. "Are *you* seriously using laces to hold up your pants?"

"It's iconic."

"Debatable." I teased, shutting my laptop.

Beth's ensemble consisted of a flashy lime green tank with low-rise jeans. I guess it was trendy this time around, wearing pants that you could only style if you had a flat stomach. Couldn't be me. But it was definitely her.

"You look great, Beth."

Meeting Dr. Praigale — Marie-France Leger

"And you haven't changed out of your sweats."

I glanced down at my oversized Bruins crewneck and leisure pants. "What's wrong with my outfit?"

Her head fell slightly as she examined me head-to-toe. "You look like a hermit who hasn't seen daylight."

"I'm still not seeing the problem."

"Then fix your eyes, girl." She bent down, collecting loose dresses off the floor. "Tonight, you're going to take someone's breath away."

The itch to lift my screen prodded at my fingertips. I ignored the temptation and set it aside completely. "I'm not typically in the habit of killing people."

She giggled, then threw a black dress at my face. "Put this on."

I uncrumpled the fabric and laid it across my legs. It was a simple black halter with an open back – no designs – and an asymmetric hem. "Kind of plain, don't you think?"

She took out a silver dress, plastered in sequins. "What about this?"

"Why do you even own that?" I swallowed down a laugh. "That's a Dollarstore disco ball."

She gasped. "It's one of my favourite outfits."

"I'm sorry to hear that." She charged at me but I cowered behind the black dress in my hands. "Fine, fine! This'll do."

Meeting Dr. Praigale — *Marie-France Leger*

"Well it has to because we're leaving in five. GO!" She urged me to the bathroom, shooing me in. "Vamoose."

Inside, I surveyed the array of Beth's soaps and skincare and took the liberty of straightening them out. The first time we met had been in one of our online Zoom tutorials. We'd been paired for a creative writing project where we had to explore nature for one hour – no technology – and document our findings in thick description.

Besides Ruby, I never really had a good experience with anyone up until that point, especially friends. It wasn't that I was unpleasant or unapproachable, just misunderstood.

And damn anyone who tried to understand me.

When Beth and I were tasked to work together, the bond was almost instant. I'd heard people talking about soul ties, two halves of the same whole – the poetry bullshit – and called it a hoax. But there was no denying the safety I'd felt in her presence, the comfortability I hadn't found, well... ever.

Before Malcom, I was brittle.

After Malcom, I was ruined.

She accepted me as both and loved me all the same.

Even still, I kept her in the dark about certain things. It was impossible to trust anyone wholly. Even if I wanted to.

Because I wanted to before. I *had* before.

And look where it got me.

"Is this the new product?" I lifted one of Beth's creations for her soap company and sniffed. "Is that –" and sniffed again, "vanilla and pumpkin?"

She swiped it from my grasp. "Yes and it's in testing so paws off, girl."

"You can't tell me not to touch something if it's out in the open like that."

She rolled her eyes, wrapping the oval bar in parchment and sealing it in a drawer. "So you'd drink acid if it was just sitting there?"

I shrugged, sampling another soap. "Depends on the day."

"E-NOUGH." She poked my ribs, throwing a towel over her soap tray.

"Is business booming?" I chuckled, shimmying into the dress.

A growing smile stretched across her face. "It's booming so hard that shots are on me tonight."

"I'm not taking shots." I hiked up the fabric a little higher so it hit above mid knee and turned to her. "Do I look okay?"

Her eyes were on her phone, presumably rapid texting Alan. "Ravishing," she mused, quickly taking a glance at my attire. "A star in the sky, Astra."

The mirror reflected my lifeless complexion, the dull, dark waves tucked behind my ears and I sighed.

A star in the sky.

But I couldn't find my sparkle.

***

"It's so fucking loud in here!" I yelled, doubting she heard me in the dim lit space of Tav's Tavern.

What seemed like an amateur rock band was shredding on the small marble stage, wearing fishing hooks as clothing.

Fishing. Hooks.

Aside from the band providing entertainment, the place looked exactly how I pictured it: various iconic artists lining the exposed brick walls, an L-shaped bar in the corner and rows of stand up tables tucked behind a horde of cheering people.

Scratch that.

Cheering wildebeests.

My fingers latched onto Beth's wrist as I pulled her near. "This demographic is terrifying!"

"Hush!" she commanded, her eyes zipping to more spacious areas. There were practically none. "Let's see if we can sit near the bar!"

"That's the worst thing we can do!"

"Well, we're trying anyway!" Sharp nails dug into my skin as Beth dragged me near the back tables, searching aimlessly for a place to sit.

"What can I get for you ladies?" An enormous man asked, his whole frame occupying two barstools.

Meeting Dr. Praigale *Marie-France Leger*

"*Fucking hell*," I uttered under my breath, taking in the Texas Chainsaw Massacre in front of me, food-stained beard and all.

"Oh, do you work here?" pepped Beth, completely naïve to danger.

"Nope," he smiled, exposing yellowing teeth. "Just wonderin' what I can get for you two Bella-Bots."

Beth grimaced. "That's an odd thing to –"

"Move." I spat, shooting daggers at the Hulk. "I'm ordering a drink."

"I'll order one for ya, lass." He bumped the bar with his fist. "What d'you want?"

"To order my own drink, and I'd love some fucking space."

Beth grabbed my shoulder. "Astra –"

As if things couldn't get any worse, he let out a belch before inhaling his pint, then burped again. "Yous two strike me as a sugar n' spice type. Sugar n' spice and everything –"

"Enough, Chris." A booming voice overpowered the goliath. I didn't even think that was possible until I set my eyes on the bartender, all brick and muscle, shooing the creep away like a fly.

Beef chunks cursed under his breath, glaring at me with glossy, lemon-tinted eyes before disappearing into the crowd. The bartender waved us over, setting square menus atop the counter.

"Sorry about that," he apologized, slinging a towel over his shoulder. "Nights like these attract the crazy ones."

"He come here often?" I questioned, glancing over the list of cocktails and beer.

"Chris, yeah. He tries to be a regular but can't handle his liquor enough for anyone to remember his order." Bartender cleared a glass from the couple next to me. "It's different every time."

"Oo," Beth cooed, settling her freshly manicured fingers on a splayed napkin. "So you're a gossip?"

"No ma'am," he extended a hand, "I'm Rourke."

A bolt of electricity shot up my spine. "Rourke?"

He peeled his eyes away from Beth, clearly more interested in her ballerina charm, and looked my way. "Rolls off the tongue nice, eh?"

"It really does," Beth tried, propping her elbow on the bar – a sign she was flirting for free drinks. Kudos to her, honestly. By the way Rourke was checking her out, it was definitely working.

I ignored her attempts and pushed my menu aside. "Do you know Susan DuPont by any chance?"

Almost instantly, his cheeks reddened. The dark atmosphere couldn't even hide it. "Why?"

"Just wondering."

Meeting Dr. Praigale *Marie-France Leger*

"I went out with her a few times," he avoided eye contact as he dried a wine glass, "nothin' more than that."

"Huh," I huffed. "Interesting."

Mom had told me that they'd still been going strong, that this Rourke Flance man could potentially be the one. I don't know why I believed her.

I believed her every single time.

A part of me just wished she could settle happily. Mom's own mother was exactly like her, mind you, I never got the chance to meet dear-old granny before she kicked the fan. And despite the neglect and instability, I knew Mom just wanted to be loved.

At the end of the day, that's what all humans craved, regardless of the impossibility. For the first time in my life, I found myself sympathizing with her situation.

"Rourke!" A guy just as tall as the bartender called, dressed in a brown cow-hide vest and jeans. Rope bracelets covered both of his wrists, concealing whatever tattoos were stemming from his forearms.

"Gimme three old-fashions, per Durk's request. Hi Jill," he waved at one of the women sitting next to Beth, then turned his attention to her partner. "Cindy, how's the cat?"

I could barely hear anything beyond my radius, but managed to make out her response. "*Dr. Praigale's a wizard, stitched her right back up.*"

My entire body froze.

Meeting Dr. Praigale

"Make sure to tell him that," mystery cowboy chuckled. "He might unstitch your cat again if you call him Doc."

"Noah's quite the character," the girl, *Cindy*, added.

"I'll take that as a compliment." A voice sounded from behind me.

That voice.

His voice.

My muse.

I swallowed hard, gripping the menu, refusing to turn around. *There's no way.* That couldn't be him.

"Ah!" Cowboy raised an arm, swatting Rourke's shoulder. "Right on cue, Big Bone!"

No -

No, no, no, no...

There was no fucking -

"What are we having tonight, Astra?" said Dr. Praigale.

Chapter Eleven
Noah

I wedged my body between Astra and the man next to me, leaning over the counter to square my shoulders. "Tight in here."

She stared at me, lips parted slightly, completely silent.

"We've got to stop meeting like this." The line came out smoothly, but I truly meant it. These coincidences were particularly unnerving.

"What –" she shook her head. "How?"

"I'm starting to wonder that myself."

"I'm just really fucking confused –" she placed a hand over her mouth – "sorry."

"For?" I held up a finger to call Tav's attention, then returned mine back to her.

"My potty mouth," she laughed. "Not very *author-esque* of me."

I stared at her in amusement. "I'm familiar with curse words, Miss DuPont."

"I don't doubt that," her cheeks reddened, "but I'm trying to cut back on my vulgarity."

"I'd say this situation calls for it," I teased. "Are you a fan of standup comedy?"

She shook her head. "Not particularly. My friend dragged me out of my cave."

Meeting Dr. Praigale   *Marie-France Leger*

I eyed Tav as he spun bottles of liquor, trying to impress a forming crowd. "We have that in common, it seems."

"What does your cave look like?" she asked.

"Bland, grey," I shrugged, "but quiet. I enjoy my alone time."

She smiled. "Sounds like your haven needs some colour."

I smiled back. "Maybe you could help me with that."

Her cheeks were flushed with colour. "I got your book," she cleared her throat. "Ruby gave it to me."

My grin was wide. "I know you've read it, but after our conversation I just thought..."

"It was a nice gesture, really. Thank you, um," she dipped her chin, "you didn't need to that."

"I wanted to."

Astra turned away shyly, glancing around the bar. "I've never been here before. *Very* different to Cloud Café."

"Tav's sort of a Metalhead. Loves all things rock n' roll."

"And you don't, clearly." Her eyes roamed up and down my body, taking in the navy sweater and light jeans I wore. "You're classy," she added.

A laugh burst from my throat. "Classy?"

"Classy."

I moved closer. "So we've got Mr. Classy and Ms. Vulgar, a match made in heaven."

She blushed, crossing her heart. "I promise not to swear again."

"Why? Are you afraid to cuss in front of me?"

"Cautious," she supplied, her shoulders easing back. "You're just super professional and well-natured. A true doctor."

I bit my tongue. "I'm still a person."

"Yeah I know, but –"

Tav approached, interrupting the conversation, and slid a glass of brown liquid my way. "Surprised you're drinkin' tonight, Big Bone."

I glanced at Astra. "I'm just really *fucking* tired."

She smirked and shook her head, the corner of her lips tugging up. I liked that.

Tav ran his fingers through his thick curls. "Be tired every damn weekend, you're startin' to bore me."

"What's this?" I took a quick whiff before pushing the glass to Astra. "Whisky?"

"Tav's Tranq, I call it." His chest raised in pride. "Got a whole blend of shit in there."

My hand instinctively grabbed the medley of poison from Astra's, our fingers brushing together before I secured it in my palm. "Absolutely not."

She cocked a brow. "Think I can't handle it?"

Those brown eyes twinkled with amusement, the creases of her smile lines deepening with her taunt.

I physically could not contain my breath. "I'm not doubting you."

She swiped back the drink. "Then give it here."

The blonde behind Astra perched her head in the crook of her neck. "Can I have a sip?"

"I'll get you something, sweetheart." Tav addressed, sliding another glass of his *special* drink my way before engaging with Rourke.

"I'm Beth!" The blonde kept her chin on Astra's shoulder, coiling a hand around her body to exchange greetings.

"Noah," I nodded, wiping my palm on my pants before meeting hers. "Condensation, my apologies."

"A man with manners," she drawled.

"Easy Beth," Astra said pointedly.

"So you're a doctor?" Beth asked me.

My smile hurt. "Not tonight I'm not."

That was my cue to turn back to the bar. I twirled the glass cylinder in my hand, taking a full swig of liquor.

It never got easy, the burn of spirits going down my throat. I wasn't much of a drinker, only the occasional beer or two at dinners or celebrations.

My sister, Bridget, had checked into rehab a few years prior due to her alcoholism. It was a case of bad friends, bad company, and they pressured her to experiment with all kinds of nasty stuff that fried her brain.

Meeting Dr. Praigale *Marie-France Leger*

Alcohol was the one that stuck.

And no matter how hard she tried, the people around her never did.

Regardless of Dad's protests, Mom and I sent her to rehab, per Bridge's request, and when she got released ninety days later, some of my sister's colour returned.

She still had cravings, which is why every activity since then I made sure to center around pure adrenaline. A fun detox outside the confinement of a rehabilitation center.

We went skydiving, tubing, whitewater rafting – the typical outdoorsy activities that I'd never normally engage in.

But I did.

And I loved it.

Because I loved my sister, and she started to love herself again.

When you see someone in your family struggling with an illness such as alcoholism, it changes your perception on everything and everyone.

I don't know when drinking became a mere requirement for social outings, that without booze in your hand you were deemed a social pariah.

Of course there was nothing wrong with indulging once in a while, but more often than not, people drank to distract themselves from *themselves*. Besides the physical and mental impairment it brought, there was bliss tethered to the central nervous system that made us function.

Meeting Dr. Praigale   *Marie-France Leger*

The numbing of pain.

Who wouldn't want that?

And as the liquor settled into my stomach, the desire for more danced across my tastebuds.

"How come you don't like it when people call you 'Dr. Praigale?'" Astra's voice drew me back to reality.

It would be easier to explain the anatomy of a Greyhound than discuss the aversion to my title.

"Like I said," taking another sip, "I'm ordinary underneath the scrubs. I'm still Noah."

"Well you once told me, *Noah*," she leaned in, "that just because I choose to play a character doesn't mean I'm not that same person in real life."

I chuckled lowly. "Did I really say that, M. D. Pont?"

"Shh, not too loud." She lifted her drink, clinking her glass against mine. "I'm undercover."

I watched her take a sip, perplexed and mesmerised all at the same time. This woman, an enigma in my brain, that fate couldn't shake away from me.

And the longer I was in her presence, the happier I became.

To that foreign feeling, I drank.

And to the art of forgetting, even for a moment, I downed the rest of Tav's Tranq.

Chapter Twelve
Astra

For the rest of the comedy show, Dr. Praigale and I didn't speak.

Not that we even had the chance to.

As it turned out, him and the owner of the bar, Tav Miller, were actually best friends. He escorted Noah – *Did I just say, Noah? I must be losing it.*

He escorted *Dr. Praigale* to some V.I.P section near the front of the stage, while Beth and I sat in the corner of the bar with Rourke and the rest of the crowd.

"Surely there's space for the girls?" I heard the doctor argue.

But Tav insisted that the closest vacant spots were reserved for Durk's team and photographers.

So that left us here, sitting like chewed up birds, underneath a poster of Elvis smoking a cigar.

"Great idea this was, Beth," I nudged her elbow. "I can barely see the show."

"It is a bit tough..." She swirled her head around, pinching Rourke who was just behind us lining shot glasses. "Any way we can sit on this bar?"

He shrugged, lifting a hand. "Be my guest, just don't hit the cups."

"Gotcha." Beth yanked me backwards and hoisted herself up onto the sticky counter. I followed suit, making sure to smooth down any creases in my outfit.

"This is his closing act," she murmured into my ear, tittering with joy. "Crowd work."

I only looked at her with shy envy. Beth was one of the very few people I decided to let into my life, which was shocking considering our differences.

I'd never wish for anyone to experience the life that brought me up, the circumstances that made me into who I am. When you relinquish control for so long and finally gain it back, you do everything in your power to hold on to it. Beth, well, she was so... *untouched* by the world and all its grievances.

She got excited about birds walking by her feet, munching on stray bread and pinecones. When it rained, she'd dance in the puddles like she was a mermaid refilling her life force.

I simply welcomed the downpour.

That sense of drowning was calming to me – the weight of nature, refreshing and cool, paralyzing my bones.

Beth was sunshine and butterflies.

It was good to have her around, to remind me that people like that still existed.

And as I spotted Dr. Praigale glancing my way, sporting a gentle smile paired with deep-set dimples, I began to think that maybe Beth wasn't the only sunshine to exist in this world.

Meeting Dr. Praigale *Marie-France Leger*

***

"How did you not laugh once, Astra?" Beth frowned as she called upon Rourke for another round of drinks. "Durk is literally the funniest person alive."

My shoulders lifted. "I hadn't noticed."

"Okay, well," she slid a freshly poured shot of tequila my way, "what's your idea of comedy?"

I thought back to Durk Dillon's crowd work, where he spotlighted a man wearing overalls and assumed his drink of choice was breast milk. "Definitely not farmer jokes."

"That was the worst jab of the show, he had better ones, I swear."

"Beth, I heard them all." I turned to my drink, squeezing lime into liquid. "I was sitting right next to you."

She took her shot ahead of me. "Maybe you just need more alcohol in you."

"Not a chance. I'm seeing stars."

"Funny, so am I," Dr. Praigale smirked, eyes planted on me as he approached the bar with Tav. "How did you like the performance?"

I placed a palm to my cheek, attempting to hide my flushed skin. "I wouldn't call it that."

"You didn't like it?" Tav interjected, shouldering Mr. Pringle. "I liked it," then turned to the doctor, "Big Bone liked it, too."

Goddamn *Noah* smiled. "You're the odd one out it seems."

The buzz shot straight to my head. "I'm perfectly okay with that, *Big Bone*. Lotta names for you."

He chuckled, taking the barstool next to me while Tav entertained Beth and Rourke.

"What other nicknames are there?" he asked.

I folded and refolded the napkin in my hand. "For one, you're Doctor Praigale, and then there's Noah, Mr. Classy and Mr. Pringle, then, um, Big Bone?"

A laugh, smooth as butter, escaped his throat. "*Mr. Pringle?*"

"Praigale, Pringle, all the same."

"Not quite, but I like it." His dimples indented his cheek, as prominent as that golden smile. "Stargirl and Mr. Pringle."

I pushed a lock of hair from my face, rubbing my temples to ease the forming headache. "Why do you call me that?"

"Call you what?" he sipped from his drink. "Stargirl?"

"Yep, that."

He shrugged. "Why do you call me Mr. Pringle?"

"Because it's funny."

"I agree."

"You're not answering me," I pushed, flicking his knee.

I froze, retreating my fingers. *Where the hell did that come from? What the hell, Astra?*

Meeting Dr. Praigale *Marie-France Leger*

His line of sight followed his leg, then my hand, and rested on my face. "Do that again."

"No." I frowned, though I felt a little lighter. "You avoid questions like the plague."

"The plague should be avoided. People died."

"A single question isn't going to kill you."

"Then let me ask one of my own, Astra," he turned to face me, "what's your story?"

I almost choked. "My story?"

He nodded and I laughed at the absurdity. "That's pretty vague, Doctor. Don't they teach you to be more specific in vet school?"

A hardness settled over his face. "Missing info's a missing limb."

Well, uh... "I wouldn't go that far."

People started to shuffle out of the bar while the set lights dimmed and the stage began to fold into the wall. A guitar clock hung from the ceiling that read: 11:56 p.m.

"Why not?" he questioned. "Why not take it that far?"

"Because that's so... medical." My ring finger circled the edge of my glass as I let my tipsy thoughts wander. "Sometimes saying nothing says it all."

"And do you do that? Keep quiet to avoid trouble?"

Something stirred inside my chest, a blooming confidence ready to erupt. "I'm not quiet now, am I?"

Meeting Dr. Praigale — Marie-France Leger

He smiled. "No." Then, he signaled for someone behind me. "Tav, is the roof still under construction?"

From the look on Dr. Praigale's face, he seemed content with the response. "Come on," he lifted out of his seat, placing a gentle hand on my arm, "I want to show you something."

And that's when the wasps came, swallowing my joy, encircling me with darkness.

I couldn't have it normal. I couldn't have it easy.

Everything in me screamed to stay put. I was wary, of course I was fucking wary to let a stranger lead me somewhere unknown.

I'd been there before.

And my skin still harboured indented handprints beneath it.

But looking at the vet – *Noah*, the kindness in his stature, allowed me to move an inch.

I watched as he collected a set of keys from Tav, whispering something to Beth that prompted her look of approval, and nudged his head to the wooden door near the phone booth.

Beth got out of her seat and pushed me forward. "I'll be fine with these guys, babe. Go on, he's nice."

How do you know? I wanted to scream. God, I felt like such a fucking idiot hesitating to go somewhere with someone who did nothing wrong, nothing to hurt me.

But this was how the world made me. How Malcom, and Liam, and every man who went through the revolving door of my life taught me to be. One of life's testy games to challenge my ability to trust.

"A shell ain't for livin', Starburst." Ruby had told me after I rejected one of the regulars at our café. He never came back again.

Taking in a few staggered breaths, I stepped towards the door. *One. Two. Three. One. Two. Three.*

Dr. Praigale had no idea what kind of downwards spiral was happening in my mind right now. I didn't want him to know.

He didn't deserve to be pulled into the eddies of despair.

"Where are we going?" I swallowed, my voice softer now to control my breathing.

But his answer didn't come, not right away. He stared at me for a few moments, as if assessing my entire demeanour. His lips pressed into a thin line as he shook his head, cupping my shoulders, and steering me back around. "Absolutely nowhere."

In a daze, I watched him return Tav's keys, patting Beth on the back quickly and nodding at her response. Now, her expression held nothing but solemn understanding.

I seemed to be the only one left in the dark.

He eventually made his way to my side, leading me to a tucked away table near the billiard set and sat down.

Meeting Dr. Praigale   *Marie-France Leger*

"Dr. Praigale?" I inwardly panicked. "What... What was that about?"

He lifted two pool cues off the wall and handed me the shortest stick. "We're going to play a round."

"But the roof –"

"You don't know me, Astra," he replied, shaping his cue tip. "And until you do, we won't be going anywhere alone."

Every single word died in my throat.

Did he...

Did he know?

Did he see me struggling?

Was I that obvious?

Instead of explaining, I felt the need to ask for pardon, to express regret and guilt and shame. "I'm really sorry, it's just –"

He waved a hand, making his way around the table. "You've got nothing to apologize for, love."

Love.

A well of emotions pulsed through my veins, homely and overpowering.

Love, the sentiment I wrote about in books, an intense emotion scattered between hundreds of pages but rarely ever announced.

And Dr. Praigale used it.

Used it... to address *me*.

"Now if you're up for it," he tapped the red-velvet billiard table, "how about we get to know each other over solids and stripes?"

Chapter Thirteen
Noah

She was nervous.

Anyone with eyes could tell.

It pained me to believe she was unable to walk a rooftop terrace with someone in privacy. That something, or *someone*, affected her so badly that she simply couldn't.

Nonetheless, I wasn't about to put her in a situation where she felt uncomfortable, let alone frightened.

Whatever happened to her... *whoever* did that to her... they deserved endless misfortune.

"Shall I break, or do you want to?" I offered, removing the triangular rack from the table.

"Go ahead." Her voice was slightly guarded, but I understood. Who knows what she went through, what feelings resurfaced at the thought of seclusion.

Protectiveness was engrained in me. Caring for my family, my animals, my staff – that was second nature. Maybe it extended to her. And maybe that's why I let that one word slip.

Love.
I'd called Astra 'love.'
A girl who was not mine.
A girl I barely knew.
And yet –
It snuck past my lips like fresh air.

Meeting Dr. Praigale — Marie-France Leger

That was wholly unexpected– a puzzle I'd figure out later, but for now, I would get to know this woman simply because I could.

And most of all, because I wanted to.

Leaning over the pool table, I steadied my aim and hit the cue ball to break formation, sinking two stripes: a twelve and a ten.

"You're solids," I told her, scouting for my next target. Number thirteen was in my sights, and I missed by a fraction of an inch. "*Shit.*"

"Were we not just talking about vulgarity?" She swatted my pool stick gently before positioning herself to my left.

"You were" – I thumbed my chest – "this guy made no promises."

She chuckled warmly and relaxed into position, sinking number one in a clean hit.

"Beginners luck," I joked, taking a sip of beer. "You'll miss this."

"And here I was thinking you'd cheer me on."

The corner of my lips tugged into a smile. "What gave you that impression?"

She shrugged, missing her original shot but landing a seven. "You seem to be the town's favourite."

"Which town?"

"This one." Her third attempt was a scratch. "Crap."

"Good word," I winked.

She shrugged. "Told you I'm trying to change."

My gaze drifted to the eleven, almost impossible to sink without hitting her five but I welcomed the challenge.

"So how am I the town's favourite?" I asked, watching her from the corner of my eye.

What a mistake that was. I completely fumbled my chance, missing the striped ball entirely. *Damn distraction.*

She cleared her throat. "I overheard some woman talking about how you stitched up her cat or something?"

Most likely Cindy Cumberbatch. Her Siamese had a bladder stone. "Well, it is my job."

"You could brag you know," said Astra, surveying the pool table for her next move. "Your name is certainly praised."

I snorted in amusement, countering her compliment. "Yours could be too if you decided to use it."

She kept quiet, sniping the five into the middle pocket. I had yet to determine if her silence was due to my comment or concentration, but in my best efforts, I scrambled to keep the peace.

"What's your favourite colour, Astra?"

She cocked a brow. "Seriously?" Then sank number two. "Blue."

Conveniently, the colour of the ball she just hit. It sent a warm feeling to my stomach, diluting the concoction of alcohol nesting within.

"Problem?" I asked.

She scuffed her next shot. "That's just such a typical question."

"We're getting to know each other, aren't we?"

"Sure." Her back rested against the brick wall, head tilted to the side. "Why?"

I sharpened the point of my cue. "Why what?"

"Why do you want to get to know me?"

"Why not?"

"See, that right there doesn't help." A full laugh escaped her lips. "You answer my questions with questions."

I noted the glossy change in her eyes, even in the dim lighting. "And you don't answer mine at all, so it looks like we've hit an impasse."

She watched me for a moment, pursing her lips before saying, "Have you heard from your ex-girlfriend?"

The beer nearly tumbled from my hand. "Straight to the deep end, okay."

Astra crossed her arms, setting the stick aside carelessly. "This is how I get to know people," she started, flicking a finger back and forth. "I don't care about icebreakers or favourite foods and colours –

Meeting Dr. Praigale *Marie-France Leger*

that stuff changes every day. The real shit, like exes and mistakes... you can't undo those things."

Looking at her now, I knew she'd crossed the line between sobriety and inebriation. A pained expression stamped her face, flashing away in an instant.

"Maybe that's why I'm hard to get to know," she whispered inwardly. "People don't see things the way I do."

Something told me she regretted her words, but I responded all the same. "Then hand me the binoculars."

"What?" she laughed.

"Hand me the binoculars, let me see it your way."

She took a moment to respond, her gaze heavy on mine. "I don't have any."

"Then how do you expect anyone to understand you?" I moved towards her, closing the distance between us until we were a mere few feet away. "To see things your way?"

Her fingers found the chain of her necklace, toying with a beaded, golden strand. "It's easier to keep people at a distance."

"You really believe that?"

"How do you not?"

"You could be missing out on good things." *Good people*, I thought.

"Oh, Dr. Praigale..." she snorted sardonically, "I'd much rather someone misjudge me, hate me and leave, than open up and have them walk out anyway."

I sucked in a breath, staring at this girl who unwittingly handed me the crumbs to her past.

Who was Astra Meredith DuPont?

One thing was unmistakeably so, she had quite the story.

And it involved a lot of hurt.

Distant chatter faded into the background as the ambiance shifted. Hanging, overhead bulbs melted to a pale orange and cherry red.

My attention turned back to her. "My ex and I don't talk," I disclosed, allowing Astra through the cracks of my foundation. *I'd earn her trust. If that's what it took.* "We haven't since that night at Cloud Café."

She exhaled, her shoulders slackening. "Do you miss her?"

"Like I said before, I'm happy it's over."

"That's not really an answer," she contended. "Some people may not be right for you, but it doesn't mean you're above missing them."

I pushed my tongue against the inside of my cheek, pondering her logic. In a sense, she was right. The way my father raised me was to see things in endings and beginnings, no in between. A grey area did not exist in contrast to black and white. When things concluded, there was no sense in revisiting

Meeting Dr. Praigale *Marie-France Leger*

them. No, that was unnecessary, according to Mitchell Praigale.

However, that never applied to Annika. Because in his eyes, she was my match.

A vet, like his son.

Graduated with highest honours, like his son.

Earned good money, like his son.

But unfaithful...

Unfaithful, like *him*.

"I don't really miss her, Astra." That was all truth. "The relationship ran its course."

"How do things just..." Her gaze found the floor. "End?"

I stood up straighter. "What do you mean?"

"How do you know when it's time to walk away?"

"I think –" A million thoughts crossed my mind as I searched for the right words to say. "Sometimes feelings fade and life starts to pull you further apart rather than closer together."

"But do you not work on it? Or at least try to keep the love alive?"

"Love can't die, Astra. And if it does, then it never lived."

A stretch of silence filled the gaps between our bodies, allowing shallow, slight breaths to drift on by. The words I released hovered in the air, words I never expected to say, but believed all the same.

I only loved Annika in the way she loved me.

Meeting Dr. Praigale   *Marie-France Leger*

And maybe, that was not love at all.

"Do you always get this deep with your clients, Dr. Praigale?" Astra teased, wearing a tight smile.

My jaw twitched, a growing ache reminding me of the responsibilities that awaited me once I left this atmosphere and the depth of her company. "You're no ordinary client, Astra."

She stood up, shaking away the knots in her shoulders, and snagged her pool cue from the wall. "Then what am I?"

I opened my mouth to say something, to formulate the words I'd been feeling this whole night, when Tav called from behind the bar. "Closing in ten, Big Bone! Finish up the game!"

Beth was leaning on Rourke, clearly out for the night. Tav slid over a glass of water her way, shooting me a thumbs up.

My eyes fell on Astra, any words I could have said receding back into its box. "Right now, Stargirl, you're toast."

She nodded with a faint look of disappointment, and followed me to the pool table.

This wasn't the way I wanted to communicate with her; in the presence of drinks and strangers shuffling in and out of barstools.

Whatever this emotion was, it could wait. And glancing at her now, ruminating in the feeling of forgetting, I knew I'd be patient.

Meeting Dr. Praigale *Marie-France Leger*

"Here's an idea," I proposed, lifting the beer to my lips and finishing off its contents. "Whoever sinks the eight ball buys dinner next Friday."

Confidence thrummed through my veins at the sight of her lighting up, a shy look-away, and her gentle laughter. "I'll make sure to avoid it, then."

Game on. "Me too," I lied, leaning over the table and lining up my cue.

My grandfather taught me to play pool before he passed away. To say I was a decent player was generous, but I knew a good outcome when I saw one.

And I was determined to score the prize of this game.

In one direct hit, my cue ball collided with the eight, sending it directly into the top left pocket. "Ah, looks like my hand slipped."

Astra covered her mouth with one hand, shaking her head. "Technically, you lost."

"No, love." I unlocked my phone, handing it to her for contact details. "I think I won."

Chapter Fourteen
Astra

Last Edit - 11:49pm: No Title
She didn't want to think about <u>him</u>. Someone good was coming, someone who seemed to care about her. It was in the air and Taylan could feel it, but she couldn't quite reach out to the tall, masculine figure with elegant brown hair and chestnut eyes. And the harder she tried, the more that apparition blurred, those eyes fading to an awful, mossy weed. She hated the colour green. It reminded her of ~~him.~~
[REVISE]

I woke in a startle, my breaths heavy and thick with dread.

Instinctively, I reached for my throat, curling around the pressure points that Malcom had grabbed in my dream – *my nightmare.*

Two years.

Two fucking years that felt like yesterday.

The damage he left behind planted thorns beneath my flesh, feasting on my psyche.

And for this reason alone, I needed to cancel my Friday night dinner plans with Dr. Noah Praigale.

People can't hurt you if you keep them out.

Meeting Dr. Praigale *Marie-France Leger*

I'd done some thinking that led me to this decision. Not some, but *all* my thinking trying to wrap my head around his proposition.

We were tipsy, for one. He wasn't in the right headspace. He couldn't have been. That's why he tanked the game on purpose.

On purpose, to buy our date.

I raised my knees to my chin, burying my face in the comfort of my arms.

God, what would he think of me? A grown woman who couldn't even commit to dinner. *One normal fucking dinner.*

Talk about ridiculous, idiotic, damn near immature but I would've rather been the disappointer than the disappointed.

And yet, for some inexplicable reason, he wanted to get to know me. He tried. I noticed. I didn't understand it. But I noticed.

Isn't that what I wanted? For someone to see me, and I mean, really see *me*?

The characters in my books jumped at the sight of affection... and I ran from it. How could I possibly write these romance novels, spew ballads and bullshit about love when it didn't exist to me?

I was a hypocrite. This was nonsense.

And I wouldn't change.

Falling was easy. Heartbreak was easier.

I'd never let myself get attached again. I couldn't. Dr. Praigale would have to stay my muse from afar, at least until I finished this book and said goodbye for good.

"Astra, he's stunning." Beth had gawked the entire walk home. "Not to mention he's totally infatuated."

The thought made me ill. "What did he say to you?" I'd asked.

"When?"

"When he leaned down?"

"Oh," her cheeks reddened. "He wanted to show you some greenhouse on the roof, I guess? But when he saw that you weren't about it, he changed his mind."

When he saw that you weren't about it.

If only he knew how much I wanted to go with him.

How badly I wanted to reach out and take his hand, to thank him for considering my hesitation.

But what would have happened then? Would he have used me as a rebound to forget his ex-girlfriend, the woman he claimed to feel nothing for?

Men promised a lot of things, knowing promises were the easiest to break.

"*Fuck*," I uttered, wanting to explain myself to someone – anyone – him, even, but there was only one person I knew would listen. One person who fully understood me.

Since my sister had her baby over a year ago, she rarely got any rest. Her sleep schedule was so messed up that I figured she'd be awake. When she

Meeting Dr. Praigale *Marie-France Leger*

answered my call on the second ring, it proved me right.

"Can't sleep?" Eva's voice was tired, but that was the new normal. On the rare nights we did talk, it was always between the hours of one and three.

"I tried but, you know me."

The distant patter of footsteps sounded through the line. "I just moved to the couch so I don't wake Ty and Becks. What's eating at you, sis?"

Even though Eva was three years younger than me, having a child really yanked out her maturity. She stayed in and read books – books I'd recommend to her – and bounced between remote jobs while supporting her child... and Mom.

Same category, I suppose.

"How is she? And Ty?"

"They're good," she yawned. "Becks took her first steps the other –"

"Mom told me," I interjected, smiling at the thought. "Did you get it on video?"

"We did, I'll send it to you in the morning."

"It's the morning, Eva," I jested, glancing out my window to the navy twilight.

She chuckled. "We have to start picking appropriate hours of the day to talk. I'm running out of juice."

"One day we'll figure it out. How's Mom?"

"She's um, got a new man apparently."

I let out a sigh. "So nothing new."

"Nothing new." A bridge of silence passed before she spoke up again. "But tell me about you. How's the writing?"

"It's... steady."

"Steady, huh? Spill, Astra."

I chewed on my bottom lip, smoothing my sheets. If there was one person I never wanted to hide anything from, it was Eva. We'd been through too much together.

"I think I met someone."

"You *think* you met someone," she reiterated, "or you actually met someone?"

Noah's warm features came to mind; his lean build and dimpled smile. Those burnished eyes and turned ears eager to listen.

I puffed a breath. "It's Snowball's vet."

The line went quiet, until it didn't and Eva yelped, "Shut up! Dr. Praigale?"

"Shh, you're going to wake your kid."

"How?" She ignored my concern. "When? I need all the details. Oo, he's real cute Astra."

Explaining was the hardest part, because I, myself, had no idea what to make of the connection. If there even was one.

"You were in Wonderland celebrating Becks' first steps and Mom was going on a date with –"

"– the bartender, yes. I remember. You took Snow to the vet, right? That's when you met?"

"Yeah, but..." I thought of the coincidence at the café, then reuniting with him by sheer luck at

Meeting Dr. Praigale *Marie-France Leger*

Tav's Tavern. "We just kept running into each other, again and again. It's weird... like, I had no idea he existed and now he's everywhere."

"Astra!" she practically shouted through the phone. "What's with all the monotony? Are you not excited? This is exciting!"

"How?"

"Because it's new and fresh, and something different from –"

"Malcom." His name was hard to digest, like nails cutting my spleen.

Eva lowered her voice to a softer tone. "I was going to say your past, sis. It's about time you start anew. Take the jump."

"What if there's a catch? It's never been this... *normal* before."

"Normal?"

"Yeah, like, I don't know. We met, and we talked and then he asked me on a date and it sounds stupid but it just feels too good to be true."

My sister took a pause before saying, "You know Astra, not every story has to be dramatic or sad or tumultuous, right? Ty and I met at a pub after I'd just broken up with Ronnie. Remember? He just came up to me, bought me a drink and now we've got a kid together.

"Look, I've never been happier. He's my person. And he didn't come with all the qualms and woes of the past. Some stories don't need to set off a bomb before they get their happy ending. They don't need baggage."

I sighed. "Well sadly, I carry a lot of that."

"Then let it go."

Three simple words.

Let it go.

As if it were the easiest thing in the world.

Erasing the scars that painted my heart, the bruises that inundated the layers of my skin.

"And if I can't?"

"You wouldn't be talking to me about this if you didn't feel some type of way. I say go for it."

"Eva –"

But she cut me off. "I know you're guarded, and you have every reason to be. Malcom was a shitbag. A living, breathing, piece of garbage. And Liam –" she groaned, "don't even get me started on that worm. But not everyone's going to hurt you, Astra. And at the very least, let people prove that they won't."

I processed her words, allowing a sliver of hope to light a spark inside my heart. "You really think I should see it through?"

"I really do," she exhaled. "Life doesn't make mistakes, Astra. But you might, if you choose to let this opportunity slip."

It was easier said than done; to let someone through the cracks, allowing them to see your vulnerable side. But one quick glance at my phone, the device that Doctor Noah Praigale plugged his

Meeting Dr. Praigale *Marie-France Leger*

number into, told me that maybe some things were worth pursuing.

Even if the end result could cost me my heart.

Chapter Fifteen
Astra

Last Edit – 2:32pm: No Title
Maybe this was it for her. Maybe she found something worth holding on to. And maybe, just this once, she shouldn't cut the rope that tethered her to hope.

I wasn't big on surprises.

My personality didn't call for it. Like pecan pie and olives – two things that just didn't make sense together.

However, that beacon of hope, (A.K.A my sister Eva), pushed me into seeing Dr. Praigale today – an hour and a half from now – for Snowball's vet appointment.

And guess what?

He had no idea.

That was about as far as I took surprises.

"It's nice of you to come." My mom said as we pulled into the far right parking spot at M & N's Vet Clinic. "A little bonding experience."

"This is your idea of bonding with your daughter?"

She rubbed her eyelid, a trickle of cheap mascara fibres tumbling down her cheek. "I'm trying to be nice, Astra. What've I done to you?"

Meeting Dr. Praigale — *Marie-France Leger*

Right then and there, I wanted to hurl a hammer through the glass. God, was it ever patronizing.

It's like she wanted me to retaliate, craved for the fight that wasn't in me to give. *Her best weapon*, I thought. To challenge the woman who birthed me, fed me, clothed me until I could manage myself.

She'd never let me forget the things she's done. Even if she rarely did a thing anymore.

"Let's just go inside." I strapped Snowball to my chest and hugged him tight, petting his white coat before stepping into the clinic.

The smell of disinfectants hit me like a truck as the receptionist, Vern, asked, "Appointment for?"

"Snowball DuPont," Mom responded, smiling proudly at the fact she gave her dog – *our* dog – my father's last name.

Bile and regret inched up my throat at the thought. An animal was a much better companion than Andre DuPont had ever been.

"Ah, right! Let's check his weight first." The jolly old secretary scampered around the desk and directed us to a large scale. "Just place him up top and hold him still."

It took a few seconds for the machine to stop beeping, then she scribbled something onto a piece of paper and led us to patient room number two. "Dr. Praigale will be with you shortly."

Meeting Dr. Praigale   *Marie-France Leger*

Upon her leaving, my mother settled in one of the two blue plastic chairs in the corner, flinging one leg over the other. "Smells like shit in here."

"I mean, it is a vet clinic." I retorted, leaning against the wall with Snow in my arms. Riding side by side with my mother in her vehicle was enough *bonding* for one day.

"Fucking foul," she scoffed.

I rolled my eyes. "Should've brought an air freshener, then."

"Watch your mouth," she scolded, glaring at me with venom.

I resisted the urge to combat. "It's not even that bad. Just smells like sanitizer."

Then came the exaggerated groan. "Must you argue with me on everything?"

I had no energy left to dispute. I zipped my lips and threw away the key. It's what she taught me best. To shut my mouth when her opinion was correct.

It was always correct.

She made damn sure of that.

Two soft knocks sounded behind the door, followed by a soft creak. I took in a sharp breath as *he* stepped inside. In that moment, I was face to face with my savior.

Dr. Praigale was dressed in all black scrubs, that ridiculous dog bandana pushing back his hair. He wore black Crocs on his feet, with an added accessory of a silver watch around his wrist.

Meeting Dr. Praigale *Marie-France Leger*

Heat bubbled in my chest, swirling in circles around my heart. What was this feeling? If not pain, *what was it?*

That warmth spread up my neck when he startled back, noticing my presence.

Those russet eyes took me in, full of wonder.

I returned the gaze, gripping at this feeling.

Hope, it seemed to say. *This is hope.*

"Susan," he breathed. I watched his fingers tighten around the edge of his clipboard. "Astra."

And then he smiled.

That genuine, dimpled smile that begged me to smile back. It was contagious. It was kind.

I was instantly transported back to a few nights ago, under the dim, heated lights of Tav's Tavern, when Dr. Praigale asked me to dinner.

A flicker of recognition in his eyes told me he felt it too; the brewing tension, the unspoken words in the presence of my mother. But it still lingered, the sizzle of happiness radiating off his body. An energy, an aura of some sorts, passing onto me with each secretive glance.

If this is what surprising someone felt like, then I'd bathe in this feeling forever.

"Apologies for not showing up last time Noah," Mom started, drawing out her syllables. "Hope my daughter didn't give you a hard time. Or my dog."

Meeting Dr. Praigale — *Marie-France Leger*

A tinge of pink floated beneath his cheeks as he set down his clipboard, and stepped towards me. "Snowball is always cooperative. As for Astra..."

He towered over me now, his body just a foot away, as he ran lengthy fingers through Snowball's hair. My heart hammered in my chest, his proximity sending my nerves into a frenzy.

I glanced up at him then, that same, gorgeous smile stamped across his face as he released, "I managed just fine."

Lord, save me.

"How's our little guy doing?" he asked, prompting me to place him on the examination table.

"Seems alright," Mom responded, cleaning grime out of her acrylic. "Old boy, but still kicking."

Could you not give any less of a fuck? I wanted to say. *At least pretend to care.* But I guess in some backwards way, taking Snowball to the vet was her way of showing affection. The bare minimum of it, but still something to note.

Dr. Praigale glanced at me, the corner of his lips tugging upwards before he carefully removed the bandana on his head and put it to the side.

"A couple loose threads," he released, whispering in my direction.

I looked down, hiding a smile. "I didn't see any."

"I'll be sure to check later."

Meeting Dr. Praigale   *Marie-France Leger*

Mom cleared her throat, pulling me out of the moment. "What's the update, Noah? Any new meds? What do I need to do?"

So *helpful* of her. So *convenient*.

He took hold of his clipboard and flipped a page, trailing a line of words with his finger. "Snowball dropped a pound and a half which is good, not quite what I wanted but it's a start."

Her face beamed with pride. "Been walking him."

"Have you?" I couldn't help but interject. I knew she was lying.

She scowled. "Duh. How'd you think he lost the weight?"

Me.

Since his last vet appointment (and the day I met Dr. Praigale), I went over to Mom's house every three days to give him a walk. That didn't count the times he stayed over and we played fetch for at least two hours a day.

My mother was absent.

Last week, Eva told me she didn't come home for two nights in a row, barely a third but finally stumbled in drunk off her ass.

"How'd job hunting go?" Eva had asked from the couch, rocking baby Becks.

I don't think Mom realized she was still awake, realized that Eva could barely sleep nowadays.

Don't think Mom realized all that much unless it concerned her.

Meeting Dr. Praigale   *Marie-France Leger*

"If I get a job, you'll know I got one."

That's all she said to my sister, her daughter – the one holding her grandchild. A dismissive, careless response.

I guess Mom's recent fling had fled, meaning no poor sod could provide for her share of rent at the time being. Eva and Ty basically took care of everything, even though Eva was a fucking *mom*, unlike ours.

"Regardless of how he lost the weight," Dr. Praigale sliced the tension, "I want to change his diet, get him on something nutritious."

"We feed him good at mine," grunted Mom.

The doctor stood up straighter. "And what qualifies as good, Susan?"

I hated to admit that seeing my mother struggle for an answer had me overjoyed. She was a ball of feigned calculation that always missed the mark, even if she didn't see it.

But now it was showing, and she was well aware of her impotence.

"Um," she began, "chicken n' shit. Peas. Lots of peas."

"Peas," he stated, reiterating her words flatly. "Chicken and shit."

I barked a laugh, flinging the back of my hand over my mouth. This really was a sight to see. And as they continued on about health and weight management – Dr. Praigale petting Snowball's mane

Meeting Dr. Praigale *Marie-France Leger*

while peppering my mother with knowledge – I kept quiet in sheer admiration.

Suddenly, my decision to come today felt all the more right.

***

"I just need to give him his vaccine and he's all set." Dr. Praigale picked up a needle, flipping off the cap and collecting a small vial of clear liquid.

I hated calling him that. *Dr. Praigale.* I hated how I felt the need to after so many personal conversations. We played a game of pool for Christ's sake, he... he asked me to dinner.

And yet, watching him in his element, so professional and collected, I felt odd addressing him in any other way.

"Astra," he called, willing my attention. "Do you mind sitting with him to keep him steady?"

"Sure, do I just..." My ass hit the plastic chair beside Mom, the chair I immediately yanked two feet away to have a bubble of space.

He lifted Snowball off the table and into my arms, positioning his head so it was buried underneath my arm, his backside facing the exam room.

"Perfect, okay. Just hold him. Make sure he doesn't wriggle out."

"I'll try." My finger dug into the sides of his fur, keeping him in place.

Meeting Dr. Praigale — Marie-France Leger

Dr. Praigale stepped forward and bent his knees, his face now eye-level with mine.

There it was again, that swell of emotion gnawing at me under the intensity of his gaze. He let out a breath and I followed suit, watching his throat bob before he positioned the needle.

"It's okay," he cooed, placing a large hand over Snowball's hair. I don't know if he realized it was resting over mine, or if he felt the warmth of my skin underneath his palm.

I don't know if he did it on purpose.

But I'm glad he did.

After a few seconds he retracted his fingers, lifting up Snow's bushy tail and pushed in the injection. The dog attempted to thrash between my arms, but my grip was strong.

And the next thing I knew, there was... *liquid*, on the inner thigh of my leggings.

"Um..." I coughed. "What is –"

Dr. Praigale cursed under his breath, moving quickly to the napkin rack and positioned himself in a crouch between my legs.

"I... I – missed. I'm so sorry," he murmured, folding two cloths. "I'll clean this for you."

In the matter of seconds, Dr. Praigale's calm demeanour shifted as his frantic hands moved up and down my thigh, wiping vaccine residue with a quilted napkin. The contact was instant, and I froze.

Meeting Dr. Praigale *Marie-France Leger*

"I'm sorry," he kept repeating. "Sometimes this happens. Not often, but," and he chuckled nervously, "sometimes."

"It's okay, it's okay," I directed to myself more than anyone else. I reached for the napkin in his hand, "I got it."

He stopped then, staring up at me with gleaming, chestnut eyes. In the dark hue of Tav's Tavern, I never got a chance to see them up close. The golden flecks that encompassed his pupils, turning brown irises into rays of sunshine.

"I didn't know you were coming..." he said softly, barely a whisper.

I wanted to see you. That was the truth I couldn't bear to give. Instead, I settled on, "I had the time."

In that moment, staring at the fluidity of his movements, memorizing the deep lines indenting his cheeks when he smiled, the twinkle in his eyes when he looked at me – I could see something, feel something... Something worth holding on to.

And with that new realization, I corrected my answer to: "I made the time," and watched two beloved dimples pierce his cheeks in appreciation.

***

"Weird," Mom clicked her tongue. "Weird, weird, weird."

Meeting Dr. Praigale   *Marie-France Leger*

"What?" I didn't want to hear it. I knew it was coming as soon as we exited the exam room, but I still didn't want to fucking hear it.

"You and Noah shagging or something?"

She popped her gum and I flinched. Snowball felt the involuntary movement and whined in my arms, looking up at me with concern.

I didn't answer her. Even if it wasn't true, not a pinch inside me wanted to speak to that woman right now.

I pet him silently and watched as she pulled out her purse and paid the fee that Dr. Praigale *didn't* waive.

"How was the appointment?" Vern smiled my way and gave Snowball a little wave. "Hi cutie."

Mom simply slapped her card down on the table and slid it to the receptionist. "Fine. Bit of third wheel, though."

I wanted to scream. I wanted to lunge at her and drag her out of this place by the hair. She hated clinics because she thought they were dirty? Well Susan DuPont was by far the crummiest thing to walk into this goddamn establishment.

"Ah, well, Dr. Praigale has that effect with animals. Always snuggles them up in a way that you almost feel like you're intruding," Vern joked, handing over the card machine to my mom.

As if she wanted to dig the knife further, to *ruin* me, she glanced my way with a smirk. "Wasn't talking 'bout the dog, sweetie."

Meeting Dr. Praigale   *Marie-France Leger*

My feet propelled me forward, red, hot fury boiling beneath the surface of my skin, but just before I reached my Mom, a figure came out of the staff door.

Dr. Noah Praigale.

"Astra?" he called. "Can I talk to you for a minute?"

As I made my way towards him, another person trailed behind him. He was about an inch shorter than Dr. Praigale, handsome as well, with wavy golden hair that poked out of a red cat bandana.

"Big Bone, do you have a second?" the man asked, pushing a pen into his scrub breast pocket.

Big Bone.

That nickname again.

Tav called him that, I remember. And they were friends. Looking at these two men now, roughly the same age and surely working here together... there must've been a connection between all three of them.

Dr. Praigale looked between me and the other veterinarian, holding up his index. "Hold on," he told him, then moved towards me.

"Noah," the other man pushed, "Mitch is on the line. He's pissed."

It was a visceral reaction, almost instant, that Dr. Praigale gave. Blood drained his face, his jaw ticked and hardened. Something set him off. Something about *Mitch*.

I took a step back, silently excusing myself from whatever conversation the two veterinarians were about to have. If Dr. Praigale needed to say something to me, he could text me.

He had my number now.

God, I'm never going to get used to saying that.

"Stay put, Astra. Can you? Just –" he scratched his temple – "I want to talk to you, I just have to deal with this first."

"I have to drive –" but he was already next to the other doctor, engaged heavily in discourse. I could make out the words "playmate," "adoption," and "unorganized." Nothing else.

"Done here?" Mom said, coming up to stand beside me. She popped a mint into her mouth and grabbed Snowball out of my arms. "I'll take him to the car if you got... business." She eyed Dr. Praigale.

For the first time, I didn't protest. "This won't take long, I promise."

Mom didn't so much as look back before exiting the clinic, leaving me to sit by a window seat next to a pile of *Doggy Digest* magazines.

The heavy tension radiating off Dr. Praigale was apparent. I couldn't help but watch both vets shaking their heads and waving their arms in concern. It made me want to question, to ask what got them so heated, but I reminded myself it wasn't my place.

It wasn't my problem.

Well, that's not true anymore, is it Astra? That similar voice returned. *You're starting to care.*

No, that couldn't be true.

Meeting Dr. Praigale   *Marie-France Leger*

Or maybe...

After a few moments, Dr. Praigale took a seat next to me, exhaling deeply. He kept his lids shut, titling his head back briefly before looking at me through tired eyes. "Hi, Astra."

I swallowed. "Hi," then tucked my hands between my knees. "Are you okay?"

He kept his arms crossed. "Do I look worse than I feel?"

I scooted towards him. Just an inch. "You still look classy."

He laughed out loud, ruffling his hair. "God, love."

Those damn butterflies.

They banged against my insides.

Bang, bang, thump.

"I'm sorry for keeping you. I had things to say," he straightened out, "but now I just feel like sitting here."

I opened my mouth to speak but he interrupted by adding, "With you."

Now I was full on blushing. I was full on blushing but I didn't give a damn. For some reason, I wanted him to see it.

And when he noticed, he too, moved a little closer.

The question escaped my lips too fast. Too soon. "Did I stress you out by coming here?"

Meeting Dr. Praigale   *Marie-France Leger*

His neck craned back, as if the question shocked him almost as much as it shocked me. *Why the hell did I ask that?*

"Astra" – he let out a strained laugh – "*what?*" Confusion swam beneath his eyes. "You were the best part of my day."

I gulped as the air combusted from my lungs. "Oh."

"It was a nice surprise," he smiled sincerely, then swiped a palm down his face. "It's just clinic stuff and hiring and pressure. *Lots* of pressure."

Again I tried to speak, but he carried on.

"I'm not trying to put this on you, really. I'm glad to see you..." Then he glanced down. "Even if I ruined your pants."

I snorted, rubbing away the residue of the vaccine stain. "Not a very good shot, are you?"

"Well Astra," his lips curled slightly, "if you put a beautiful woman in front of an archer, even they'd hit the grass."

Bang, bang, thump.

I glanced away quickly, ignoring my rhythmic heartbeat. "Can I um, do anything to help your situation?"

He drew out of the moment, his posture sagging once more. "Not unless you have the time to play with animals every Tuesday and Thursday."

My eyes twinkled with wonder. My head spun in thought.

What if...

Meeting Dr. Praigale — *Marie-France Leger*

No. No, surely not.
But it could be good inspiration?
I didn't have the time.
Make the time.
Make the fucking time.
"Astra?" Noah's voice. He noticed me considering.
"That was a joke," Dr. Praigale stated. "I didn't mean to suggest –"
"I'd love to." The words tumbled out before my brain could protest. "When do I start?"
"Astra," he leaned in, letting out a disbelieving laugh. "It's okay, we're in the process of hiring an adoption assistant for the clinic. I can't ask that of you."
"Why not?"
"Because you're busy and you have a life, a *job*, you're – you're an author," he pushed, "and I don't want you messing up your schedule. I'll find the help, seriously."
I chewed the inside of my lip, pondering over the empty nights I had staring at my computer screen with no story in sight. Writers needed inspiration, needed *something* to grab on to. To believe in.
I believed in Dr. Praigale.
At least to the extent of my art. My next book would have been a failure had I not met the vet, I knew that for certain.
He was my inspiration.
His proximity made me *feel*.

Meeting Dr. Praigale — *Marie-France Leger*

And every author needs to feel in order for their characters to come to life.

"Hey." Dr. Praigale placed a gentle hand over mine, his skin warm at the touch. I froze at the contact.

"Thank you," he whispered earnestly. "Thank you for offering."

I swallowed back the disappointment, standing up a moment later. My hand went cold the second it lost his grip.

"Well," I started, rubbing the back of my palm, "if you need me, let me know by Friday."

An honest smile stretched across his face. "Our dinner."

"Our dinner," I repeated, planting the seed of truth in my brain. *I can't escape this*, I accepted. *I don't want to escape this.*

Just then, I heard the familiar rumble of an exhaust engine – Mom's exhaust engine – skirting out of the parking lot and fading into the wind.

I ran to the window.

My jaw dislocated, hanging by a singular thread.

I watched as her blue Subaru pulled onto the two-lane street.

And then it was gone.

Just –

Gone.

What.

The.

Meeting Dr. Praigale *Marie-France Leger*

FUCK.

"Astra?" Dr. Praigale's voice was a muffled caw at my ear. "Astra, what's wrong?"

I was left unresponsive, a hardened shell – debilitated beyond belief until I could muster up one word. "Why."

"Astra." *His* voice. Again.

"Why..." I muttered, over and over again. "My mom just – she left me."

Left me.

Like a useless bag of trash, expendable.

Disposable.

"Why..." I don't know how long I remained in a dazed, pitiable state of being.

There it was, behind my back, the sixth sense of a weighted presence coming up behind me. I saw the shape of Dr. Praigale's shadow towering over mine as he too, surveyed the parking lot for my mom.

He wouldn't find her.

"She left me." It was a painful admission.

"I don't understand." He moved towards the door, angling his head out into the open, then came back to my side. "Why would she do that?"

The list of reasons was long, I'm sure. Maybe I looked at her the wrong way, belittled her comments, made her feel inferior for once in her goddamn life.

Maybe she didn't like the way Dr. Praigale educated her on something she didn't know.

FOR ONCE.

Meeting Dr. Praigale — *Marie-France Leger*

IN HER GODDAMN LIFE.

This, *her* – she was my mother.

That woman gave birth to me, held me in her arms at one point and stared at me lovingly.

She kissed my forehead and wrapped a towel around my shivering, naked body. Taught me how to smile with teeth, how to close my eyes and shut out the world.

"It's okay, Astra," I'd have her say. "I'll never leave you."

See?

How easy it is to construct a narrative?

See?

How blissful the art of fiction can truly be?

Because no one wants the truth.

No one wants to know that my mother got knocked up by a deadbeat when she was twenty, stole baby clothes from Walmart and canned goods from the Dollarstore.

That's not poetic.

That's not romantic.

But that's real fucking life and that woman – that *abandoner* – left me in pieces.

Just like Dad had.

Just like Malcom had.

And... just like Dr. Praigale will.

People can only hurt you if they get close enough. Don't let them get close enough.

Meeting Dr. Praigale *Marie-France Leger*

I turned to the vet, looking at him through bloodshot eyes, and betrayed my heart. "I don't think dinner is a good idea."

Without waiting for his reaction, I swiped out my cell, calling an Uber.

I was doing it again.

I knew I was doing it again.

Isolating my happiness, yanking it back into that cold, dark room of comfort and solace.

But I didn't want to be abandoned. I couldn't do it again.

I wouldn't survive.

"Wait –" his shoes squeaked against the marbled floor. "Wait, wait – Astra –"

I didn't bother to glance back as I exited the clinic, embracing the wind's breath into my lungs.

One. Two. Three…

One. Two. Three…

The staccato of my heartbeat recoiled at a touch, *his* touch, forcing me to face him.

"Please tell me what happened," he begged, frantic eyes scanning my face. "I want to have dinner with you. I want to spend time with *you*, and get to know *you* and –"

"– and then what?" Tears sprung to my eyes. "Where do you expect this to go?"

"Astra…"

"No, tell me." *Fuck.* "Tell me your intention isn't to leave. I won't believe you."

Meeting Dr. Praigale *Marie-France Leger*

"Leave?" Those soft, golden brown eyes searched for something within mine.

I knew they were vacant.

They have been for some time.

Heat burrowed itself beneath my cheeks as I craned my neck to the side, glancing at the whole of his staff watching our exchange from the window.

And then it came. The fatal blow. "You should get back to your job, *Doctor* Praigale."

That sealed our fate. At least I could imagine so. *Who would want to be with a girl like me? Battered and broken, so void of light and hope?*

I knew I was in the wrong. Projecting. Reacting. I knew I shouldn't have been treating him like this.

He did nothing to me.

But he *could*.

If he mattered enough.

He *would*.

And the shittiest part of it all, he started to matter. A whole damn lot.

That power – to hurt and to heal... I would never give that away again. I couldn't do it.

My phone pinged as the Uber, a black sedan, pulled up two parking spaces down.

The wetness of tears cascaded down my face. The thought of my mom leaving with no warning, no words, just pure *instinct*, pierced the walls of my caged heart.

Meeting Dr. Praigale *Marie-France Leger*

"For Astra?" the driver asked as I rounded the car, opening the backseat door.

"Yes –"

"For Noah, actually." *His* voice overlapped mine as he leaned into the passenger window, speaking with politeness. "I won't be needing a ride anymore, thank you."

His palm slapped the car door shut, tapping the backside of the trunk as if it were a horse, and sent the sedan off.

He faced me, his expression stoic, as he pulled out a twenty-dollar bill and flattened it into my palm. "To cover the cost."

"Why?" I griped, watching my *second* ride of the day drift off into the sunset. "Why did you do that?"

"I changed my mind." He crossed his arms, voice stern as stone. "I want to hire you."

Chapter Sixteen
Noah

"What the hell happened out there, man?" McLean followed me to my office, blabbing like a baby bird. "Who was that?"

"A client," I responded, flipping through my files until I found the adoption assistant contract.

"That was not a client Noah, don't fool me. Is she one of Annika's friends? An angry sister or something?"

"Annika doesn't have a sister, you know that."

He moved to block me from exiting the door, leaning back on the wood. "You caused a scene, and I want to know who's responsible for that."

"Me," I pointed at my chest, eager to get to the waiting area before Astra decided to leave again. "I am responsible. And now, I'm going to hash out that responsibility so, excuse me."

Pushing past McLean, I caught sight of Astra's frame in the reflection of the glass window, a disgruntled frown plastered on her face.

She was still here.

Angry, but here.

Good enough for me.

"Follow me, Astra." I called, waving her into the staff entrance.

Meeting Dr. Praigale *Marie-France Leger*

She followed my direction tentatively as I led her to the back of the clinic where the adoption centre was located. There was a small office at the entrance, rows of spacious kennels and toys, plush bean bags chairs and a turf area filled with water bowls and treats.

I remember the first time I pitched the idea to my father about having an adoption centre. No other clinic possessed one until we were able to get this one running, until my father saw that it was foolproof and possible.

"Lots of expenses," he told me. "But I'm sure we can manage."

He gave me a look then, one that translated to "good work" without him having to utter the words. It was one of the only times that I earned his approval, his respect.

Even though all my life that's what I fought to do.

We had rescuers comb the streets for strays, hired trainers who specialized in animals with PTSD, and caregivers to tend to their needs. Volunteers aided in playtime, but we were expanding. We needed permanent help.

I looked to Astra as she waited in the doorway of the small office cove, inspecting the filing cabinets, the hanging bulbs... anything but me.

"Sit, please." I pointed to the navy loveseat in the corner. "No one's ever really in here so I apologize for the lack of chairs."

She didn't answer but sat all the same, staring at the cream-coloured walls. They must've been really captivating, if she was gazing at them like they were the more interesting part of this room.

Not the human trying to talk to her.

I don't know where I went wrong, what I did. But when her mom left her... I mean, seriously left her at the clinic... a pain lodged itself in my chest.

Suddenly this quiet, careful Stargirl made sense.

And in that moment, I wanted to protect her. *Needed* to protect her.

Whatever reasons Susan had for leaving, she didn't run them by Astra. She left her without caution. Without explanation. And by looking at Astra, it didn't seem to be the first time someone close to her had done that.

"*You'll leave*," she'd said. She believed that with all her heart. And out of all the things you could believe, leaving was by far the most painful.

I could tell that she struggled with the idea of vulnerability, allowing strangers in. I was like that too once, when Annika cheated and left me heartbroken.

But who broke *her* heart?

And why did I suddenly crave, so badly, to want to fix it?

"So this is a job interview?" Astra finally broke the silence, her gaze firm on mine.

"It can be," I simply replied.

"What if I don't want the job anymore?"

Meeting Dr. Praigale *Marie-France Leger*

I almost laughed. "Then you can walk out that door and call another Uber. Here," I slid out my wallet, pulling out another twenty dollars. "On me."

She opened her mouth to say something, then pressed her lips together. "Keep it."

I sighed, folding the bill back into my pocket. "I'm not going to force you to have dinner with me. I won't do that."

Her eyebrow quirked up but again, she said nothing.

"And this contract," I slid over the agreement form, "is purely temporary."

She picked up the piece of paper, reading over the checkboxes and expectations for being an adoption assistant. I only circled the playmate portion for her, a mere two sentences detailing health and safety and *fun*, but she scanned everything else anyway.

Then something happened.

She cracked a smile. Slightly. But a smile nonetheless. "Seems like a tough job."

I felt elated. "There's a heavy turnover rate for a reason."

"Last assistant didn't want to play with puppies or something?"

"No, she was allergic to cats."

"Oh," she glanced back down at the paper, "that's an issue."

"Are you allergic to cats, Miss DuPont?" I tried.

She pulled a thread on her leggings. "Only if they're printed on a bandana."

The laughter came quickly, my joy beaming. She didn't look up at me, but she didn't have to. I caught her smile beneath the slits of her hair, and I trapped it in my heart.

I waited for her to say more, silently hoping to hear the jaunt in her tone, but she retreated back into her quaint, quiet mind and stared at the form.

The tension in the air was unbearable. Her sitting in front of me, unsure and doubtful – me, completely lost on how to make this situation better. Whatever this situation was.

I blew out a breath. *If she felt uneasy about showing me her vulnerable side, I'd have to show mine.* "Can I be honest?"

Her big, brown eyes looked up at me, a planet of stories brimming beneath those lids. She nodded.

"I'm sorry about your mother," I started. "I don't know the relationship between you two, but no one deserves to be left without answers."

She continued to stare, so I continued to talk.

"I didn't want you to leave here unhappy. In fact, there's a policy that states you must smile upon entry of the clinic and departure."

The corner of her lips turned slightly. "I find that hard to believe."

"Because it's untrue, but you smiled all the same."

She blushed. That too, I captured in my heart.

"You don't need to take the job, Astra, seriously –" I cocked my jaw – "I'd rather you not because honestly, I couldn't even give a proper vaccine with you sitting in front of me today."

That blush remained as she said, "Put a beautiful girl in front of an archer and they'd hit the grass."

I wanted to reach out and grab her hand right there, tell her it was going to be alright, that I wouldn't leave. But I didn't want to push my luck. Didn't want to make her uncomfortable.

"Look," I cleared my throat, "I admit, I had a hard time seeing you like that. So…"

"Embarrassed?" she muttered, "pathetic?"

"I was going to say hurt."

Her whole body tensed, paralyzing in response. She nimbly folded the corners of the work contract. Back and forth, she'd crumple and uncrumple.

And at last, she blew out a breath. "I don't know how to do this," she released, dropping her shoulders. "To have a proper, normal conversation with anyone. And it's killing me because I don't want to take it out on you." Her eyes met mine. "I barely know you."

"Astra –"

"But you've been so nice to me," she continued. "You've been so nice and for some reason you want to talk to me, and see me and it's just…"

I could feel the thump in my blood, my heart pounding in anticipation of her voice. Her thoughts. Her mind.

I'd never felt that before.

"It's what, Astra?" I prompted, softly.

She tucked a strand of loose hair behind her ear. "I've never been lucky enough to meet people like you."

I sucked in a breath of air, my eyes glued to this Stargirl in front of me, a blast of emotions combing my heart.

My first instinct was to hug her, to leave my desk and lift her into my care, banishing those fears away. But she wasn't mine, I mean, she was barely a friend.

Yes, I didn't know her. Not like I wanted to.

But this knot in my stomach was starting to bloom, the feeling of feeling *for* Astra Meredith DuPont, and I didn't want it to stop.

Two thuds at the door pushed me out of my seat, forcing me to stand and face something else – something that wasn't the careful girl nestled in the corner, cowering back to stillness.

She said too much, I could tell she was feeling. And suddenly all my thoughts began to orbit around hers.

That was until McLean stomped through the threshold, handing me a file. "Your next appointment's in five, Noah."

I swallowed down the irritation. "Very well," then glanced to Astra, pulling out the twenty dollar bill once more. "Here. Think on the job offer once you've made it home safe."

"Ah, is this the new recruit?" McLean piped, rubbing his abdomen. He stepped towards her and I felt the primal urge to pull him away.

"No –"

"Yes." Astra responded quickly, cutting me off. "Nice to meet you, um..."

"Will," he extended a hand, "Dr. Will McLean. Noah's second in command."

I stared at Astra who avoided my gaze.

Yes, she said.

She was taking the job.

Will waved a hand in my face. "Yoo-hoo."

I gritted my teeth, turning to him. "Aren't you supposed to be wrapping up a fracture in room three right now?"

"Well how would you know that, Big Bone? You've been camping in this closet for over twenty minutes." He jabbed my rib with the tip of his pen. "Anyway, Danni's got it covered. We do have vet techs for this, you know."

I rubbed my jaw, taking a quick peek at my watch. Two more minutes until my next appointment. *Two more minutes with Astra.*

Meeting Dr. Praigale — *Marie-France Leger*

"If you're the new hire, let me run you through the contract." Will held his hand out to Astra, asking for the paper. "May I?"

An infernal blaze of envy wrangled my nerves. I wasn't jealous of McLean, not even a little bit wary that he'd take the opportunity to swoon Astra at all. We'd known each other forever now; he could read my mind just by looking at me.

No, I was envious of the fact he was here, and I had to be somewhere else. With someone else.

When I could be with her.

But these were foreign thoughts, fuzzy sentiments I hadn't felt since the very beginning of being with Annika.

I have a job, I reminded myself. *A duty. This can wait.*

So with all the patience I could muster up, tightening the longing on a leash, I turned to Astra and said, "McLean will show you the ropes, should you decide to jump on board."

She nodded, giving a closed smile to McLean, and a softer one to me. "I'm on board."

It slipped my lips at the last second. "For this job, or for Friday?"

A coat of pink rushed to her cheeks, her palm flying to block the blush. I wished she didn't do that.

I wished she didn't hide the things that made her human.

Meeting Dr. Praigale *Marie-France Leger*

"For both," she released, a twinkle of light dancing in her eyes.

With that victory, I stood a little straighter, swatting the back of McLean's shoulder before ducking back into the main clinic.

For both, I grinned to myself, relishing in her promise.

In that moment I realized that even though *Dr. Praigale* wore an honest smile every day, *Noah Praigale* rarely did.

Not for a while.

Not until *her*.

Meeting Dr. Praigale *Marie-France Leger*

Chapter Seventeen
Astra

Last Edit - 5:32pm: No Title

Taylan re-dressed six or seven times, holding out a watch-covered wrist every five minutes to check the time. Josh Kahill was taking her on a date. This man, the one she finally gave a chance to, wanted to see her – spend the night with her – get to know her. What a foreign feeling, *she thought.* What a fuzzy, foreign feeling.

"What time is he picking you up?" Beth asked, the FaceTime screen idling on a houseplant.

I spent the past hour doing exactly what my main character had been doing: combing through her cluttered closet to find the perfect date night outfit.

Only Taylan Nichols wasn't real, she wasn't actually going on a date with anyone...

But I was.

And I'd be lying if I said I wasn't losing my damn mind.

"Half an hour," I responded, moving hangers this way and that, pinching silk and cotton fabric. "God, what does one even wear to a fair?"

"Ha, that rhymed." She moved the video chat to face her, nestled in bed, eating Cheetos.

Meeting Dr. Praigale   *Marie-France Leger*

I eyed the outfit options on my bed. "Want to trade places?"

"Sure," she piped. "Dr. Praigale's a hunk."

I rolled my eyes, pinching jealousy.

"What? He is" - she licked her fingers clean - "Alan would probably gobble him up, too."

"Fuck, Beth, just help me," I groaned, holding up a bright blue sundress and a skirt and tank combo. "Which one do I go for?"

"Hm, I think the sundress. Men go crazy for dresses."

"Then that settles it," I said, tossing the sundress back into my closet. "Tank and skirt it is."

"You're annoying." She rolled her eyes. "Why even bother asking for my opinion?"

"Because it matters to me." I slid out of my lounge shorts and into a white tennis skirt, replacing my NHL tee with a mauve tank. "Because I value you."

"You never listen to me."

"To be fair, I don't listen to anyone."

That pulled a laugh out of her, easing my tension by a single fucking decimal point.

"Have you thought about taking his job offer? I think you should - *actually*, I think you shouldn't." She jumped up from her bed. "Reverse psychology seems to work on you so yeah, do *not* take this opportunity. Bad idea."

Meeting Dr. Praigale — Marie-France Leger

I flat ironed my hair, chuckling. "Reverse psychology only works if you don't address the fact that you're using it."

"I tried my luck," she shrugged. "But seriously, have you made a decision?"

In all honesty, I did everything in my power to avoid talking about that day at the clinic.

As soon as I got home Monday evening, I jumped in my car and drove the half hour back into town, straight to my mom's house.

She opened the door, surprisingly, with a smug smile on her fucking face and a gin and tonic in hand.

"Why the hell did you leave me there?" I'd ripped, pushing my way past her into my childhood home.

Eva was there, sitting on the couch with Becks and Ty. She sat up straighter. I guess Mom hadn't told my sister about her little stunt.

"Answer me," I pushed. "Why did you leave?"

She waved me off like I was some seller on the street. "I was doing you a favour, giving you and Noah some alone time."

I'd opened my mouth to retaliate, but she just kept insisting, "*I was doing it for you. I was doing you a favour.*"

"What happened, Astra?" Eva had asked softly.

I didn't answer her.

Meeting Dr. Praigale *Marie-France Leger*

I couldn't look at any corner of that fucking house.

Especially at the woman who lived in it. Painted those walls an ugly shade of peach pink. Plastered picture frames of various vacations she'd scammed her ex-boyfriends for.

Every photo was of her.

Her face.

And a single, frayed portrait of a naked woman with outstretched arms.

Nothing. NOTHING of her own flesh and blood.

Before crossing the threshold to the outside world and away from my mother's prison cell, I turned around and said, "That is the last *favour* you will ever do for me."

And I slammed that fucking door and didn't look back.

Beth didn't know about any of this. She didn't need to get roped up in my family drama. Not when she would've felt sorry for me.

Screw the sympathy.

So I wiped those memories clean and resumed the conversation as if my mom's *favour* never happened.

As if she never existed.

"I told him I'd take the job, so I'll see it through. It's just a temporary position anyway."

She giggled. "I can think of far worse things than working alongside a hot vet."

Meeting Dr. Praigale *Marie-France Leger*

I unplugged the straightener. "We aren't working alongside each other. We'd literally be on opposite ends of the building, Beth."

"Same thing." She waved a manicured hand in front of the screen. "Close proximity and all that, you know, the romantic stuff you write about."

Releasing a breath, I sank into the memory of being in his office – the levelled tension, those emotion-filled glances that scraped the ridges of my heart.

"God. I feel like I'm living in one of my books." My eyes flitted to my phone, catching minute two turn to minute three. My stomach churned.

"Is that a bad thing?"

Yes, I wanted to say. *Yes*, because in fiction, there's always a third-act breakup. There's always miscommunication and something – fucking *something* that pulls the happy couple apart.

Happiness doesn't last very long.

Maybe in books, but not in real life.

"You haven't been on a date in ages, Astra," Beth continued. "You were going through the worst writers block you've ever had and suddenly, *bam*! This hot vet-doctor man waltzes into your life and flips things sideways."

I stared at her.

She stared right back.

"What's your point?" I contended, willing the nerves aside.

She leaned towards the frame. "My point is that he's supposed to be here." Her eyes softened. "He's your muse, babe, you said it yourself. And maybe he could be something more if you let him."

If you let him.

I took a second to thank Beth for the pep talk before hanging up the phone, leaning back against the wall to replay her advice.

Let people prove they won't hurt you, Eva had once told me.

I'd countered that statement, just like all the other words of wisdom I've pocketed over the years.

I wanted to sit in my suffering.

I wanted to wallow in the silence of my fears – the fears that ate me alive – accepting that love was not made for people who created it for others.

But maybe I was wrong.

And as Dr. Noah Praigale's text rang through my phone, announcing his arrival, I forced myself to crawl out of that dark hole and into a place of light.

A place of *hope.*

Chapter Eighteen
Noah

A star.

That's what she was.

She hid behind a persona but the real her called to me – the underneath.

The better part of what she couldn't see.

The extraordinary girl she refused to be.

I clutched her book *Gloria Haynes* tighter in my arm, swallowing my admiration as I watched Astra step onto her loft landing, and descend down the grated stairwell. She waved, a small wave that teetered between shyness and caution.

Little did she know how nervous I was the entire drive over. Heck, the entire week.

Apparently after McLean showed her around the adoption centre, she signed the part-time contract right away. I don't know what transpired between them, but McLean kept throwing me odd stares all week.

"Astra Meredith DuPont," he'd randomly announce, sprinkling her name over lunch or in passing. "Interesting."

I'd cut the cord yesterday and snapped. "Want to get something off your chest, Will?"

"Easy, Big Bone." He laughed. "Just wanted to chat."

Meeting Dr. Praigale — Marie-France Leger

"This is your way of getting me to talk? By chanting Astra's name like a parrot?"

He slapped my chest before walking away. "Keep this thing alive. Whatever it is."

It was then that I presumed something may have gone on in the absence of my presence, that Astra or Will may have spoken about me.

And I was fretting.

Like a spineless, twelve-year-old boy whose hormones were running rampant.

For the first time in what felt like forever, I was skittish at the thought of taking Astra on a date; a girl who opened my eyes, and my heart, like no other in such a short period of time.

I wanted to know everything about her, but slowly, cautiously. I'd never push, but I yearned to see the inner workings of her mind.

So I bought one of her books.

Gloria Haynes was a newer release, charting on the New York Times Bestsellers list for over twelve weeks.

It was a college romance between a football star and a violinist. I didn't think it would be my cup of tea, Astra had even said as much...

But I ate it up.

Her writing was captivating. A pure reflection of the woman who wrote it.

Deep, authentic, raw and real. She poured her heart into these stories, and she reaped the rewards by doing so.

Meeting Dr. Praigale   *Marie-France Leger*

It crushed me to think that she didn't want anyone knowing her real name – knowing the face behind all the love she created. The fandoms who worshipped her art.

But then I felt the abundance of luck, of fate favouring us both. We'd crossed paths, and I'd struck the goldmine.

Watching this Stargirl walk to meet me, taking the orange hues of the horizon with her, I could say with certainty she had become my yellow car.

Every day since her, yellow inched closer to my favourite colour.

***

"I want to apologize," Astra said immediately, not even a second after I pulled out of Cloud Café's parking lot.

"What?" I asked, puzzled. "What for?"

My eyes were on the road, but I could see her body shifting in my peripheral, as if trying to find a comfortable position to say something uncomfortable.

"For my outburst on Monday, for... just being weird and tense and –"

I placed a hand on her knee.

Instinctively, I touched her.

And I savoured that bit of contact, of comfort, before pulling my hand away quickly.

"Please don't apologize, Astra. I'm surprised you stayed as long as you did."

I glanced at her quickly, her eyes pinned to her knee, and cleared my throat. "I saw that you signed the contract."

"Yeah, I did. I want to work there."

I cocked a brow.

She laughed. "I mean it. I really do. At least for the time being."

"It's only a month, you know that right?"

"Obviously, I read the contract."

A quick laugh escaped my lips. "If I find a replacement sooner, it may not even be a month."

"Well," she paused, "let's hope for a struggle."

"Oh?" I turned to face her, my eyes lingering on her smiling face just a moment longer. "You love animals that much, do you?"

"More than you, I bet," she teased.

Before I could say anything, she pointed over my legs, to the book – *her* book – tucked in the driver door compartment.

"Why do you have that?" she asked, her voice small.

"I read it," I said, glancing at her. Her cheeks were red.

"Why did you read it?"

I chuckled. "Because I wanted to see what the hype was about."

Meeting Dr. Praigale   *Marie-France Leger*

"What did you..." She stopped herself. I knew what she was going to ask.

"What did I think? I loved it." Again, I stole a glance. "I loved every second of it."

She relaxed into her chair. "That's a staged response."

"I'm offended," I placed a hand over my heart. She laughed and I smirked. "Bernadette, the violinist? Quite flexible. I'm sure Lucas appreciated that."

"You're sick," she laughed, swatting my shoulder. "Of course that's the part you'd comment on."

"I mean seriously, Astra," I chuckled, "they ruined a perfectly good fiddle for –"

"I know what I wrote!" She blocked her ears. "Do not repeat it."

We chatted about different scenes in the book before I took a left towards the pier. Whether it was a good idea or not, planning for our first date to be at the town fair, I wanted a public space to make Astra feel as comfortable as possible.

Tav, on the other hand, couldn't believe it when I proposed the idea. "Do you even like rides, man?"

"I can learn to like them," I'd said.

"Does she like rides?"

"I'm... honestly not sure."

Meeting Dr. Praigale *Marie-France Leger*

He slapped a full hand on my chest, holding a guitar shaped key. "Well, if all else fails, Tavern's yours."

I nodded at him in thanks, pocketing the key even though I presumed I wouldn't use it. The whole reason I picked the town fair was because it was bustling with people, and since my last attempt at trying to talk to her alone freaked her out, I vowed to never put her in an uncomfortable position again.

Plus, a little cotton candy never hurt anyone. Right?

"Have you ever been to the Seawinds Fair?" I asked, following a train of cars.

"Once," she said. "When I was little."

"Do you like rides?"

"I used to, but I haven't ridden on anything in a while."

I glanced her way. She was smirking.

I laughed out loud.

I don't know why.

But I laughed.

And she laughed.

And it was the greatest sound I'd ever heard.

"What about you?" she piped. "Is the doctor a daredevil?"

"Horns and all," I grinned.

"Putting a little gin in a club soda doesn't count."

"It's rum and make it a double."

Meeting Dr. Praigale *Marie-France Leger*

She cocked a brow. "Does rum make you rowdy?"

"Naturally," I replied. "After a few shots, I can wrestle a bear."

She chuckled.

"But before those shots," I skimmed her side-profile, "I am that bear."

"Dangerous?"

"Affectionate."

"So you can be both, then? That's the kind of guy you are?" she questioned.

"What kind of guy do you think I am, love?"

She stared at me in contempt. "I'm not sure yet."

The traffic started to ease, and I took one final chance to graze her features before hunting for a parking spot.

God, she was pretty.

The pretty you can't even describe because it's everywhere.

Her eyes

Her smile.

Her intellect.

Her aura.

Her.

Her.

Her.

"So, tell me. What kind of guy are you, Dr. Praigale?" she asked, lolling her head to the glass window.

Meeting Dr. Praigale *Marie-France Leger*

In this moment, looking at her, only one word fit the bill. "A winner."

Chapter Nineteen
Astra

"I'm a little thirsty." Dr. Praigale licked his lips, and my eyes hovered a little too long.

Way too long.

"Do you want to get a drink?" he asked.

"Sure," I responded, catching sight of two kids slurping a gigantic milkshake out of a magic hat. "What the hell is *that*?"

He followed my gaze, eyes wide. "Looks like ten gym sessions and a spinach smoothie."

I let out a laugh. "Should we try it?"

But he was already on a mission, waving for me to follow him through a throng of people. The breeze was warm, the air smelling of candy apples and a lot... and I mean *a lot*, of fried foods.

"Do you know where we're going?" I asked, carefully avoiding the touch of strangers.

He shrugged. "I'm just following the scent of diabetes and cholesterol."

"Like Hansel and Gretel."

He chuckled. "Luckily, I'm too tall for a witch to shove me into an oven."

"Consider yourself fortunate." I frowned. "I'm not safe."

He moved a little closer. "You're safe, trust me."

I swatted his arm gently.

He smiled at me.

Those damn dimples.

"I'm going to take a wild guess and say that's our destination." He pointed to a blue shack, the roof caved into a half-moon crater called: **Magic Hat Milkshakes.**

"What gave it away?" I joked, pulling his arm towards the line.

His skin was warm, just like when he touched me in the car and I melted into a pool of lava. That skin to skin contact, so small yet so electric, forced me out of my body for a split second.

I still tried to grapple with the fact that he read one of my books. He physically went to the store, knowing my real identity, and grabbed *Gloria Haynes* off the bookshelf.

He wanted to read it.

He wanted to know every version of me.

And he enjoyed my work. Thoroughly.

There existed no higher honor than that. Talking to someone who read your book, enjoyed your book, and wanted to pick your brain about the writing process. Fuck, the biggest part of me wished, so whole-heartedly, that I could engage with my readers – that they could know how much they meant to me. But then it would be tied back to the past – to *him*, and that would... that would destroy M.D. Pont.

That would destroy Astra.

Meeting Dr. Praigale — Marie-France Leger

All over again.

I cleared my throat, focusing on the present. "Chocolate, strawberry and vanilla." I scanned the menu. "Can I guess what flavour you'll get?"

"Better yet," he handed me two bills, "just order for the both of us."

"That much trust in me?"

His eyes met mine. "That much."

I approached the cashier, a lanky teenage boy, and asked for two strawberry milkshakes.

"Would you like fries with that ma'am?" he asked, punching in our order.

My stomach growled in anticipation. "There are fries here?"

"Fries are everywhere in this fair."

Without even looking at the vet behind me, I handed him the money and scooped some change from my purse. "I'll take a large fry then, please."

As he was making our order, Dr. Praigale bumped my arm. "How'd you know my favourite flavour is strawberry?"

"Chocolate is too mainstream, vanilla is too cliché, and strawberry is the perfect mix of both."

"You think I'm perfect?" he beamed.

"Only time will tell, Doctor."

A cloud swept over his face. "Astra, please, *please* call me Noah. I'm not in scrubs anymore."

I chewed on my lip. "Sorry, I know. I just – under the circumstances of how we met, it sometimes feels weird calling you Noah."

Meeting Dr. Praigale *Marie-France Leger*

"Would it help if I said Dr. Praigale and Noah Praigale are two different people?"

"Aren't you?"

"Yes," he stated. "And you're on a date with Noah Praigale right now so quit talking about that doctor, love. You're making me jealous."

Love.

That word. It never got old. Never aged. *Fucking love.*

This damn man.

"*Order up! Two strawberry shakes and a large fry!*" the teenage boy called out.

"*Finally,*" both Noah and I released in unison.

"Jinx," I snapped first. "I win."

I melted under his gaze as he took a moment to respond. "I beg to differ."

We cruised around the fair, shakes in tow, Noah holding the fries with the wrap of his sleeve.

"I can hold it if your hand is overheating," I offered, taking a sip of heavy cream and artificial strawberry.

"No, because then we'll both burn."

"So?"

"One good hand is better than no good hands, Stargirl. Remember that." He smirked, dipping a fry into his shake.

I stared at him in wonder. "You like sweet and salty?"

"Of course." He chuckled, handing me a crisp fry. "I'm not a total bore."

"Okay, convince me," I grabbed two extra fries and swirled them in the pink cream. "Tell me something that makes you interesting."

He placed a wounded palm over his chest. "Have I not convinced you already?"

"Nope," I savoured the taste of salty sweetness as the fry hit my tongue. "Go on. Excite me."

We stepped over a puddle of *questionable* substance and trailed the pier. A barrage of roller-skaters passed us with a shout. "*Woohoo! Tiny, titty, tinted windows out the backyard bazooka!*"

Huh.

"I want whatever they're on," Noah gaped, watching them fly down the walkway.

I snickered. "You want to get plastered and roller skate?"

"You said to name interesting things." He leaned the fry bag towards me and slurped his shake. "Alright something exciting... let's see."

I watched the shoreline, awaiting his answer.

He cleared his throat. "When I was twenty-one, Tav, Will, the uh – the other veterinarian who showed you around –"

"Yeah, William McLean, I know."

"Right," he continued. "We all got pretty drunk one night after class, and Tav had the bright idea to steal dog treats from our professor's lab table.

It was for some exercise we were supposed to do the next day."

His smile widened, as if getting lost in the memory. It made me happy.

"I don't know why I went along with it, but he snagged these squishy chicken bones and said he'd give us a hundred dollars each to swallow it whole."

My mouth flung open. "You didn't."

He cracked a genuine laugh. "Oh I did. I was so broke back then, Astra. Will tapped out the last second but I dunked those bones in gravy and I made the money."

A chorus of laughs bubbled from my throat. "Did you feel sick afterwards?"

"Not really," he wiped his eye. "I mean, it couldn't have been good for me. Tasted pretty funky too."

"I'd imagine."

"But that's how I got the nickname." He wore a proud smile. "Big Bone."

"That's why they call you that?"

"Yeah," he wiped cream off the top of his shake. "And then I spent that hundred dollars on a week's worth of Arby's curly fries."

I gasped. "Out of all the things."

"I was young," he shrugged. "I was broke and had no concept of anything, especially nutrition."

My eyes swept across his torso, down to his long, lean legs and toned arms. I swallowed. "You definitely learned some things over the years, then."

Meeting Dr. Praigale *Marie-France Leger*

He caught my lingering gaze and smirked. "Is that a compliment, Miss DuPont?"

Yes. Very much so. I thought to myself. But aloud, I said nothing, just knuckled his hand gently and grabbed a fry.

A crowd cheered from one of the game stands, where a happy couple was being handed a gigantic pink giraffe.

"Want to play?" Noah asked, tossing his milkshake in a trashcan.

Before I could answer, he fished two toonies out of his pocket and handed it to a walking water vendor, purchasing a bottle.

"Here, give me your hands," he said, unscrewing the cap.

I didn't protest, just held out my fingers. With my wrist in his hands, he pulled me closer to an isolated area, and began pouring the water over my fingers. With the bottle cap secure between his teeth, he rinsed the fry grease and seasoning off my skin, then did the same for himself.

"We could've just found a bathroom," I ribbed, still reeling in the warmth of his touch.

He hesitated to let go. "I know."

The words lodged in my throat. But the butterflies were dancing.

Bang, bang, thump.

He disposed of the water bottle and led me towards the game stand. "Come on, I want to win you something."

Meeting Dr. Praigale *Marie-France Leger*

His enthusiam, the atmosphere, everything about this evening had been too good. Too surreal.

Too easy.

I couldn't help but think about Taylan Nichols, the main character in my book, and if she had been real – would she be enjoying her fictional date just as much as I've been enjoying this real one?

Would that bliss last?

Would it, Astra?

That voice.

That fucking voice.

It wasn't hope, no. It was something else. Something vile.

Malcom's twisted tongue popped into my head like larva, wiggling its way in and out of my psyche, tempting me to fall back into the pit of doubt.

It's too good to be true, isn't it?

He's just going to hurt you.

Trust me, you're worth hurting.

I choked on the poisonous air that flitted through my lungs. Those words pushing me further and further away from this moment – from happiness.

My thoughts and fears were drowning me, so much so that I didn't realize Noah had been holding out his hand with three darts in palm.

"Astra? You okay?" He looked worried. I must've given him a reason to.

Fuck. Fuck. Fuck.

"I'm fine," I forced a smile. "You go ahead and play, I'll just watch."

He tilted his head, examining me with softened eyes. Then he nodded once and turned towards the dart board.

I wanted to turn my brain off.

To shut out any wicked presumptions I had of serenity and hope.

I was here.

In this present moment.

With someone who made me very happy.

You don't have power over me, Malcom. You're gone.

And I repeated that, over and over and over again as I watched Noah extend a hand and send the dart flying.

It landed sharply between the outer bull and the twenty. "*Not quite what I wanted,*" he murmured to himself.

I took a step closer to him, needing to blanket myself in his proximity.

The next dart landed right in the outer bull, a hairline away from the bullseye.

"Well jumpin' jaguars, aren't you a pro?" the shack owner whistled.

Noah grinned my way, tugging a smile out of me.

"Not so bad a shot this time, am I?" he drawled.

"Stick to darts, not vaccines," I jested.

He smirked and lifted an arm, never taking his eyes off me, and released the dart with one firm flick of the wrist.

It happened in an instant.

The dart flying.

The shack owner gasping.

My eyes in complete and utter disbelief as I fixated on the dart stuck to the red velvet of the bullseye.

Noah's stare was entrancing. He was fully aware that it landed where it was supposed to.

And his eyes never left mine.

"How..." I couldn't even come up with the words as the shack owner chimed a bell frantically.

"WINNER! WINNER!" he yelled.

People glanced our way, but I was transfixed on him.

Noah. Fucking. Praigale.

"As they say," his grin was ear to ear as he pointed out a yellow star and handed the winning stuffy to me. "Eyes on the prize."

Chapter Twenty
Noah

"I can't believe you hit that," Astra gawked as we walked back to my car.

"Must've been a stroke of luck," I winked.

"Well give me some of that luck," she said, hugging the yellow star stuffy to her chest. "I want to win the lottery."

"What would you do? If you won the lottery?"

She took a minute to respond. Then, "I'd open my own bookstore. Have a café like Cloud and I'd sit by the window, in my rocking chair," she smiled, "and I'd throw eggs at teenagers."

My neck swerved to her. She still held the star stuffy tightly, but her grin was ear to ear.

"Didn't expect me to say that, did you?" she smirked.

"I must confess," I rubbed my chest, laughing, "not in the slightest. Seems very thought out."

"Well, I've always wanted to own a bookstore, I mean, that's every author's dream. And coffee? It's in my blood."

"What about the egg throwing?"

"Right, that," she shrugged. "Some brats deserve it."

Meeting Dr. Praigale *Marie-France Leger*

"In that case, I'm in." I chuckled, "Brown or white eggs?"

"Both," she smiled, bumping her fist against mine.

The sea breeze brought our bodies closer together. She spoke again. "What about you, though? Why be a vet when you got a killer dart throw, hm?"

I caught her watching me with innocent wonder. It felt... like the best drug in the world.

"Back in college" – I cleared my throat – "Tav and I used to go to the games room between classes and practice darts. We'd play for hours and hours and when we got really good, we started taking bets from people at bars.

"We pretended we were terrible, throwing darts at the wood beside the board." I laughed, thinking back to our piss poor acting skills that no drunkard could catch. "And when it was time for the final round, we challenged double or nothing. Honestly, I think we hit bullseye every time, and by the end of it all, we made a few hundred dollars every weekend."

Her jaw dropped. "So you were a con-artist."

"The best in the business."

She took a step closer to me. "Here I was thinking you spent your evenings reading *Doggy Digest*."

I shrugged. "It's interesting material."

"So I've heard."

I cocked a brow. "Talking to other vets, Miss DuPont?"

She laughed. "I think I've had my fill with you, Dr. Praigale."

"Good."

As we approached my car, I made a quick stride to open the door for her. "I hope you saved some room because the night's not done yet, Stargirl."

And as if all the light in the world powered her smile, she replied, "I was hoping you'd say that."

***

The sky had turned to a light shade of midnight by the time we arrived at Tav's Tavern.

While Astra had been in the bathroom earlier, I shot him a text to ask for a favour - one that I knew would make or break the evening, should Astra decide to stay.

Astra stepped out of the car and onto the parking lot, where the dim lights of the Tavern were shut off. "Seems pretty empty for a Friday night."

"Tav closed it down."

"Permanently?" Her eyes widened.

"No," I led her to the entrance, "just for tonight."

"But why -"

She stopped, pausing at the threshold of the doorway, taking in all that Tav and I had planned out.

Meeting Dr. Praigale *Marie-France Leger*

A table and two chairs sat in the middle of the dance floor, the whole perimeter illuminated by battery powered candles. The scent of something sweet filled the air, a mixture of roses and baked goods - both of which were perched atop the table, per my request.

Jeez, I thought to myself. *Tav can be useful.* I chalked down a mental note to thank him later and made way for the speaker playing soft rock in the background.

"Noah..." Astra whispered, covering her mouth. "What is all this?"

I smiled. "My attempt at a romantic gesture."

"This can't be real," she murmured, a twinge of shock and appreciation in her voice. "This isn't real."

"It's as real as it gets," I responded, switching the tune to something classical. "I know we just ate some fries and shakes but I thought we could have -"

"Are these Ruby's Cloud muffins?" Astra gasped, holding up the box of six I requested.

"I hope so." I walked over to the table and sat down, peeking inside the box to make sure Tav got the order right. "I know you probably eat them all the time, but I figured it may give you a touch of home."

Her lip quivered and I fought the urge to pull her close, and for the first time... to kiss her.

It was a firework feeling, a tug on my nerves, drawing out all my wants and desires and fusing them into this moment.

Meeting Dr. Praigale — *Marie-France Leger*

She needed someone.

And I wanted to be that someone.

"I don't know where home is for you. You haven't told me and you don't need to," I said softly, holding out one of the muffins, "but you're safe here. I promise on my life."

She slowly took the muffin from my hand, her shaky fingers gripping the wrapping, and released a breath. "Empty."

"What?" I asked, lowering the music.

She took a seat and exhaled. "My home was empty, it's always been this... this void. Of nothing."

I shifted back at the realization of what was happening, of Astra finally letting some walls down, of being... open.

She shook her head, ripping off a piece of the muffin. "What you did tonight, all of this –" she waved – "this has never happened to me before. I'm still... I'm sorry, I'm speechless."

"It was nothing," I swallowed, watching her smooth out some kinks in the tablecloth.

But she glanced up at me and said, "It's everything."

I took a muffin of my own and waited for her to continue, carefully peeling away the wrapping and taking a bite. I chewed softly, as if any other noise or distraction could drown out the chances of her speaking further.

Meeting Dr. Praigale *Marie-France Leger*

She took a small bite, and a kernel of happiness blossomed inside of me. "These are so damn good."

I chuckled. "I'm surprised you're not sick of eating them by now."

"You can't get sick of these. They're addicting."

"I know" – I licked a crumb off my finger – "does Ruby ever have leftovers?"

"Barely," she took a bigger bite, "I swear a hundred people a day come in and sell them right out. I'm surprised you managed to get some."

I shrugged. "Tav's a charmer."

"And McLean? Or Will?" she asked. "What's he like?"

"A bit of a shit disturber, I'd say," I laughed. "How was it when you two spoke at the adoption centre?"

"Nice, he was really nice. Persuasive," she nodded. "He wanted me to sign that contract."

"And you did."

"I did," she beamed. "He said you'd be thrilled if I got the job, and you know, I didn't want to disappoint."

We shared a laugh and I could see the lightness in her eyes, the crease in her smile lines.

"So you did me a favour?" I teased.

"Oh, absolutely. Now you owe me."

"Okay, let's cash that in." I leaned forward. "What do I have to do?"

Meeting Dr. Praigale — Marie-France Leger

"You..." she tapped her chin with her index. "You have to answer three questions."

"That easy?" I smirked.

"You haven't heard my questions," she retorted.

"Whatever you want, Stargirl."

Her smile was sincere. "And because you're *Mr. Romantic*, you can ask me three questions too."

I snorted, then sighed. "It doesn't need to be a trade, Astra. I wanted to do this. I wanted to plan something nice for you."

"This is a once in a lifetime opportunity," she chuckled, but there was hesitation in her voice. "I want to let you in, Noah. I want to try."

The urge to take her hand buzzed at my fingertips. "Well then, I'm honoured. Ask away."

She stared at me intently. "That phone call you took, at the clinic on Monday –" she cleared her throat and I sat up straighter, tensing at what was to come – "You just seemed really overwhelmed. What was that about?"

I let out a breath, holding back the bite in my tone that I knew always came out when discussing my father. This would be the first time talking about it – about *him* – with Astra. I needed to level myself.

"That was..." A lump of coal lodged itself in my throat. "That was my dad. The owner of M & N's Vet Clinic."

Meeting Dr. Praigale — *Marie-France Leger*

"I read that on your website, the famous father and son vet duo. Great reviews," she added with splendor.

I couldn't find it in me to reach for joy. "That's us, yeah. The best service, the best staff, the best... the best everything."

Her brows furrowed. "You don't agree?"

"I do. I do agree. I love my staff and I love the people I work with, I mean, most of them were my classmates and Vern – my receptionist – she's been a treasure to my family for decades."

"Then why the long face?" Two of her fingers extended outward, but she quickly folded them back into her palm.

I wondered what might have happened if she didn't. If she let herself touch me. *Does she feel the tug like I do?*

I sighed, backing away from the thought. "My father isn't the easiest person to get along with, to put it lightly."

Concern flashed across her face, but she kept silent.

"He's a very hard man to please." I shook my head. "Honestly, I don't think anything impresses him except achievement."

"But you both share the success of this clinic –"

I stopped her. "In his eyes, M & N's is his. Only his. I'm just the doctor he hired."

"You're his son."

Meeting Dr. Praigale   *Marie-France Leger*

"I don't know that he sees it that way, Astra." My eyes met hers. "His standards are impossible. He's a... a great veterinarian. He cares about his clients. That's about all he cares about."

"That can't be true." Again, I watched those fingers twitch in my direction before she hid the motion.

"Why can't it be?" The words tumbled out of me numbly. "I'm sure to him he has his reasons."

"Yeah, to him, but those reasons don't make it fact."

I took a bite of my muffin. "I guess we'll never know."

"Do you not get curious about what he thinks? How he feels?"

I leaned in closer. "I'm more curious about you."

There was a sudden shift in her demeanour, a mannerism I began to catch more frequently when she was spotlighted.

"What about me?" Her voice was hushed, small. Timid.

It was as if an invisible, impenetrable wall buzzed around her – an electric fence that kept people out.

I wanted to know why.

I needed to reach her.

"You fascinate me," I admitted, setting down my muffin.

Meeting Dr. Praigale *Marie-France Leger*

"That's not a question." She crossed her arms, lips slanted in tease.

"It's not. I'm just trying to read you. To figure you out."

"I don't get why," she shook her head. "I'm nothing spectacular."

"Do you honestly believe that?"

A slow nod. "It's not self-deprecating if it's fact."

"Astra, come on now."

"It's not just you." She sat up straighter. "I have a hard time believing anything nice doesn't come with a cost."

There were so many things I could've said, so many answers I craved to hear. But this girl, sitting so guarded across from me, needed fortitude, not fear.

"Help me," I said, laying out a careful palm. "Help me figure you out."

Those brown eyes, reflecting like golden rays in the orange hue, were fixated on my gesture. As if a foreign object was placed in front of her - equal parts captivating yet terrifying – she inched her hand closer, fingertips grazing mine.

"Can I hold your hand?" I asked softly, wishfully.

I watched that delicate throat bob, the curl in her wrist, before she gently rested one finger above my own.

I couldn't help the smile on my face, the beaming grin from ear to ear and the flush in my

Meeting Dr. Praigale — *Marie-France Leger*

cheeks. This was big for her, touching me, being here with me... This wasn't easy.

Something had made this human act of intimacy impossible for her.

And that hurt me.

I couldn't imagine what hurt her.

I retracted all my fingers except the one she was holding, my index, and tapped her fingernail gently.

"That's okay, love," I released, "baby steps."

She gazed at me as if I was an anomaly. "How are you so kind?"

I raised my shoulders. "If you can be anything, why not be kind, right?"

"I guess," she sniffed. "I wish I felt that way."

I watched solemn grief cloud her eyes. I couldn't stand it. I needed to know what broke her. I needed to know how to help.

"What's your fatal flaw, Astra?" I asked, chipping away at the surface of vulnerability.

She glanced up at me. "What?"

"Your fatal flaw. Everyone has one."

She hesitated. "What's yours?"

Sadly, an easy answer. "I'd say perfectionism."

Her laugh was curt. "Of course it is."

"You could've guessed that?"

"It's a very textbook answer, that's all."

"It's the truth," I replied, forcing away the thoughts of my upcoming schedules, tasks, and my father's demands.

She tapped her finger against mine. "I wasn't trying to be insensitive. If anything, it's a compliment that you need things in order. Structure," she continued. "Stability."

"Well then," I leaned in, "what's yours?"

"I guess..." A loose thread of hair fell over her eyes. "Wishing for someone to understand me without letting someone try."

I opened my mouth to speak but she cut me off.

"Noah, I want to let you in and – I..." Her tentative eyes looked up. "Have you ever heard the name Malcom Matheson?" she asked, barely a whisper.

Matheson... Malcom – Matheson... "Sounds familiar." I nodded before the tragic recognition hit me all at once. My voice lowered. "Matheson. The football star from Woodstock? He passed away?"

Astra's stare was hollow. She said nothing. I didn't know what that meant, but it couldn't have been good.

"Was..." I chose my next words carefully, a coiling pit of dread forming in my stomach. "Was he a friend of yours?"

Her features contorted sourly, as if the word *friend* was almost painful to hear. She turned over her right forearm, pointing at a long white scar that extended along the crease of her elbow.

"A few nights before Malcom died, he shoved me against a fence at a home-game party." She couldn't meet my eyes. "They um, lost, that night. The team. Him."

He shoved me against a fence.
He shoved me against a fence.

The words slithered through my ears like barbed wire.

"He was mad, he blamed himself, and when he blamed himself... he blamed me."

My knuckles curled into a fist as I pleaded for a sense of control I knew wouldn't come. "Malcom Matheson was your boyfriend?"

"Unfortunately." Her laugh was sarcastic, tired. Worn. "For about five years."

Oh my God.

"And he hurt..." I couldn't say it. I couldn't say the words. I couldn't believe them.

"All the time." A tear dripped down her cheek. "All the fucking time."

I felt paralyzed, watching her break like this. Watching all that suppressed suffering bubble to the surface. It started to make sense, all of it – all of *her*. And I hated that these were the pieces that made Astra, *Astra*.

Five years.

Five years with an abuser.

"I don't want pity," she started, wiping away the sadness with the back of her hand. "It was a long time ago. But sometimes it feels... it feels like yesterday. Sometimes," she swallowed, "when I write,

I feel like he's there, grabbing my neck, squeezing the life out of me again.

"Everyone loved him. That funeral... *his* funeral, everyone just kept saying he was a good boy, a good person and I stood there - like a fucking broken doll, rubbing all these injuries and pleading for someone to see me... for someone to notice what he'd done to me."

"Astra you don't have to -"

But she pressed forward. "You need to understand, Noah," she glanced up, eyes bloodshot in gloom, "that I've only ever been alone. Even in the company of others... I've only felt emptiness.

"Because I'm conditioned to love people who leave me, hurt me. And... I don't know how to love someone who won't."

The ringing in my ears intensified to something wrathful. Vengeful.

I couldn't do it anymore. I couldn't do it.

This time, nothing held me back.

Nothing stopped me.

One second I was in my seat, the next I had Astra in my arms, her small frame locked into mine, safe - safe from Malcom, safe from the horrors of this world.

Safe. Safe. Safe. The word took on a whole new meaning, being with her now, learning bits of her story.

I didn't need to hear any more to keep her secure, protected.

Meeting Dr. Praigale *Marie-France Leger*

"I've got you," I repeated, over and over, allowing her tears to coat the collar of my shirt. "You're safe now."

She tensed. "I'm sorry – I don't know why I'm telling you this –"

"No." I cupped the dampness on her cheek. "You have nothing to apologize for. Nothing. Never. Not with me."

"Noah –"

"I'm not going to leave, okay? I will never hurt you. All that pain, that stops with him." I stared into those beautiful, brown spheres, unable to hold back the intensity of my emotions. "Your happiness starts with me."

She blinked at me then, eyes blanketed in tears, and produced a small smile.

My heart grew two sizes.

Beneath all the breakage was a world unknown, a plot she was terrified to tread, but I knew – I damn knew that I'd be right by her side.

It was unlike any feeling I'd ever felt.

A gravitational pull, a tug in the cosmos, an unbreakable bond that seemed to exist before Astra and I had even met.

Written in the stars, as the poets say.

Maybe they were written for us.

I don't know how long we sat there, arm in arm, chest to chest. I could've held her for one more minute, or forever.

Whatever she wanted.

"My question..." she whispered at last, wiping a tear from her cheek. "I have a question."

"Anything." *Anytime. Always.*

Her voice cracked. "Do you still love your ex-girlfriend?"

"Astra –" I breathed, shaking my head in absurdity.

"I need to know," she insisted, widening her glossy eyes. "I need to know before I say what I'm about to say."

With her body cradled in mine, her head angled to me, those lips, her beautiful lips calling out to me, I spoke in truth.

"I haven't thought about Annika since the moment I thought about you. And every moment after, it's only been you."

A sole tear dripped down her cheek, melting into the skin of my fingertip, dissolving into stars.

"I don't know what to do with these emotions." She shook her head. "We haven't known each other that long and yet..."

I placed her hand to my heart, speaking the unspoken. "It beats for you too, love."

She scrunched the fabric of my shirt into her tiny palm. "Do you like me, Doctor Noah Praigale?" Her gentle laugh was a love song. "Because I really hope you do."

Moments like this rarely existed. I knew that now. In my twenty-nine years of living on this planet, I'd never felt this way before.

Meeting Dr. Praigale — *Marie-France Leger*

Unlocked. Bare. Swirling in a state of complete and utter limerence.

She asked me a question – despite it all – if I liked her.

Doctor Noah Praigale.

A mechanical brain, void of arts and literature. Someone who studied anatomy and medicine for a living, not stories or works of fiction.

And yet, it was adoration that came to mind, when looking at her. Passion behind pages, secrets between sentences.

I want to know what you're thinking about, I'd say. *At all times of the day, you wander off and I want to know where you go. With eyes so warm and welcoming despite the chaos you've lived through. I want to talk to you, when the skies turn to shades darker than night and when the sun rises to unreachable limits, I want to talk to you about how we can reach the stratosphere together. I don't know you, Stargirl. Not in the ways I'd like to, not yet. But I can wait. Because I like you. I'm really starting to like you. And the beauty of falling is the journey of flying. The beauty of you, Astra Meredith DuPont... is everything.*

I cleared my throat, smiling at the thought of pouring my heart and soul into someone who needed this love more than anyone else. But with time, these parts would be revealed.

And we had nothing but time.

"That's one way to put it," I released, prompting her towards the empty dance floor.

"What are you doing?" she followed, folding her arms around her middle.

"I have a question," I said, pulling out my phone. The soft hum of *Apocalypse* played through the speaker, growing louder with each step I took towards Astra.

Toe to toe now, I gazed into those starlit eyes.

"What's your question?" she grinned, head tilting to the side.

I knew that she knew.

But there was beauty in saying exactly how you felt – requesting exactly what you wanted, from the person you needed.

I cleared my throat, bowing to her height, and extended a hand. "Will you dance with me, Stargirl?"

Chapter Twenty-One
Astra

He held onto me with such carefulness, his hands resting at my waist, his tall frame blanketing me in embrace.

I'd never been held like this – never been held by someone who knew how to hold me.

No bruises.

No rough edges.

Just... tenderness.

Every part of me ached; my mind, my soul, my fucking heart and yet this... this man, who had me tucked in the net of his arms, alleviated some of that pain.

Did that mean something?

Could it?

I wrapped my hands around the back of his neck. "So this is what you listen to. *Cigarettes After Sex*."

He pulled me closer. "Novo Amor, Bon Iver, you name it."

"A true melancholic man, Mr. Pringle."

"Without a doubt," he supplied. "I'm also huge on crying into whiskey bottles and writing sonnets at midnight."

I chuckled. "A man of many layers."

"As far as the eye can see, Stargirl."

Meeting Dr. Praigale

"What happens now?" I asked, pushing my face closer to the fabric of his shirt. He smelled like cedarwood and sage. Two scents I knew I'd never forget.

Cedarwood and sage.

"What do you want to happen?" he responded, his chin dipping against the top of my head.

We swayed silently for a few more moments, the faint sound of chords filling the empty spaces around our bodies.

What do you want to happen?

If it were that easy, I'd say everything. *Everything, all at once, right now.*

But it wasn't simple.

Nothing about this was simple.

Feelings and emotions... they seemed like a walk in the park until you had them. Until they consumed you, elated you, diminished you and tore you to pieces and then you were left with nothing but a hole in your fucking heart that never went away. Never filled.

A heart that slowly dies.

I thought my ability to feel earnestly was abducted by Malcom, stolen, even before he left this planet. And learning to trust again – to love again – that would take an absurdly long time.

Noah didn't deserve that. To wait for someone like me to be ready for someone like him.

And yet, selfishly, I wanted to take the chance.

"Should we go slow?" I swallowed, almost immediately regretting the question, but his fingers tightened around my waist.

"If we go any slower, I'd say we're living statues."

I poked his chest softly before looking up at him, feeling so naturally calm in this moment.

Safe.

"I know you meant us, love," he smiled down at me, those sunken dimples peeking through. "I'll go at any pace you want."

"Everything moved so fast, so intensely." I admitted, adjusting my arms around his neck. "I feel like I just met you and now you're..."

"Everywhere?"

"Yes, I hate it."

His shoulders shook in amusement. "You hate it?"

"It's not supposed to be like this..." My mind wandered to my novels, the slow-burn of it all. Friends to lovers, enemies to lovers, all the tropes that made up a good story.

We were none of those things.

We just...

Met.

"What is it supposed to be like?" He pulled my body closer, two fingers grazing the skin beneath my tank top.

Meeting Dr. Praigale *Marie-France Leger*

A shiver ran through my spine at his touch. So gentle and warm. Nothing like Malcom or Liam. And yet, that pleasure made me shudder.

I cursed the dead, for once in my fucking life. That he left me with scars only I could see. Only I could feel.

If that made me a bad person, then I'd go to hell.

Because for the rest of my life, I'd never be able to tell the difference between love and hate, bliss and pain, serendipity and sadness.

Everything blended together.

I tried, so hard I tried to savour the moment, but I couldn't do it. I felt too much. I yanked my body away, shutting my eyes in shame. "I'm sorry."

The music was off in an instant.

My ears were ringing.

"Astra," he took a step closer. I moved back. "Talk to me."

It was Malcom there, stalking up to me, eyes feral like a hyena.

And then it wasn't.

And then it was.

And I couldn't – *I can't fucking breathe* –

I gripped my hair in my hands. "I just need a second," I murmured, finding the closest chair.

The scrape of wooden pegs came a second later as another chair appeared in front of me. Noah leaned forward. "It's a weird feeling, I know."

I kept my head low, avoiding his gaze.

"Whatever this is, you know, between us... It's something I want to hold on to. And I mean it, Astra, when I say we can go at whatever pace you want."

I felt his hand on my knee, briefly, before he pulled it away. "Is it okay if I cash in another question?"

I nodded slowly, catching a breath. That stupid voice kept returning. Kept chanting.

Shame. Guilt. Regret.

Shame. Guilt. Regret.

But then it was replaced by something else, something kind.

Something safe.

"Do you think you're lovable, Astra?" Noah asked, his words a blanket of comfort in my ears.

I wanted to say yes. To believe that, with all my flaws, someone could love me. So I nodded. An auto-pilot response, coming from someone exposed to many, many affirmation posts. That if I told myself I was worthy of love, I'd receive it.

"Yes." And it was the greatest lie I'd ever told.

Noah paused before saying, "But you don't think anyone can ever love you."

It felt surreal, knowing that I couldn't be dishonest with him. That he could see right through my mistruths. Noah didn't ask the question, he formed a statement. I took it as such.

And again, with pain, I nodded.

He sighed. "Why do you think that?"

Then came the saddest admission. The worst acceptance. The simplest answer of all. "Because no one ever has."

The silence that followed was deafening, forcing me to cower back to the moments of my past.

It was over. Malcom was gone. He couldn't hurt me anymore.

But wishes were words, and just because you said them, didn't mean they'd come true.

I wished it was that easy to let go of.

I wished I was easier to love.

Noah's chair scraped closer to mine. He bowed forward. "The first time my dad ever really looked at me was when I got accepted to vet school." He planted his elbows atop his knees, brows cross. "We never had a good relationship, him and I. I don't know what I did. I don't know what my mom did, or my sister but...

"It's like he hated us from the start – saw us as a part of this game of life, as if we were just accessories, not a family."

All I could do was watch him, hear the strain in his voice, as the hazy feel of my emotions dulled out quietly.

I wanted to listen. To hear his story.

To shy away from mine.

"But when I got in, when it was clear I'd be following in his footsteps, it's like he was proud of me. For the first time in my life, my father looked at me with pride.

"He said, '*Everything happens for a reason, son. Make no mistake of that.*'"

Noah grimaced, and I nudged my chair forward, tempted to take his shaky hands in mine.

"That was the day he cheated on my mom." His brown eyes turned a shade darker. "She knew it all along. Apparently it wasn't the first time."

My tongue went dry. For the first time, I spoke. "How did you find out?"

His laugh was oil. "The old man told me. Just straight up told me. Said it was about time we had a grown-up conversation."

A flicker of rage lodged itself in my temples. "That's his definition of grown-up?"

He tilted his chin. "I asked my mom about it. I said, '*How can you put up with this? How can you stay with someone who doesn't treat you right?*'"

A hollow pit formed in my stomach.

"Astra, I didn't understand back then." He shook his head. "My mom came from an abusive home, a toxic, terrible backstory. You said that everyone loved Malcom?"

I nodded, a sour taste hitting the back of my throat.

"Everyone thinks the same of my dad. That he's this amazing vet, which he is, I'm not downplaying that. But he never showed us an ounce

Meeting Dr. Praigale *Marie-France Leger*

of love. Not my mother, not my sister when she went to rehab, and especially not me."

My heart hammered in my chest, seeing the sadness in his eyes, a mirrored pain of mine, and it slowly came together.

That phone call, at the clinic. His tense shoulders, the constant need to prove his devotion and intelligence. He'd earn his worth. He needed to show that he was successful in order to be loved.

It was a miserable existence. To live in the shadow of someone who'd never let you shine.

I knew that all too well.

"My mom stayed with my dad because she never thought it could get better." Ragged sympathy radiated off of him as he spoke. "To this day, I think she's scared to walk away because he conditioned her to feel like she can't be somebody else without him."

The ghost of Malcom called to me, reminding me of his presence. Reminding me of this exact feeling.

"It's not too late for you, Astra. People make choices: to be happy, or to live in fear of happiness."

He held out his hand, pressing two gentle fingers underneath my chin. "I know how it feels to live in a lack of love. But it doesn't stop me from wanting to give it."

I closed my eyes, leaning into his touch, allowing his words to flow in and out of me like a gentle breeze.

Meeting Dr. Praigale — *Marie-France Leger*

For the first time in my life, I felt it. The spark of understanding. The stars colliding.

Meeting Dr. Praigale had been no accident.

And the longer I fought that feeling – that he was a muse to my masterpiece and nothing else – the longer I'd live in this lie.

I didn't want to do that anymore.

I just... I just wanted peace.

He was up before I could respond, extending a hand out for me to take. "Let me drive you home, it's getting late."

Everything in me wanted to fight for this moment to last, to spend every second getting to know all there was to know about him.

But my energy had been depleted, he'd seen that even before I felt it. And I could tell he was using every ounce of his in an attempt not to break.

The car ride back was quiet. Not tense, but rigid. As if a stone wall had formed between us, one we spent all night breaking down.

I wasn't the only one suffering.

I wasn't the only one shattering.

Everyone had scars beneath their skin.

Some wore it visibly, and some hid it within.

Who were we both if not shadows of our traumas? Of our past chains and shackles?

Would we overcome this together? Or was this too much? Opening up... letting out the demons. Could it have overwhelmed him? Me?

Was this a mistake?

"What are you thinking about?" he asked, pulling into the parking lot of Cloud Café.

If only he knew. "Just wondering how we went from *Magic Hat Milkshakes* to divulging our traumas."

He chuckled then clicked out of his seatbelt. Before I could open my door, he rounded the car and opened it for me. "Maybe the sugar made us high."

"Remind me to never drink that shit again," I replied, matching his pace towards the loft stairwell. "What time is it?"

"Close to two."

"In the morning?" I gasped.

His lips curled. "Some first date, huh."

I snorted as we made it to the front of my door, a stinging feeling of goodbye looming over our heads.

"Thank you," I started, above all the things I could've said. "Thank you for everything you've done tonight, Noah."

He smiled. "I'd ask when I'll see you again but you have work on Tuesday."

"That's right," I snapped my fingers. "And you are now my temporary boss."

"Nervous for your first day, love?"

I crossed my arms, leaning against the doorframe. "Careful Dr. Praigale, some may say you're acting unprofessional."

"It's my clinic." He took a step forward, towering over me. "Do *you* have a problem with it, Miss DuPont?"

Meeting Dr. Praigale   *Marie-France Leger*

My breathing hitched. "It just seems very cliché."

"Ah, would it count as a workplace romance?" His posture dipped lower as he too, leaned against the doorframe, confining me to the small space between him and the wood behind me.

"So you're familiar with the trope?" I fought my nervousness. My intrigue.

He smirked. "I can be."

Fuck. "You know, mixing business and pleasure never works out."

"My pleasure would be working with you, Astra. And working alongside you, is business. I see nothing wrong with that."

"We'd be co-workers, in a sense," I blushed.

He looked me up and down. "In a sense, I suppose we already are."

"Then we can't do..." I swallowed, glancing down to his lips, then back to those honey-brown eyes.

"Do... this?" The back of his knuckles grazed my cheek, so featherlight and gentle.

"Friends." It came out before I could sheathe my brainlessness. "We should stay friends."

I didn't mean it.

Of course I didn't fucking mean it.

But I was exhausted. Scared. Fragile.

And if Dr. Praigale was to be my boss, then we had to maintain a level of professionalism that did not involve late night dates and Magic Hat Milkshakes and... well, *this*.

A pained expression crossed his features but he said nothing, pushing away from the brick wall, granting me a moment to breathe.

"I'll see you on Tuesday, Miss DuPont." His long legs descended the grated stairwell. "Looking forward to working with you."

I stood in a static state, watching him wave goodbye before driving into the night. His headlights disappeared. His presence was gone. And yet that familiar scent wrapped around me like an impassioned hug.

Cedarwood and sage.

Chapter Twenty-Two
Astra

Last Edit – 6:34am: No Title
Taylan tossed in her sleep, dreaming of a long bridge, separating the light and the dark. One side called to her, lured her in with breathless kisses and ferocity. The other, a calm, kind aura. So alien to what she's come to know. And yet, she dipped her toe into the dark, wondering if those broken promises could be redeemed. And if somehow they could, would those promises mean anything anymore?

"Ring-ring, Astra. Pages, I need pages."

Teresa's voice was the first I heard this morning. I'd woken up around six a.m., midway through writing Taylan's revelations, when she called an hour later.

"I'm just finishing off this paragraph," I grumbled, typing out the last few sentences with a slice of toast between my teeth. "Can you give me a minute?"

"Parker needs them in for edits. Half the book is done now, no?"

"Erhm…" I glanced at my page count. Two-thirty-two. "I don't know how long I want this book to be."

Meeting Dr. Praigale *Marie-France Leger*

"You don't know how it's going to end? *When* it's going to end?" There was a pinch in her tone; one of the main reasons I chose to work with her in the first place. She gave me legroom to write, not to procrastinate.

"I don't typically plan the endings, they just sort of... come to me."

A huff. "Well, tell this ending to come fast. It's been nine months of zero from you. No interviews, not since *Leafing Through Liv*. People need product, Astra. Otherwise, you'll blend into nothing."

"I doubt that's true." I bit back. "Plenty of authors publish two or three years at a time."

"Yes, and they're also in the limelight. You, my dear, refuse to be."

I didn't have an answer to that. Teresa was right. With everything that happened in my past, I couldn't fathom having my name out in the public. There would be... talk. People linking my name to *his*. If M. D. Pont was revealed to be Astra Meredith DuPont, my success would be tied to the death of Malcom.

My worst fucking nightmare.

"I expect you to be writing all day." Teresa added. "Parker wants the book finished by the end of the month."

My jaw dropped. "That's impossible."

"It's your career, Astra. It's possible."

A blush coated my cheeks. If Teresa and Parker, my agent and editor, found out I'd taken on

Meeting Dr. Praigale   *Marie-France Leger*

another job – albeit temporary – they'd lose their damn minds.

"I'll get it done."

"Good," she piped. "Now email what you have so I can update the team. We have to work on some cover designs too so if you can draft a synopsis, that'd be great."

I sighed, rewiring my brain to new timelines. "Yeah, I'll send something over by the end of the day."

"Great." And she hung up.

I slumped back into my seat, staring at the unfinished story of Taylan Nichols, wondering how in the hell I'd manage to finish this book in just under four weeks.

On one hand, if I were to pull out of my commitment with Dr. Praigale, then he'd be screwed over – *royally*, because I made a promise. But on the other, if I couldn't devote all my time to writing, then my deadline wouldn't be met.

It's a temporary position, I told myself. *Just Tuesdays and Thursdays. I can do this.*

After all, Dr. Praigale was my muse, and quite literally the only reason I'd written something readable in the last nine months.

But after our date, after opening up to him and seeing his own vulnerability, the lines of inspiration blurred.

Because Noah wasn't just my muse anymore, he was a chance. A man who promised me happiness.

A man who – I cringed to admit – I wanted to see again.

And in just one hour, I would.

As friends.

Co-workers.

Professionals.

I couldn't afford it to be anything else, not now anyway. And if I accepted the darkest parts of me, they were terrified of commitment. Of allowing the dam to break, and letting light flourish.

This was something good. The start of opening a new door, while slowly closing another.

But that scared me. That fucking terrified me.

And I refused to lose it – *him* – by jumping headfirst into uncharted territory.

Walls kept me safe – kept the pain away.

So as long as we were hiding in the shadows of our identities, everything would remain exactly the same.

If we were no longer M.D. Pont and Dr. Praigale then...

We were simply Astra and Noah.

And I haven't been that girl in many, many years.

***

"Good to see you again, Miss DuPont."

Vern, the receptionist, greeted me at the door with a wide grin.

"Hi... Vern. Can I call you Vern?" I asked.

Meeting Dr. Praigale — Marie-France Leger

"'Course hon." She laughed. "That is my name."

I welcomed her warmth. "Some people prefer titles."

"Not around here, Dr. Praigale insists on a first name basis."

"So I've heard," I smiled.

"Anyhow," she slid a keycard my way, "door's down the hall. He should be in there getting everything ready for you."

I nodded in thanks and trotted the familiar path down the corridor, narrowly avoiding carts filled with syringes and clear vials. Before I found the entrance to the adoption centre, I was intercepted by Dr. William McLean, cross armed, leaning against the keypad entry.

"So you really did come back, huh?" he started, lips slanted in glee.

"You expected me not to?"

"Wasn't sure."

"I signed the contract in front of you."

He hummed. "Could've been anyone."

I flicked up my wrist, ogling the watch – *yes the watch* – I wore for the day. "I'm ten minutes late."

William let out a low whistle. "Boss won't be happy."

I took a step forward. "And if I tell him you're the reason why?"

He matched my stature. "Then you're a snitch."

Meeting Dr. Praigale *Marie-France Leger*

"Enough McLean," Noah's stern voice came from an intercom above. An intercom I hadn't even noticed was placed there.

William just smirked, unlocking the keypad himself, before jaunting away.

Shit disturber indeed.

I glanced up at the camera I found in the corner ceiling, blinking red, watching me. I gave a smirk of my own, knowing who had access to this recording, and stepped through the door.

Reaching the entrance to the office, I spotted Noah smoothing out some papers. He was dressed in burgundy scrubs, a brown, plastic headband pushing back loose threads of his hair, and black Crocs.

"Don't you clean up nice?" I teased, knocking softly on the doorframe.

I could feel him smile even before he turned to me. "It's the Crocs, isn't it?"

"They're mesmerizing."

He wiggled his feet then stood up, handing me a paper. "Your to-do list, Miss DuPont."

My eyes scanned the sheet. "And here I was thinking I'd be playing fetch all day."

He took a step closer, the scent of him wrapping me in momentary bliss.

"That's number four on the list, if I remember correctly."

At my side, he leaned down, grazing his hand gently over mine, and pointed to the task. "I remembered correctly," he smirked.

My heart stalled.

He moved aside, grabbing a stack of files before making way to the exit.

"I'm on line one, if you need anything, love," he added, half in, half out of the door.

I swallowed. "I thought we were being professional."

The corner of his lips curled, his eyes roaming over my face, down my body. "Thick walls, Miss DuPont" – he knocked on the wood – "no one can hear a thing."

And with that pocket of information, he was gone.

Leaving me utterly stripped, bare –
And completely fucking smitten.

Chapter Twenty-Three
Noah

Two weeks of civility.

Four shifts of professionalism, keeping Astra at a distance, when all I wanted to do was learn every inch of her mind and forget the world existed.

She told me she wanted to be friends, that this – *whatever this is* – could wait.

I never understood that concept. When two people, so evidently connected fell for each other, how they could wait to unite the spark.

But I wasn't Astra.

And there was beauty in patience. That, I understood.

Even though she signed the part-time contract, two days a week still felt like plenty. A bolt of lightning that struck every part of this clinic.

She was that lightning.

I'd sometimes walk by the adoption center, pretending to grab a file or call log, and see her playing with the kittens and puppies. She never noticed me, of course, not when her attention was on the animals.

But my attention was on her.

Wholly, fully. Entirely. On *her*.

I thought it would be a good idea, thought I could work with her nearby and feel somewhat steady.

What a huge misjudgement.

Her presence was everywhere, overwhelming.

Between surgeries and appointments, I'd think, '*Why not just pop in and chat? No harm in that.*' But as my feet carried me towards the kennels, McLean would stop me every time.

"You've got a job to do, you know. Mitch is supervising next week and if he catches you slipping, this clinic's never going to be yours, Big Bone."

And that was the push I needed to take a step back, to respect not only what she wanted – a *friendship* – but also a reminder of my position, the job I had to do.

I was Doctor Praigale.

But I was acting like some lovesick Noah.

We had a few promising interviews for the permanent position of playmate and adoption assistant, but until Astra's contract was up at the end of the month, she would remain in my company.

She would be the one to meet Dr. Mitchell Praigale.

My father.

The idea of that swam laps around my mind for days on end.

She seemed to be doing well. We'd interacted just as much as I did with my usual staff. The occasional question here and there, a few stolen glances that transcended the professional setting of my clientele, however she never rang my line.

Until now.

Meeting Dr. Praigale *Marie-France Leger*

As I walked to meet her in the office, my mind contemplated different avenues of conversation. Since our date, I never brought up anything surrounding feelings or the possibility of another outing. She hadn't so much as texted me unless it involved a computer issue or clarifying tasks.

I had to commend her on her work ethic, though I wasn't shocked. She was a writer after all, as well as a part-time barista and now...

My part-time distraction.

"Knock-knock," I tapped the doorframe, stepping into the small office space.

She hadn't made any changes, though I didn't expect her to. She wasn't staying. I had to remind myself of that.

But seeing her now, slumped over the wooden desk, fingers flying across computer keys and hovering over files, she appeared to fit right in.

Right into my world.

"Hey," she started, seemingly distracted. "Sorry to bother you."

"Never a bother, love. What can I do for you?"

Now her eyes met mine, wide and eager, but she didn't address the sentiment. "I can't seem to access this one file for um" – she scanned the screen – "Adam Lee. He wants to adopt the eight-year-old Corgi."

I walked over to the desk, hesitating to lean over the chair, then carefully lowered myself to her height. "Can I take a look?"

"Please," she shifted the laptop, "that's why I called."

She smelled like lilac and roses, the scent of her shampoo so near it wrapped me in its embrace.

We said nothing as I clicked from tab to tab, glancing over scanned documents that prompted a recurring error.

"Hm," I scrolled, "he may have pulled out of the adoption."

"Why?" She looked almost pained.

"It happens often enough." I glanced at her, a few inches above me as I balanced on my knees. "Owning a pet is a lot of work. A lot of people see a cute dog or cat and make rash decisions."

"It's not fair to them though, the animals" she frowned. "To promise a home and not deliver."

"That's why we make it as comfortable as possible for them here."

She chewed her lip, eyes facing the screen. "Don't you get attached to them?"

"Of course," I shifted back. "It's hard not to. Especially with the lives some of them had to endure."

"Then why don't *you* adopt them all?"

I laughed. "Every day, Astra. Every day I wish I could."

Meeting Dr. Praigale   *Marie-France Leger*

She turned to me. "One day, I'll do it. I'll have a home designated for all the animals that need one, and they'll be my children."

The swell in my heart grew a fraction further.

When I met Annika, she'd retorted a similar speech. It had won me over, and considering we were in the same field, I respected her more for it.

But this, seeing Astra distraught over Brandy the Corgi, it was a whole new feeling.

A feeling that I now realized, was lacking in Annika.

I fought with all my might to resist asking the question, but it was a battle I couldn't win, not when I needed to know everything about Astra Meredith DuPont.

"Do you ever want kids?"

I thought she'd react, shut me out entirely, call me ridiculous for even asking, but she didn't. Instead, she looked at me inquisitively, drumming her fingers.

"I don't know," she responded. "I'm afraid of the world we live in. I don't want them to experience the same things that I have."

The thought of Malcom Matheson's hands on her sent a coil of dread to my stomach. For nights it kept me up, passing her in the hall, the quick but sweet goodbyes she'd make, I saw it everywhere. *Him* everywhere. Following this poor woman like a ghost, concealing her from the light.

If I could burn a shadow, I'd turn his to ash.

Meeting Dr. Praigale — *Marie-France Leger*

"And I really don't want to end up like my mother," she finished, shaking her head.

"You wouldn't," I added swiftly. "You couldn't."

Her eyes twinkled with a plea. "How do you know?"

"Because you're nothing like her."

"I try not to be," she sighed. "But what if there's some part of me that is? What if I become the very thing I hate?"

"Astra" – my fingers curled around the base of the rolling chair – "we make a conscious effort every day to be a better human. We make a choice. Despite your mother's upbringing, and hers before, you are your own person. You dictate your fate..."

My eyes subconsciously flitted to her lips. She drew a breath. I saw it too.

"You dictate what you want," I swallowed, forcing my gaze upward.

Her pupils dilated. She was reacting to me. She didn't want to be friends. And even though deep down I knew that I had to be patient, this feeling satiated me enough.

My eyes flicked to the laptop once more, seeing an empty tab at the bottom. A word document, an untitled page.

Instinctively, I clicked it, and a train of pages covered the screen.

"Don't look at that!" she blurted, tilting the computer away from me.

Meeting Dr. Praigale *Marie-France Leger*

I held up my hands. "Was that your book?"

Her cheeks were pink. "Just a few passages I wrote during lunch. Trust me, I was working."

"I don't doubt you were working," I laughed. "Hell, this isn't even the position you signed up for. Go out there and play with some puppies, Miss DuPont."

She relaxed. "Dr. McLean showed me the ropes around tech."

"I bet he did," I grinded out.

She looked puzzled. "Is something wrong?"

"I think he's got a bit of a crush on you," I admitted, though I didn't want to believe it. Never, in all my years of friendship with Will did I doubt him.

But with the flirtatious remarks, the way his eyes would trail her as she left the clinic, him blocking my path to see her... I couldn't help but wonder if he was infringing on my territory.

Oh.

No.

I did not just say my *territory.*

Astra's expression was a mix of confusion and ridicule. "You're joking, right?"

Then, she started to laugh.

"Noah, I've seen him get into different girls' cars every shift I've worked here. And that's four. Four shifts. Four girls. Four cars."

Well, he did tell me that.

Meeting Dr. Praigale *Marie-France Leger*

There was Caren from the gym, Blake from... I don't know, actually. Sab, a friend of a friend, and I suppose the new one he'd yet to inform me of.

Regardless, I couldn't shake the feeling. And that bothered me to no end.

"He's a serial dater," I shrugged.

She rested a hand on my shoulder, our first contact in weeks. Though small, I savoured the touch.

"Are you sure you're not overreacting?" she asked, softly.

"Well, I'm not underreacting, Stargirl."

At the sound of her nickname, she stared at me with intention, a soft glow growing within her eyes.

"Are you jealous, Dr. Praigale?"

Jealous.

I could've laughed at the thought.

I was never a jealous person. Protective, yes. But there was a difference between the two.

I'd felt the need to comfort Astra before, to shield her from pain and peril, and that feeling never faded.

Maybe I was reading into it because of my longing, my eagerness to keep her in my life. I was self-aware enough to realize how deeply I'd fallen through the cracks of infatuation.

Yet another distraction I'd have to face while she worked alongside me.

"I'll have to talk to him," I said, more to myself than anything else.

Jealous. *Ridiculous.*

Her gaze never faltered. "You didn't answer my question."

"It's a skill." I shrugged in jest, placing a hand over hers. "If I'm allowed to be anything, then protective is what I am."

"Of..." she goaded.

I squeezed her fingers. "Of what's mine."

She retracted her hand, smiling with victory. "So now I'm yours?"

"Informally," I smirked, teasing. "Don't think I've forgotten what you told me, though. Friends, right?"

A cloud passed over her face. "Noah..."

"You don't need to explain. I understand."

And I did. Even if it burned a hole through my heart.

She had a battalion of demons locked away in her mind, a band of struggles to work through before opening up to the concept of togetherness. Intimacy.

I'd wait. There was no question of that.

Because there was no question of her.

She enraptured me, faster than I thought humanly possible.

"Can I read that?" I nudged my head to the open word document, filled with her writing.

That same blush returned to her cheeks as she closed the laptop, checking her watch. "Maybe when it's on the shelves next month."

"Next month?"

"My agent and editor want the book done in two weeks. I -" she paused. "I've been writing day and night and in between shifts at Cloud and, well, *here*."

I shook my head. "Astra, why didn't you tell me? This a huge commitment, a huge deadline. I can find a replacement, we have people on the go -"

"I need to be here." She cut me off, unable to meet my eyes.

I stood up, sinking into my heels. "Why?"

"Because..." she swallowed. The intensity in her gaze could have powered the sun. "Because you're my muse."

Chapter Twenty-Four
Astra

This wasn't the way I wanted to tell him.

I mean, how does anyone properly say, '*Hey, you inspired the book I'm writing so I have to stick by your side until it's finished*' without sounding like a complete stalker psychopath?

Mind you, the novel wasn't exactly centered around either of us, but I'd be lying if I said that crafting Taylan and Josh's characters didn't have any semblance to real circumstances.

Dr. Praigale helped my art. Whether consciously or not, it didn't matter. This was the first time I'd written something substantial in months, something authentic and real. Unlike all my other cheesy romances, this one had meaning - feeling.

This one was all me.

"I'm your..." he stalled, searching for the words. His expression was incredulous.

I put up a shaky hand. "It's not - um, serious. It's just, inspiration."

"Astra..."

The sudden urge to explain myself came out in verbal word vomit.

I fucking panicked.

"I know it sounds weird and you probably think I'm obsessive or creepy but it's a writer's process and it's not uncommon -"

"Astra."

"– but I knew I had to tell you at some point, and I don't want you to think anything was fabricated between –"

I stopped.

He stopped me.

I…

I was staring at him.

Right in the face, I know I was.

I was fumbling and stammering trying to explain myself – the reasons for being here, the proximity and then –

And then he was –

He was *kissing* me.

His lips.

Doctor Noah Praigale's mouth –

Was on *mine*.

It happened so fast, like a gust of wind – a pleasurable, sweet escape of desire and ecstasy – that came and went within a split second.

One fucking second.

A heartbeat, that I would pay anything to return to.

Because before I could pulse my lips, get lost in the feeling that *was* Noah Praigale, he yanked his body away, a look of utter shock and reverie on his face.

"What…" I couldn't speak.

Meeting Dr. Praigale *Marie-France Leger*

I couldn't even register the moment, the brief collision of bliss, before the illusion of his mouth danced in echo.

"I'm sorry, I –" He staggered back, as if physically restraining himself from coming any closer. "You are... You are *not* my friend, Astra DuPont."

And without warning, he left the office in a rush, abandoning me with the memory of his warm lips against mine, and the unspoken words that lingered between us.

You are so much more.

Chapter Twenty-Five
Noah

... what have I done?

Chapter Twenty-Six
Astra

"So he just kissed you and walked out?" Beth stopped mid-bite, crumbs of Cloud muffin tumbling down her fingers.

"I'm so confused," Eva added, spooning banana pudding into her mouth. "Did he go into shock or something?"

I invited my sister and best friend over to the Café exactly four days after Noah had kissed me. *If you could even call that a kiss.*

After he left, we hadn't spoken.

He hadn't texted me.

He hadn't so much as said goodbye when I left my shift that evening. Just a curt nod, and a swift dismissal.

Obviously I had to think the worst. Even if he had kissed me – or rather, planted his mouth on mine for a millisecond – even if there *was* affection, I didn't feel it.

Not when he fucking left.

"Are you okay, Astra?" Eva asked, pushing a chocolate croissant my way. "Eat. You've done nothing but write these past couple weeks."

"Yeah girl, how many calories have you consumed in the last seventy-two hours?" Beth questioned.

"Enough." I responded, tearing a piece of crust off the top. "I can't even deal with anything right now. That deadline is a week and a half away, and I'm fucking stuck."

"You're not stuck," said Beth.

"Noah's my muse, you know that. And now, where is he? Gone." I shook my head. "I shouldn't be surprised."

"You have to see him tomorrow," Eva reminded me.

I wish she hadn't.

"Yup, and then next week I'll be free and bookless." I glanced up to see Ruby unfolding her apron. "Hey Rubes."

"What're you sulking about?" She marched over, a cup of coffee in hand.

"I'm not sulking, this is my natural face."

"It is, actually." Eva said.

"Just pure gremlin, all the time." Beth chimed.

My finger flew up at both of them. *Can you guess which one?*

"A boy kissed Astra and ran away." Beth pointed at her muffin. "This is amazing, Ruby, I need a box to go."

"Twenty-four-fifty," she charged, then tilted her head to me. "Which boy, Starburst?"

I sighed. "The one who took me to the fair."

Meeting Dr. Praigale — *Marie-France Leger*

"Ah, right. The vet." She grabbed the closest chair and slid it over to our group. "Tell me all about it."

I crossed my arms, leaning back in my seat. "Shop's still open."

Ruby smiled. "Beth, be a darlin' and unplug that neon sign."

"It's only eight," I retorted.

"And it's my damn shop, I close when I want to."

"God, from an outsider's perspective, you two look like enemies." Eva laughed.

I bumped my elbow against Ruby's. "Who says we aren't?"

"Details, Astra. Old Lady Ruby wants some details." Her crystalline blue eyes twinkled with glee.

"You're really referring to yourself in the third person?"

"I ain't livin' in no damn storybook, unlike you."

Normally, I would've taken her jabs. Ruby's wisdom extended beyond my years, and I never fought her for it.

Maybe I was overwhelmed, exhausted or just flat out brittle... But this one hurt.

It really fucking hurt.

And when things hurt, I leave.

So I slid out of my chair, but not before she caught my arm.

Meeting Dr. Praigale *Marie-France Leger*

"I'm sorry, Starburst. I was out of line." She patted the cushion. "What'd the vet do?"

I let out a long exhale, staring into those kind, aged features, and sat down. "I confessed to him that he was my muse and he kissed me, sort of, then walked away. I haven't heard from him since."

She wrinkled her nose. "And that makes you sad?"

Heat swirled beneath my cheeks. "I mean, yeah, that. And my book deadline's in ten days."

Her stare never faltered. "Wan' know what I think?"

"I do!" Beth and Eva piped in unison.

But Ruby held my gaze. "Starburst?"

I nodded. "Sure."

She adjusted her position. "You've got all that creativity in your head. It doesn't come from the vet, or the wind, or this damn table" - she rattled the wood - "it comes from you. Don't you dare say you can't write a damn thing if he's not around, cause he's just a person. And you, Starburst, you're the writer."

I swallowed hard, letting her words soak in.

"And Astra," she continued, "what d'you except the poor man to do? I've seen your walls fly up for less than some date. Poor guy's probably head over heels and can't do anythin' cause you won't let him."

"I don't have the time or the -"

"The what? The courage to let someone in?"

I blanched, suppressing years of untouched pain. "I'm not a coward."

"No," her face hardened. "But the longer you let the ghost of Malcom haunt you, the closer you are to becomin' one yourself."

And with that, she slid out of the chair, plugged in the OPEN sign, and escaped to the backroom kitchen.

***

Last Edit - 12:02am: No Title

Taylan fought with her heart every single day. Her mind wanted something from her, a prison – a cage. It was comforting, isolating herself in the caverns of her pain. Pain was the poison she was willing to drink if it meant keeping out the heartbreak.

Josh Kahill was a shining knight. He promised to take care of her. But promises never sat right with Taylan. Nonetheless, he made her happy. Despite the odds, her world was lit on fire.

And for the first time in forever, she was ready to ignite.

Meeting Dr. Praigale *Marie-France Leger*

Chapter Twenty-Seven
Noah

"Do you like Astra, McLean?"

I couldn't stop myself. I had to know.

Jealous. Ridiculous.

Maybe a little.

He turned to me, muting the morning news, and let out a staggered laugh. "Pardon me?"

I grazed the edges of my yogurt cup with my spoon, scooping out the granola. "Do you?"

"What kind of question is that?"

"A valid one."

"A stupid one," he countered, rounding the table. "You're my best friend."

"I didn't ask if you were my best friend, I asked if –"

"If I had a crush on *your* girl? No, Big Bone. Far from."

"Then why do you get all, you know, extra *McLean* around her?"

He let out a gruff laugh. "Because I want to see if she can handle the heat, man. I want to see if she can take the company you keep. I don't want you hurt again. I'm tired of seeing you hurt, Big Bone."

I exhaled a sigh of relief, though I felt far from calm.

"What's going on with you lately?" He moved closer. "You ditched me and Tav Saturday, misplaced

Meeting Dr. Praigale *Marie-France Leger*

three prescriptions, and now you're asking me if I like your –"

"She's not my girl, McLean." I shook my head, biting back the sting in my next words. "I kissed her."

He let out a laugh. "Well that's contradictory."

"You kiss girls all the time that aren't yours."

"It's not the same and you know it. Look," McLean checked his watch, "if you want to talk about it later, I'm game. But your dad's coming in about ten minutes and you've got to put on a good face. Succeed now, sulk later."

The thought of Astra being down the hall, probably chipping away at the mindless tasks I handed to her while she could be writing her book didn't sit well with me.

The book that I, supposedly, inspired.

What a sentence.

That fact alone was just as unbelievable as her being so close, yet so far away.

I had no defense for my actions – for kissing her, for leaving abruptly.

All of it was too overwhelming, too complicated.

She liked me.

And I liked her.

But it wasn't enough. And in that moment, I couldn't handle that.

Meeting Dr. Praigale — *Marie-France Leger*

I was ashamed, so ashamed that I let those impulses drive me to the point of what I'd done. I couldn't form the words, not even in total isolation for the last five days.

And what's worse, I wouldn't have the time to, now that my father requested a whole staff tour since his last visit over two years ago.

Changes were made.

He wanted to approve them.

Whether I liked it or not.

McLean was right. I could attempt to explain myself and my absence to Astra later, but right now, I had to greet my father.

And ruin the start to my day.

***

"Hi son, you look..."

Here we go.

"Weathered," he settled on.

My father was dressed in all black scrubs, sunglasses still on head. He didn't come from the Guelph clinic, no, he just wanted to look the part.

The owner. The boss.

The best.

"Dad." I gave him a curt nod, leading him to Vern. McLean was leaning over the receptionist desk, talking to Courtney, when he realized who was approaching.

"Dr. Praigale," Will addressed, straightening out.

Meeting Dr. Praigale — *Marie-France Leger*

In the presence of my father, nicknames did not exist. It bled onto my functionality when he was around – turned me into something less than *me*.

"William," he nodded. "Getting a lot of work done?"

"Always."

He noted Courtney, the kind-faced intern, his eyes analyzing every bead of tension between both employees and scoffed. "I'm sure."

Before Will could defend himself, my father marched along the corridor, judging the state of ~~my~~ his clinic.

"Sanitary, clean. Sterile." He mumbled more to himself than anyone else. "Who's your janitor?"

"Same as always."

"George..."

"Guran, yes."

"Ah." His tone was clipped. "Who are the recent hires?"

I swallowed the rock in my throat, glancing over to the entrance of the adoption center. "Soon to be Courtney, the young woman you saw speaking with –"

"She'll be gone soon enough," he interrupted. "I'm sure William will see to that."

Quiet rage hid beneath my eyes. "She's a very good intern. I'm positive she'll be an asset."

"To some, I suppose," he hinted at Will. My stomach rippled in anger.

Meeting Dr. Praigale — *Marie-France Leger*

"Who else?" he prodded, disregarding my annoyance.

I trailed him through the staff room and the hallway, listing off Danni's new vet tech assistant, Rose, and our recent groomer, Jerry.

"And the playmate position, it was filled, correct?" He made way for the adoption center and my heart folded in half.

I didn't want my father to meet Astra. Or rather, I didn't want *Astra* to meet my father.

In a perfect world, I'd have a supportive parent, a humble, soft-spoken, amicable guide who would show me the ropes without pressure and pride.

This wasn't a perfect world.

And my father was not that person.

"Who is it?" he asked, plugging in the four-digit keypad password.

I didn't want to say it.

I couldn't say it.

Despite all his flaws, Dr. Mitchell Praigale was one of the most observant men to walk this earth.

He'd know in an instant that she meant more. Meant *too* much.

He'd use that against me.

The door clicked open and standing right behind it, as if waiting for the disaster of this run-in, was none other than –

"Astra Meredith DuPont," she smiled broadly. "Pleasure to meet you, Dr. Praigale."

Chapter Twenty-Eight
Astra

Call it a sixth sense.

I knew he needed my help. I saw the look on his face through the camera monitors, the tension in his shoulder blades, the lines creasing his forehead.

His father was a spitting image of him, mind you, an older version with deep set wrinkles and an aura made of stone.

Dr. Mitchell Praigale looked like Noah if he carried the world on his back with complete and utter disregard for humanity.

But who was I to judge?

He hadn't said a word to me.

Dark brown eyes, almost black, peered into my soul with contempt. The coal-like stubble along his cheek flexed as he cocked his jaw, assessing me.

"Dr. Mitchell Praigale." He extended a hand. "But you were already aware."

"Of course," I smiled sweetly. "Your son speaks highly of you."

The corner of Noah's mouth curled, but he remained silent. *It was that easy to lie to a man who couldn't fathom being contended.*

He cleared his throat. "So you've been speaking to my son, then?"

"He's my boss," I replied.

Meeting Dr. Praigale — Marie-France Leger

"Technically, Miss Meredith DuPont," he took a step forward, "I am."

I glanced at Noah, his throat bobbing in discomfort. Of course, he wouldn't rival his father, there were too many skeletons in that closet.

But me?

I had nothing to fucking lose.

"Respectfully, Dr. Praigale, your son shares a name in this clinic."

He snorted. "So it seems."

The points of my nails burned holes in my palms.

When Noah told me his father was a jackass, a part of me couldn't believe it. How could Noah – *Noah Praigale*, the kindest man on this godawful planet – come from his seed?

"So what have you done for *my* clinic, Miss Meredith DuPont?" Dr. Mitchell demanded, stepping aside. He surveyed the adoption center beyond me. "Besides... clean."

A string of curse words peppered my tongue, begging to come out, but Noah interrupted me.

"She's done plenty. More than what was outlined in the temporary contract, Dad."

But Dr. Mitchell just smirked. "I'd like to hear it from her, Noah. A grown woman can surely speak for herself."

I stepped up to plate, unable to quench my bubbling frustration. "Every five-star review of this clinic is because of your son, Dr. Praigale. I don't

Meeting Dr. Praigale *Marie-France Leger*

know if you're above reading reviews, but if you took a second to see that he does damn good work here, you'd hand this place over to him entirely."

A nerve in his jaw twitched. There was a crack, a singular crack in the mask Dr. Mitchell wore, but he didn't let it show for more than a second. It was almost frightening.

What Noah said proved to be true, then.
A man of stone. A callous man of stone.
"Interesting," Dr. Mitchell released.
One word.
Filled with malice.
God, this man was fucking insufferable.
He tightly clapped Noah on the shoulder then dipped his arrogant, haughty chin to me. "It has been the highest pleasure, Miss Meredith DuPont."

Noah followed him out the door, without being told, and I couldn't bear to watch. All the guilt I felt came back like a tidal wave, and I knew that Noah was about to take some form of punishment for my outburst.

The air was stale and uncomfortable. Dogs whined in the distance. I pressed my body against the wall, ducking behind a metal post.

I could hear yelling from beyond the door, in the quiet, isolated corridor of the clinic. I moved further into the shadows, attempting to overhear.

I needed to do something
I needed to know *he* was okay.
"Dad –" Noah's pleading voice.

Meeting Dr. Praigale   *Marie-France Leger*

"I could fire you," Dr. Mitchell spat, flinging a finger at Noah. "For hiring some inadequate tramp to work beneath me. To share my name. To employ someone with tasteless manners…"

There were words, a lot of words, most of them harsh –

And yet, I heard nothing.

But I saw it all.

I saw Noah move, so quick – so fast – shoving his father against the wall.

The yelling returned.

The arguing.

The pushing.

But the ringing in my ears blared out the noise.

Inadequate tramp.

Tramp.

TRAMP.

"Only use I've got for you is a good fuck, Astra." Said Malcom.

"Why don't I let my friends have a turn with you? You're shit at blowjobs, you know. Alex could put it in your ass, Declan could put it in your pussy and me, because I'm such a good boyfriend, I'll take your disgusting ass whore mouth. Take one for the team."

"That's who I am, baby. A team fucking player."

"A captain."

"You'd never understand, baby. You're too weak. Too spineless."

"Come here, baby, let me have at you."

(DON'T TOUCH ME!!!!!!!!!!)

"Astra, baby –"

"Astra..."

"ASTRA!"

It felt like a zap of electricity.

One second, I was floating in my past, drifting through a nightmare... and then I was here.

Present.

Alive –

Where I now sat on the floor of the office, backed up against the concrete wall. Shaking.

Noah crouched in front of me, eyes brimming with heat. Worry. "Astra..."

Where was his dad?

What happened?

How did I get here?

"Dr. Mitchell –" My voice crumbled.

"He left, love." A gentle thumb caressed my cheek. "He's gone."

I'd been crying.

"Noah," I whispered, bracing myself for the worst. The guilt. "Did he fire you?"

He continued to stroke my cheek, rubbing the hot tears from my eyes. "No."

"But he can?"

"He won't."

"Noah –"

"He won't, Astra." He leaned forward, the scent of cedarwood and sage flooding me with bliss and safety and warmth and protection.

Meeting Dr. Praigale   *Marie-France Leger*

"How much..." Noah's voice broke. "How much of that did you hear, Astra?"

I lied. I needed to lie. "Nothing."

He rubbed a stressed palm down his face, shaking his head. "None of those words were true. Nothing he said, Astra," he swallowed, "I'm so sorry you had to hear that."

Looking at Noah, I felt like a shell. But he too, seemed broken.

Exposed and vulnerable.

Irreparable and brittle.

We both came from hurt. In some ways, that made us stronger.

"I'm sorry he's your father." I shut my eyes. "I'm sorry I embarrassed you."

This made Noah flinch. "He embarrassed himself. In a professional setting – in *any* setting – the things he said were..." He shook his head, pinching the bridge of his nose. "Outrightly disgusting. Unfair. God, fucking *untrue*, Astra."

"But what if..."

"You are none of those things. Do you hear me?" Noah took my chin in his hands. "My father is a bitter, bitter man, Astra. Do not let his senseless insults cut you."

I didn't speak. Couldn't speak.

"There are no words in the world –" he choked, clearing his throat – "there are no words in the world to convey my apologies."

Meeting Dr. Praigale *Marie-France Leger*

My tongue was dry. "You've done nothing wrong."

"That's not true Astra, I could've done something more -"

The weight of his emotions hit me like a truck. "Noah..." I started, grabbing hold of the chain around his neck. "You don't need to bear the responsibility of other people's faults. They aren't your flaws."

Tears clouded his eyes. "He's my father."

My hand rested steady on his cheek. "And you are more of a man than he will ever be. More of a man than he ever was."

His brown eyes met mine with softness. He said nothing, yet his gaze told me everything. Our foreheads touched. Our breaths melded together.

"You are incredible, Astra DuPont." He whispered, his lips inches away from mine.

This should have been the moment to tell him, to pull him close and embrace his warmth and security. To open up. To start over.

But fairytales didn't exist in real life.

And choosing pain was easier than choosing love.

Silently, I retreated blindly back into the space of torment, the locked cavern of my mind that housed me for too long.

I knew how to deal with bad people.

I didn't know how to deal with good.

"I can't get any closer to you." My words were a whisper that didn't want to come out. "Even if I want to."

"Astra…" His whole body went frigid, leaning away. "Why?"

Don't say it. Don't you dare fucking say it. "This will end badly."

I don't believe that. I don't believe that.
YES, YOU DO.

"You'll hurt me," I swore, "and I'll hurt you and – I can't get hurt again. And you don't deserve to go down with me."

My heart banged against my chest, begging to let it out. To let it free.

To let it love.

When I met Noah's eyes, they were filled with raw emotion.

Since the very beginning, I'd been avoiding the story behind those beautiful, brown irises. Eyes are the window to the soul, as some say. They mirror the ugly in you, and the beauty you want to see.

I've only ever believed that beyond the eyes of the soulless, were empty, empty promises. Years of pain. Torture. Displeasure.

I always hated my eyes.

An endless puddle of brown, extending onto a highway of infinite mud and decay.

But looking into Noah's eyes, a chocolate honey with warmth so sweet you could taste it, I couldn't help but see redemption.

Meeting Dr. Praigale *Marie-France Leger*

Paradise. Hope.

And all those fears slowly melted away, taking the darkness of Malcom with them.

He knelt forward, ever so slowly, placing a gentle hand behind my head and pulled me into his arms.

I don't know how long he held me for, only that he did.

And that was enough.

His breath was a tender kiss against my ear as he released, "I've never hurt more than seeing you like this, love."

It broke me.

To hear those words.

To know someone cared and fully, for once in your life, believed it could be true.

Malcom had tainted the portrait of me. The artist that lived behind the pages of her book because she was afraid to experience the real thing.

Afraid that love could exist.

Because if it did, then it would be better than the illusion of it.

It would be better than fiction.

It would be infinite.

It would be mine.

Not a tale of M.D. Pont's.

But Astra Meredith DuPont's.

The girl behind the stories.

The girl who documented romance for those who craved the experience of passion. Of forever.

I'd create my own story.

And it would start with Meeting Dr. Praigale.

I pulled away, shyly, rubbing dried tears from my stained skin. "Does this mean I'm fired?"

Noah let out a genuine laugh, holding me close. "Consider this your last day."

"That's fair," I shrugged, forcing a smile. "I guess I have to make it count, then." I moved out of his grip and grabbed the list of to-do tasks before the end of the day.

"You don't need to do anything, Astra," he said.

"No, no. I never leave things unfinished." I squeezed his hand. "I'm okay, I promise."

"If you need me, if you need anything –"

"Later." I smiled. "I'll need you later."

And when Noah finally left, I didn't feel emptiness or pain, or the hollow ache I've been so accustomed to.

I felt a blossom of hope coiling itself around my heart, with the tenderness of a dove, and the brightness of a star.

***

It was nearly eight p.m. when Noah called me into his office.

The staff had shuffled out some time ago, I could tell by the lack of cars in a now empty parking lot.

With all the strength I could muster, I forced the interaction with Dr. Mitchell out of my mind, relishing in the fact that I'd never have to see that immoral man ever again.

The world polluted his heart.
But I had nothing to do with it.
It wasn't my problem.
He wasn't my problem.
People had two paths in life.
They could become the very thing they hated, or transform into the best version of who they always were.

If I lingered in the darkness that haunted me, let it consume me, there was a possibility that I could turn out like Dr. Mitchell – a sad man, unable to form attainable connections, living in fear of the power he could lose, or the power he could gain.

What a horrifying thought, a horrifying sight. I almost felt empathetic.

Almost.

And I never, ever wanted to become someone who let the darkness of the world consume them. Not anymore.

So I turned to the kennel, doing a final round of cuddles and pets before saying my last goodbye.

Over the course of the past few weeks, I'd bonded with so many animals. I'd even had Snowball keep me company for two days last week. He wasn't big on the other dogs, but he didn't hate them either.

Meeting Dr. Praigale *Marie-France Leger*

Old boys rarely wanted new friends. He had me. And I had him.

But I still couldn't grapple with the concept of being a veterinarian. Having to put down animals, see them sick, rehome them while simultaneously loving every single one.

How could Noah's heart be so big? How could he come from Dr. Mitchell Praigale and be... everything his father was not?

It was unfathomable.

To people like me, it was admirable.

I didn't need to be near him to feel his tenderness, the kindness that touched every single nook and crevice of this clinic. It was my fuel to write, and in between breaks, I took every advantage to do so.

I'd grown an attachment to one dog in particular, a dachshund named Roger. He had one working eye – the other had cataract – and the owner simply abandoned him. When I asked Dr. William McLean about it, he'd told me they never found out who dropped off Roger, just that he was placed in a box on the clinic's doorstep over a year ago, with a note saying: "*my treat*."

Roger had followed me everywhere since I got here. He was only six, and his stout, tiny legs trotted around like raindrops against cement. He was my shadow. Even Snowball didn't mind him. *That much.*

I didn't want to say goodbye.

Meeting Dr. Praigale

Marie-France Leger

But there was so much left to do. And knowing Noah, he'd find a good home for Roger.

Because Noah was the epitome of good.

And I trusted that statement more than anything in this world.

I knocked twice on Noah's office door, glancing down the adoption center hallway one last time before entering the space.

"You wanted to see me?" I asked.

"Take a seat," he said, pulling off his glasses.

I did. He extended a paper.

"Can you sign these forms?"

I took them from him, scanning over the parting agreement. "Sure."

As I initialed the checked boxes, my mind wandered to the what ifs.

What if this is it?

What if I can't write anymore because he's not around?

What if the proximity kept us alive? And the distance kills us?

I couldn't help it.

I wasn't used to... reassurance.

"Signed and ready for departure," I teased, handing over the form. I stood, wiping off the dog hair from my jeans. "I'm going to miss this place."

He smiled, leaning back into his chair. "This place will miss you."

Meeting Dr. Praigale — *Marie-France Leger*

"I should've taken this route, you know. Animals are way more appealing than manuscripts and edits."

"Every career has its challenges, Miss DuPont," he chuckled.

"Oh, we're back to formalities?"

He smiled. "I like the sound of your name when I say it."

I swallowed, a surge of heat shooting up my spine. "Anything else you need from me, Doctor?"

He kept his eyes secure on mine, gaze darkening. I'd written tension before, the intensity of it, but I'd never felt it. Not with a desire like this.

His eyes were a pool of melting honey, trailing every curve of my silhouette. Suddenly I became very aware of the seclusion, how alone we were in this vacant building.

Me and Noah Praigale.

And the vigor of a thousand stars.

He stood up and leaned forward, planting two firm hands on his desk. I could envision the blood pumping in his veins – the adrenaline painting every wall with this friction.

My heart hammered in my chest.

"There's plenty," he released, rounding the table. "Plenty I want from you."

My legs were boneless, paralyzed by want. Nothing else – *no one* else – could take that from me.

This was a pivotal step of trust, of allowing someone to prove their good intentions. But Noah wasn't just anyone.

And this...

This felt like the beginning of fucking everything.

Because when Noah positioned himself in front of me, gazing into my eyes with the intensity of the sun, I couldn't help the burning desire, the *desperation* I needed to have him close.

To have him now.

To have him always.

"This isn't a good idea," I let out, shutting my eyes against the desires.

"Mm," he clicked his tongue, stepping closer. "Not very friendly."

I couldn't answer, not when his hand snaked around my waist, and he spoke again. "The second you signed that parting agreement, we stopped being colleagues..." He dipped his chin to my ear, his breath grazing my neck. "And now that we're no longer professional, tell me, Astra... What is it that you want?"

I closed my eyes, holding back the want – the desire to feel him. But all I could focus on were his hands around my waist, his breath against my skin.

Noah. Noah. Noah.

"I'll ruin you," I choked out, a final threat to let him flee. To run for the hills. To keep the potential of pain away.

Meeting Dr. Praigale *Marie-France Leger*

    His hand travelled from the base of my spine up to the nape of my neck, the other pulling me close. And then he whispered, so smoothly against my lips, "Then ruin me."

Chapter Twenty-Nine
Noah

Our lips collided with a lifetime of longing.

There were no breaths to breathe in but each other's. No moves to make unless I took her with me.

This was infinite bliss.

This was euphoria.

"*Noah*," she moaned softly, her tongue melding into mine as if it were my own. Her whole body, her whole *being*, was entangled with my soul.

I lifted her up, leaning her carefully alongside my desk, feeling her legs wrap tightly around my middle.

Good. She liked this.

She was comfortable. She was okay.

I kissed her. Everywhere, I kissed this beautiful woman, trailing every inch of her mouth, her jawline, her neck like it was a map I could never tire of exploring.

"This was what I should've done" - I spoke breathlessly - "this is what I wanted to do before I kissed you and fucked it up."

She pulled back with a smile, cheeks flushed. "My potty mouth rubbed off on you, Doctor."

"You make me dizzy." I guided her further onto my desk. "It's disorienting."

"Why did you leave?" she asked, tugging at my collar. "When you kissed me."

I pulled back and studied her expression, hesitating to explain the unexplainable. "No one's ever, I don't know" – I shook my head – "written with me in mind, I suppose. No one's ever written about me at all."

"That's not really an explanation, Noah," she wrinkled her nose. "I'm still lost."

I sighed, allowing my lips to brush the curve of her ear. "It was a lot of emotion. Let's just say that."

"So you kissed me because you were shocked? And then..." she chuckled, "and then you left because you were shocked that you kissed me?"

Well... "I've been wanting to kiss you for weeks. At the time, it seemed like an opportune moment."

"And then what? You psyched yourself out?"

I accepted my defeat and planted my face in the crook of her neck. "Just call me an embarrassment."

Her whole body shook with laughter. "Your words, not mine."

I pulled back, lacing both my fingers behind her waist. It felt so natural. Her being here with me, laughing, smiling... being human. Those chocolate brown eyes gleamed with playful innocence, and I melted.

"I'm happy we met, Stargirl," I said, meaning it with my whole heart. "Even though our worlds are very different."

She drifted closer. "And yet, here we are."

I placed a gentle kiss on the corner of her mouth. "Here we are, love."

She said nothing, only devoured me with her doe-eyed stare, her fingers finding the loops of my scrubs.

I swallowed. "Astra..."

"Noah," she released, but I engulfed her in a lust-fueled kiss.

Her face fit perfectly in my hands, the tickle of her eyelashes dancing across my own. I let a lone hand linger down her spine, allowing my fingers to graze the bare skin above her hipbones.

A soft hum escaped her lips, her fingernails scraping the hem of my pants. "Astra," I said again, kissing her once before taking a slow step back.

Her face was red, a mirror of mine, I could only presume. The taste of her still lingered on my lips.

God, she was so beautiful.

So beautiful I could spend forever memorizing the pieces that made her, *her*.

"You're staring at me," she whispered.

"I can't stop," I admitted.

My eyes trailed down her neck. A button from her blouse had popped off, revealing the hint of a beige bra and a...

A scar running down the inside of her cleavage. "Astra, what is –"

Meeting Dr. Praigale *Marie-France Leger*

I stepped forward, but she caught my hand and covered her chest. Instantly, she shot up.

And I bloody panicked.

"Don't go," I pleaded, kneeling in front of her. "Don't run off."

Her fists were balled in front of her shirt, her face pale and remorseful. "I wasn't going to... I just... reacted."

What happened, Stargirl?

What happened to you?

My inference sent a tremor through my body. "Was it *him*?"

She nodded in anguish, leaning against my desk. "Well, this is a mood kill."

"I want to know," I said, pulling up the closest chair. "I want to know everything there is to know about you."

"Even the ugly?" Her smile didn't meet her eyes.

My heart tore in two. "Especially the ugly, love."

She gnawed on her lip, her whole body shuddering. This was so painful to watch. Painful to feel, I could only imagine. And yet, she maintained a brave face, and told me the hard truth.

She'd been seventeen when she opened up to Malcom Matheson about her father. How he abandoned her and her sister Eva, didn't so much as recognize his two daughters when they approached him at the counter.

Meeting Dr. Praigale *Marie-France Leger*

Malcom had worked in a different department than Andre DuPont, but they were still cordial with one another.

*After Astra had told Malcom, him and his friends got in a car and drove to Andre's house, carrying lead pipes and baseball bats. They beat his car to a pulp, spray-painted it with the word: "**USELESS**," and I suppose Andre was too scatterbrained on drugs, he didn't even realize until three days later that his vehicle was now a pile of rubbish rotting on his driveway.*

He never filed charges. He didn't care enough.

The next night Malcom had come to Astra, explaining what he'd done with shameless pride.

She said he could go to jail.

He said she should be thanking him.

And in all the ways, Malcom got his thanks in the form of forced penetration and a desire to hurt. He had sex with her in the back of his car, the seatbelt cutting into Astra's sternum with each thrust, slicing the skin between her breasts.

She didn't even realize in the moment that she'd been bleeding – that seatbelts, with the right amount of pressure and its serrated ridges, could be as sharp as a blade.

All she could focus on was Malcom. Inside of her. Without her consent.

And later, he'd grabbed her face with the force of a punching blow and said: "You're welcome, baby."

My knuckles were white.

There was a pulsing, a damn pulsing just vibrating – vibrating in my ears and it screamed at me.

Meeting Dr. Praigale *Marie-France Leger*

Thump, thump, thump.

A well of tears filled my waterline. I could feel the bile – the disgusting, putrid, acrid taste of vomit rising up my esophagus, begging to come out.

Astra was ghostly white, but remained completely removed, as if recounting a bedtime story rather than her own personal trauma.

"How are you so..." I began, but she cut me off.

"Okay?" A sarcastic snort. "I'm not okay, not really. But this happened to a version of me that died long ago. I'm just... telling you what happened."

I couldn't for the life of me understand how a single human being was capable of such atrocities.

That bastard, that *monster*, had conditioned her to believe intimacy and pain were interconnected, that no man could ever possibly love her properly. That included all the fragile parts, the brittle parts that needed the most love.

She was strong. Bright. Beautiful.

She was everything Malcom Matheson was not, and could never, ever be.

The entire weight of my body shook as I slipped forward, into her arms, and pulled her onto my lap. I shook, she shook. But we were together.

"No one deserves to die," she murmured, a mask of dismay covering the glow of her tired face.

I clutched her close. "But you deserve to live."

Her eyes softened. "You know, I never wanted you to see me the way I saw myself."

"You" – I brushed a loose strand of hair from her face – "You have nothing to be ashamed of, Astra."

She tilted her head. "What do you see when you look at me?"

"Strength." I responded immediately. "Courage. The will to turn pain into passion. You've gone through so many traumatic things, and you made it on the other side. You've created a legacy."

"It doesn't feel that way sometimes."

"It never does to the person doing it, does it?"

"That was a lot of d-words," she chuckled, a bead of a tear dripping down her cheek.

Another suggestive joke won't hurt. "I can say one more."

"Oh stop," she swatted my chest, then rested her head against my shoulder. "I've never told anyone that story, you know. Not even Beth, or Eva."

"And your mom?"

She scoffed. "My mom knows nothing about me. She never did."

"She didn't know about Malcom? The way he treated you? Abused you?"

She sighed. "If she did, she never said anything. She was always wrapped up in her own little world."

"You're her daughter." I bit out. "She should love you. She's supposed to love you."

"And can you say the same of your dad?"

"We're not talking about him right now."

"Noah –"

"I could give less of a shit about anything right now. I want you to be safe and cared for and actually believe it, Astra." I cupped her face in my hands, forcing her to meet my eyes. "Please believe that you're capable of love."

Those brown spheres, glazed over by tears, bore into mine deeply. She took a quiet moment to herself, peacefully watching me just as I watched her, then said, "No one's ever looked at me with burning desire before."

And I kissed her, so gently I kissed her lips, her nose, and her forehead, proving with the touch of my lips that someone could love her in all the ways that mattered. In all the ways she deserved to be loved.

"Then have a look at me," I whispered, pressing her closer.

"Why?" she asked.

"Because you may find what you're searching for."

Chapter Thirty
Astra

Last Edit - 1:32am: No Title
Josh ran up to Taylan's place in the pouring rain, wilted flowers in hand, waiting for her presence. She opened the door to find him smiling, despite the raindrops pooling in his shoes, the thunderclouds looming above the roof, she was all he could see, and she felt electrocuted under his gaze. He handed her the flowers, pulling her in for warmth, to feel their bodies connecting and their souls uniting. It was a soulmate attachment, Taylan knew that from the beginning, and she never believed she could find hers. Until Josh said those five words: "You are it for me".

Noah sat in the corner of Cloud Café, one week after I'd finished my final shift at M & N's Vet Clinic.

It was Tuesday night, two days before I had to submit my finished book to Teresa and Parker. I'd been dodging everyone's calls – and that included Noah – though we didn't shy away from sending the occasional text. *Or seventy.*

I didn't know what this was between us, what it could amount to, but I didn't feel afraid of it anymore. I welcomed the potential of pain, because it could also mean a potential of happiness. And right now, I needed that joy.

Right now, I was buried in the thought of paragraphs, sentences, and an unusual coffee order from an enigmatic, blue haired girl.

"You said, *pink* foam?" I clarified. "Pink foam on top of a hazelnut cream latte with *one* cube of ice?"

"Co-rrect," she slurred. "One cube."

I paused. "Right." Then plugged it into the cash. "I don't even know how to charge you for this, hold on."

She let out a sincere, loud laugh. "I'm playing a prank on my boyfriend."

"Well, that one cube of ice will really get him."

Again, another throaty laugh bubbled from her throat, and I couldn't help but laugh along with her.

"I think that'll be five-fifty?" I glanced back at Ruby, who obviously heard the whole conversation, and she nodded in approval.

The blue-haired girl leaned forward, slapping down a ten with a gum wrapper. "That guy in the back is staring at you."

I glanced at Noah who gave me a small wave, and I resisted the urge to smile back.

"He's harmless."

Blue-hair relaxed. "Ah, okay. If he was a stalker, I would've taken him out."

"I appreciate the offer." I smiled sincerely. "Can I get your name for the order?"

She popped her gum. "Blu, no E," she said, extending a hand. Her nails were painted turquoise. Christ, this girl loved blue. Even her damn name.

I took her hand, admiring the dangly beaded bracelets around her wrist. "I've decided I like you, Blu."

"Not many people do." She retorted, clearly unbothered.

I aspired to have that level of confidence.

As I made her drink, she waited on the barstool by the napkins. I thought to make conversation.

"You live around Stratford?" I asked, dropping a fat cube of ice into a translucent tumbler.

"Nah, fuck, a place like this? No offence, but my brain can't handle the isolation." She checked her phone. "I'm taking photos for a wedding so, came for the money."

"You're a photographer?"

She winked. "New thing. I've gotten two interviews for Toronto Pix, so I'm putting together a portfolio. It hasn't happened yet, but it *will*."

I chuckled, embracing the refreshing energy of this girl. "I hope for your sake it does."

"My boyfriend's waiting in the car. He didn't want to come. I dragged him."

"Oh yeah?" I swivelled some strawberry foam on top. *What the hell was pink foam anyway if not*

Meeting Dr. Praigale *Marie-France Leger*

strawberry foam? "I hope you get the position. Toronto's a big city."

"Filled with opportunity." She added. "I live in the York region. And you live here?"

I nodded, sliding over her drink. "Yep. Quiet town. Gets the job done."

"Well," her eyes slid to my nametag, "*Astra*. With a gorgeous name like that, you could be something. Really, be something out there. Try it out. Live a little more than you know, and act a little more than you do."

You could be something, really be something out there, she'd said.

If only you didn't cower behind an alias. That hopeless voice returned. *If only you weren't afraid.*

I forced away the gloom and nodded my thanks to Blu. "I'll take your advice."

She waved, "Ta-ta," slapping a personally made business card on the counter, and then she was gone.

I pocketed the card, swirling in thought, when Noah approached. "Who was that?"

"My new best friend." I teased, dusting off my hands.

"You just met her," he laughed.

"And I just met you, what was it, almost two months ago?"

He smiled. "And look at us now."

Meeting Dr. Praigale *Marie-France Leger*

"Who would've thought, Dr. Praigale." I held his gaze a little longer before asking, "What are you doing here, anyway?"

"I can't surprise you?"

"You have a job."

"The clinic closes at six every day, or have you forgotten our hours already, Miss DuPont?"

I rolled my eyes. "Do you want to buy something?"

"Yes, actually," he started, "your time."

"My time?"

"Ms. Hutchinson!" Noah called to the back, waving at Ruby.

"Hush up now, that makes me sound old!" she yelled.

"My apologies, ma'am."

She grunted. "Even worse."

"Can I capture Astra for a night? I promise she'll make up for it in the next coming weeks."

My eyes went wide. "I never agreed to this."

"Go ahead," she shooed herself further into the back. "Bout time this girl saw some sunlight."

"It's dark out, Rubes." I retorted.

"Beh." And then she was out of view.

When I turned back to Noah, his grin was ear to ear. "Come on then, chop-chop."

I unknotted my apron, slinging it over the coat rack and punched in my check-out time. "You're lucky it's a slow day."

Meeting Dr. Praigale *Marie-France Leger*

"I carry luck around wherever I go, Stargirl. And now," he leaned down to kiss my cheek, "I'm always lucky."

I blushed, still trying to fight with the discomfort of being comforted. I didn't know what Noah and I were, what we could become or anything of the sort. But this place, this state of *us* felt unchangeable. For once in my life, I wasn't worried.

I was safe.

"I'm just going to swap outfits," I said, hurrying for the loft staircase.

But he grabbed my hand, kissing the inside of my palm gently, before leading me out to his car. "No, you won't need to."

"Where are we even going?" I chuckled, sliding into the passenger seat.

He ignited the engine, placing a hand on my knee before saying, "Where it all began."

Chapter Thirty-One
Noah

We stood on the roof of Tav's Tavern, the pristine glass greenhouse shielding us with a plethora of foliage, fern and flowers. The moonlight shone through the cracks of coloured windowpane, cascading down like ringlets of starlight.

It made Astra glimmer.

"This is where I wanted to take you the first night I realized you were it."

She flinched, physically flinched, and gasped. "What did you just say?"

I turned to her, confused. "That you were it?"

She grabbed my arms, shaking me, eyes wide. "I literally just wrote that sentence – I mean, my character told my other character in my book that exact line."

A laugh busted from my throat. "Maybe I really am your muse, wow."

She squeezed my arm. "That's wild."

"You were looking pretty wild yourself just a moment ago."

"Hey, listen *pal* –"

"I'd think a writer could come up with better terms of endearment."

"Don't –" she held up a finger. "*Mr. Pringle.*"

I laughed, pulling her through the maze of greenery where I laid out a picnic basket and a blanket, directly underneath the open roof hatch.

"What is this?" she asked.

"A circus." I deadpanned. "I'm sure there's popcorn around here somewhere –"

But her lips were on mine, and I melted into her touch before she pulled away and ran to the blanket.

"You're such a romantic," she cooed, sifting through the picnic basket. "Oh my God, chocolate covered strawberries."

"One of life's greatest pleasures." I nestled beside her, leaning on my elbow.

She opened the box, taking a huge berry out and shoving it in my face. "Eat this one."

"What?" I chuckled. "Why?"

"Because it's fat and I want to watch you eat it."

"You..." I looked at her, really looked at her to search for a joke, something to signify she was kidding, but she was dead serious. "You want to watch me eat a fat strawberry?"

"Yep," she nodded. "I love watching people eat things."

"Really?"

"Do you know what mukbangs are?"

I groaned, rolling my eyes. "Oh man, Tav loves watching those."

Meeting Dr. Praigale *Marie-France Leger*

"See!" She pushed my arm. "Eat it. Don't deprive me of joy."

So I sunk my teeth into the delicious berry, watching her happiness with my own.

She popped a berry in her mouth and shook her head. "I could die happy right now."

"In my company."

She tilted her head, pausing, and leaned down to place a careful, strawberry-tinted kiss on my lips. "Especially in your company."

My chest burst at the sight of seeing Astra so comfortable. The idea that I made her safe, that *she* felt safe around *me*, was a joy I couldn't put into words.

The hazy flashback of me and Annika eating on her floor the night we cut it off resurfaced in my brain. She tried to feed me... shrimp, was it? And I was beyond irate. Her shoving it in my face, the memory of it all... It was nothing like this.

Astra could've done anything, been anything, and my heart would blossom.

"I knew I'd take you here someday," I said, reflecting on the first night we played pool. "I knew it wasn't then, seeing you nervous and all. But I promised myself we'd come here."

She stopped chewing. "I'm sorry about that night, Noah. Really."

"Don't be," I pressed her knee. "I asked you out and you said yes. We wouldn't be here now if you didn't say yes."

"Sometimes," she sighed, "sometimes I wish things were different. That I was easier to understand."

"It takes time to get to know the right people."

"I know that," she nodded. "Can I ask you something about your ex-girlfriend?"

I resisted the urge to bury my face. "Great, every man's favourite topic."

Her laugh was instant. "You don't need to answer."

"No, no, go ahead."

She sat up on her heels. "How did you move on so fast?"

I took a moment of contemplation, searching for the most respectful words. "I think that I... I think I moved on the second she cheated on me."

"She cheated." Astra said, flatly. "On *you*."

"She did, yeah. And I was heartbroken, of course I was. But when we slowly started talking again, I don't know –" I shook my head. "I felt like I was betraying myself and my core values.

"My father was this unfaithful bastard and I saw how broken my family became because of it. My sister... I mean, she turned to alcoholism and my mom's self-worth went down the drain.

"I guess by me leaving, not working on the relationship I'd tended to for so long, I felt like my father."

"That's so…" Astra crunched the blanket beneath her fingers, a plethora of thoughts spinning beneath her eyes. "That's not even in the same world, Noah. She cheated on you. You tried to make it work. You did your best."

I felt a pang of shame and release in my chest. Two opposing feelings that both made sense in this very moment. "No one's ever said that to me before."

She cupped my face. "I'm telling you that you did your best. You always do your best."

I kissed her thumb, then her knuckles. "As do you."

"Have you spoken to your dad since…"

A dull ache formed in my chest. "Since the incident at the clinic? Aside from work related issues, no. And he realizes his faults in the matter."

"He does?"

She looked shocked. I didn't blame her. I was shocked myself when he called me the following morning and sent his apologies. Mind you, they weren't directed at Astra more than his reputation, but it was still something. Even if it was nothing.

"In his own way, yes. I beg you not to take it to heart, love." I squeezed her fingers, knowing very well my father could dish out the worst of insults but was unable to take them.

She pressed her lips together. "It didn't hurt coming from him, but it definitely brought up some other things. I can't lie about that."

"I apologize on his behalf." And I meant that, sincerely.

She just squeezed my hand, gazing upwards.

"Did you date anyone after Malcom?" I asked.

A shadow crossed her face, but she didn't pull away. "No, but I'd gotten involved in something –"

"Damnit Astra, you can't catch a break." I dreaded her next words. "Something bad?"

"Just an asshole of a hookup."

She kept it short, no elaborations, and I didn't press. I wanted to keep this night as relaxed as possible, without the demons of the past coming to haunt her. We had plenty of time to get through those things together, to help each other out.

I'd learn every piece of her with time, and that is what I was most looking forward to.

"Speaking of hookups..." I started, trying to keep things light. "How do you write the smutty scenes in your book?"

She narrowed her eyes, a playful smile coating her lips. "That interest you?"

"It does," I leaned closer. "Tell me all about it."

"I write what I like."

"And what do you like, Stargirl?" My thumb circled her leg, itching for an answer.

She swallowed. "Tell me why you call me that."

"I give quirky nicknames, what can I say?" I shrugged, continuing the spirals up her thigh. "I'm a creative, like you."

She laughed. "You say that, but you don't draw, or paint or play an instrument. I mean, not as far as I know... You don't even like art, do you?"

My finger stopped just below her belt loop. I looked up at her pretty features, her angelic eyes, and smiled.

"Ad Astra, the painting by Akseli-Gallen-Kallela..." I released, noticing the flash of recognition on her face. "You were named after that painting, weren't you, Astra?"

Her eyes flitted from side to side. She moved back, shaking her head.

Well, that certainly wasn't the reaction I was expecting.

"Ruby said I was named after a painting..." she stuttered. "A few weeks after I moved in and started working for her. She calls me Starburst, because of a painting."

I sat up straighter. "You think it's the same one?

"You've never met Ruby before? I mean, before you met me?"

"Never," I placed my hand over my heart. "I swear."

She pulled out her phone, typing frantically into a search bar. She had searched the painting of Ad Astra, and her shoulders tensed immediately.

Meeting Dr. Praigale *Marie-France Leger*

She let out a quiet gasp. "You've never met my mother... You've never met her before she was your client?"

Again, I shook my head, worried.

She remained still. I could see her brain reworking something, her thoughts rotating.

"What are you thinking about?"

"I'm sorry, Noah, can we go back to Cloud? I really need to talk to Ruby."

Without question, I grabbed the picnic basket in one scoop, helping her to her feet. "Of course, let's go."

The entire journey back to the café was in utter silence. There was something wrong, I could tell, but she reassured me by placing a gentle hand on my leg, squeezing on occasion until we arrived.

She ran out of the car, unlocking the door to find Ruby sitting at the back patio of the café, smoking a cigarette.

"Home early?" she questioned, her voice raspy and filled with plume.

Astra didn't hesitate. "When we first met, you said I was named after a painting. I never asked you about it before, but I'm asking now."

Ruby sat up, stubbing out the cigarette with her foot. "Why so accusatory, Starburst?"

"When my dad left, I asked which one of my parents named me Astra. If it was my dad, I'd change my name. But no, it was my mom." She began to

Meeting Dr. Praigale   *Marie-France Leger*

shake. "Mom was drunk off her ass, and all she did was point to this painting of a naked woman.

"I didn't know what that painting was called until Noah told me. And it might be a coincidence and I could be reaching, but I need to know. I really need to fucking know Ruby."

I took a step back, feeling the urge to hold onto Astra while also giving her the space to work through whatever... whatever was happening.

This didn't have anything to do with me, and yet, I couldn't help but stick around to uncover more of who she was. Piece together the puzzles of her past.

"You took me in when you didn't know me. Gave me a place to stay, a job. You approached me. You hate everyone, Ruby. And you offered me everything." Astra clenched her fist. "Did you know me, Ruby? Did you know who I was that day?"

I watched Ruby stand, pulling down her ponytail, letting her hair drift. She moved towards Astra, extending a hand. Astra didn't take it.

"I know my paintings, that's all." Ruby sighed.

"Bullshit. I know that's bullshit. I feel it in my gut, Ruby. If I didn't, I wouldn't have come back. I can't shake this –"

"I adopted Susan for eight years," Ruby interrupted, lighting another cigarette as if she didn't just shatter Astra's world in one sentence.

I caught Astra before she could fall, her back hitting my chest like a boulder.

Meeting Dr. Praigale — Marie-France Leger

She didn't even realize I was holding her. She didn't even care.

"Her mama, Claudia, was my half-sister. Piece of work that one. I'd say a prayer for her, but good riddance." Ruby inhaled, then exhaled.

Astra remained immobile. Completely stunned. I, too... I must confess, had a hard time comprehending... anything.

"Claudia's husband couldn't – well, I won't say couldn't – didn't wan' take care of your mom no more so when she was nine, Fred gave her to me. Shoved her into my life, more like it."

"You..." Astra's whole body was in tremors. I held her still, my heart pounding.

"Yeah kid, I raised your mom. Pivotal years, poor thing had gone through it. Tough child, adopted her own mama's habits, my damn sister. I was hoping she wouldn't, but nature vs. nurture and all that.

"Your mama called me when she was at the hospital 'bout to give birth. Your ol' daddio was nowhere to be found. I held Susan's hand, and when it was over, she told me to tell her a story. I told her 'bout a woman who could reach the stars. She named you Astra on the spot, and I painted the damn thing in celebration. Shit as can be, but sentimental."

The breeze was cold, the streets empty. The wind carried nothing but icy silence.

A stretch of vacant space for miles. And miles.

Meeting Dr. Praigale *Marie-France Leger*

When Astra decided to speak, her voice was weak. "How... Ruby."

Ruby crunched a leaf beneath her shoe. "Your mom's got a problem, sweetheart. You don't think she knows that? No one hates her more than herself. She couldn't raise you, can't even raise your poor sister.

"Matheson boy died and she saw the shit he did to you. She told me that day, the day you came to Stratford, she says to me: '*Get her away from this. Save her from turning into me.*' And she hung up. She knew I'd meet you, Starburst. And I felt pity, hell yeah I felt pity for you. Her own mama hit her, Claudia - the bitter bitch - never treated your mama like anything other than roadkill.

"Sometimes, Starburst. Sometimes people aren't meant to be parents. And sometimes," Ruby exhaled a trail of smoke, "sometimes they know that the best thing to do is let someone else do it for 'em."

And that's when Astra broke.

Fell to her knees in one go.

I fell with her.

She was frantic, shaking, sobbing. "Why did you take me in? Why did you do that? How could you never tell me?"

Ruby crouched down, stubbing out the last butt of her cigarette. *How was she so calm? How could she witness Astra in such peril and be so...*

So –
Natural?

Meeting Dr. Praigale *Marie-France Leger*

"People have got to plan their own path in life, Astra," she explained, "and when I saw you, I saw a star. I knew she did right by naming you what you are."

This was all too much. All too personal.

I didn't...

I didn't know what to do. I was out of place.

Never in my wildest dreams could I have predicted where this night –

"How could you!" Astra sprung out of my arms. "How could you not tell me, Ruby! After all these fucking years, you knew me, we're fucking *family* and you let me believe I had no one!"

And that's when Ruby erupted.

And the ground shook.

And the trees cowered.

"YOU let yourself believe you had no one, damnit! You did!" She nailed Astra in the center of the chest with a pointed finger.

My jaw hung loose.

I was frozen.

"You know how many opportunities have been thrown at you? In your career, in your life, you've been given an olive branch and you lit it on fire!" Ruby didn't stop. Couldn't stop.

"I watched you, every day, destroy yourself over the past. And this man, that guy right behind you" – she nodded at me – "he finally did somethin'. He put some light into you. And time and time again, you insist on bein' alone.

"Well choosing loneliness, Starburst, that only makes you more lonely in the end."

And with that final comment, the wind stilled.

Ruby left.

And I watched as Astra sank to the ground, surrounded by a sphere of old cigarettes, and a heavier heart than ever before.

Chapter Thirty-Two
Astra

"All those times..."

I shattered to glass. "All those times my mom said she was doing me a favour... she meant Ruby. Giving me over to Ruby. Donating me like a used rag."

I thought I was alone. I could've sworn I was alone. I would've rather spoken to the vat of nothingness than any living creature that could lie to me.

Use me.

Hurt me.

Discard me.

I forgot that Noah was there.

But he was.

He was in my loft, using my kettle, making something hot and fragrant.

Something I didn't want to drink.

Something I wanted to burn my body in and melt.

And melt.

And melt.

"I'll put this here for you," he said.

Wasn't he just at the oven a second ago?

The pressure of reality hit me again, and the tears clawed their way out.

I was exhausted of crying.

Meeting Dr. Praigale   *Marie-France Leger*

I was exhausted of living.

I was exhausted of pain.

"I can't believe she never told me." I muttered. I didn't even recognize the sound of my own voice anymore. "I can't believe she never said anything."

"Maybe she didn't -"

"She gave me up..." I repeated. "My mom said she was doing me a favour, Noah... It's because she gave me up.

"She knew what Malcom was doing to me. She never..." I choked. "She never said anything. She just - she watched me suffer."

"Astra," Noah shifted. "I'm so sorry."

"Sorry means nothing. People apologize all the time."

"I am genuinely -" he paused. "This is a lot to take in."

Ripe anger bubbled inside of me.

Agony.

Ache.

"How do you think I feel?" I detonated, allowing my person and pain to unite. "Everyone lies to me, can't you see that, Noah? Everyone hurts me and I'm supposed to expect that you won't? That you never will?"

"Astra, this isn't about us -"

"Can you go?" *One... Two... Three. One... Two...* "Can you please just go?"

I needed space.

I needed time.

I needed nothingness.

The black shore began calling to me, the tide that housed the creatures of my past, pulling – yanking me in, tempting me with the promise of eternal suffering.

It felt nice, to be wanted.

To be wanted by the reapers.

I'd been surrounded by them for far too long. I was attached.

A sadness swept over Noah's eyes, but he didn't say anything. He stood, his movements languid, as he walked towards the door.

Then I saw that look.

That look of complete and utter sorrow, ruining the kindness of his features – distorting the unfeigned version of who he was... because I couldn't control myself.

He was an anchor of some sorts, the buoy that kept me tethered to life – to happiness.

To hope.

But he closed the door behind him.

He left.

And my heart was fucking pounding.

My ears were ringing.

Malcom was calling –

Liam was calling –

My mom, my dad, the regrets – the shame – the pain – the guilt –

STOP.

PLEASE. PLEASE FUCKING STOP! PLEASE.

My breath caught in a sob. I couldn't breathe.

So I ran to the person who gave me air.

I'm sorry.

I'm sorry.

I'm sorry!

My feet carried me to the door, to the direction of him, drowning out the voices – the dark hands that kept pulling me, snatching my hair – my clothes, *everything* was tearing.

My walls were breaking.

And I wanted them to break for him.

Not Malcom.

Not anyone –

But Noah fucking Praigale.

I hurled the metal door open, allowing the cold wind to slap me across the face. To ground me.

To hold me.

"Noah – wait!" I scanned the bruised atmosphere, and my heart caught in my throat.

There he was.

His back hunched, sitting on the first step of the stairwell. He turned to look at me, those downturned, kind eyes...

So soft, so understanding.

"You..." I couldn't find the words. Couldn't find the words to thank him. To apologize to him. "You didn't leave."

A weak smile painted his lips. "I told you once before that I never would."

I collapsed onto the grate, not caring about the sharp pain that hissed against my knees, or the steel cutting into my skin. "Take me away from here," I whispered, begged. Pleaded.

He stared at me for a long moment, and I relished in the care under his gaze. He merely nodded once, opening his arms. I crawled over to Noah, slowly, cocooning myself in his embrace, and I died.

In that moment, I could've sworn he died with me.

And then in a heartbeat, we both resurrected. Blossomed. Bloomed.

Into something new, something better.

Into supernovas.

Chapter Thirty-Three
Noah

We sat in my car, driving down an empty, moonlit path. Only this time it was different.

There was no laughter.

No smiles.

Just a hollow void that painted the air in broad strokes, tasing any moment of joy that tried to interfere.

I knew where I was taking Astra, a place that became my safe haven after I'd found out about Annika's infidelity – after dealing with the stress of the clinic, Bridget's addiction, my father – life.

Seventeen minutes later, we were on the cusp of Woodstock and Stratford, a gravel trail concealed by hanging trees. It used to be a park by the lake, until the overgrowth turned it into something else – a garden for shadows, a place of quiet.

It was just what she needed right now. What we both needed.

"Here." My voice cracked. The silence amplified it tenfold.

She peeled herself out of her seat, barely glancing at me as she clicked open the door and stepped onto the rocky terrain.

I exhaled, watching her briefly, before picking up a flannel blanket from the backseat and followed her out.

Meeting Dr. Praigale *Marie-France Leger*

Again, we walked in silence, her hand barely grazing mine as we pushed past cautionary signs and frail branches. It was tense, the outside air frigid, though not because of the weather.

And then the world opened up to a new climate. '*The Slope by the Sea*,' I used to call it. Only it wasn't a slope, and it wasn't the sea. Just a slight hill covered in dead grass, overlooking a deep blue lake, illuminated by stars.

In that very moment, I welcomed the calm, forgetting my past transgressions and those of Astra. We were just two young kids, sneaking away from our parents in the witching hour, neglecting our responsibilities except one another – that's all that mattered, after all.

Us.

"What is this place?" she asked, her voice crumbling.

I smiled sadly. "The Slope by the Sea," and extended my hand to hers.

She took it, hesitantly, and followed me down the dusted trail.

I laid down the blanket overtop a yellowing plain of dead grass, tapping the spot next to me. She sat, and I waited for her to take in the surroundings. No human being could deny the starlit skies that danced across a black curtain of night, or the lake that moved with the chill breeze.

It was a different world here, isolated by the business of life and problems of the past.

We could be anyone behind this forest.

We could be free.

Astra slid up her legs, resting her chin atop her knees. "I used to come to a place just like this with Malcom."

I swallowed my heartbeat. "In Woodstock?"

She shook her head. "No, somewhere further East. It was in the beginning," she paused, "before things got bad."

My head hung low. "I'm sorry, Astra."

"It's not your fault. None of this is your fault."

"I know, but seeing it all unfold..." I scraped the stubble across my jaw. "It's just, madness, I don't know. No one deserves to go through this."

She glanced at me slightly, the corner of her lips struggling to lift. "I'm exhausted."

"Tired?"

"Of life. Of just – *living,* in this constant state of guardship, not knowing when the next thing is going to strike. My mom, she knew about Malcom and Ruby and all of it is just so fucked up. I thought I made my path in life, Noah. But it was just orchestrated by something else – someone else."

"But Ruby said she made the decision not to tell you so that you could plan your life, Astra, you know, without the influence of your mom," I added, my tone gentle.

"She made a mistake, by not telling you. It's not my place to agree or disagree with that decision but" – I shook my head – "Astra that woman loves you. One mistake doesn't mean malice. It doesn't mean ill intention, not always."

She sucked in a breath, letting a loose tear fall. "I know."

"People love you," I said, wiping away her sadness. "They really do."

She looked up, eyes glossy. "How are you still here?"

"What do you mean?"

"Knowing everything, seeing me fucked up and –"

"None of that," I cut her off, leaning closer. My knee brushed her knuckle. "That doesn't scare me off."

"I'm damaged."

"You're human," I said.

"Broken."

"Breathing," I contradicted.

"I'm dead inside, Noah," she released.

I placed a thumb on the pressure point of her wrist. "But your heart is still beating."

More tears began to run. "I'm so sorry for how I've treated you. Pushing you away. I don't want you to leave."

And then she fell into my lap, wrapping her arms around my middle. "You're the only person I never want to lose."

The truth in her admission constricted my lungs, the closeness of her setting my soul on fire.

Astra.

My Stargirl.

"You're hugging me," I released, brushing dark strands from her forehead.

"I am," she murmured into my chest. "This sweater feels good."

I laughed. "Cashmere."

"The fancy degree came in handy after all."

I laughed harder, lifting her onto my lap. "Are you cold?"

"Are you offering me your sweater?"

I shrugged. "If you're cold."

She placed a hand on my cheek, resting it against my jaw. "Too Nicholas Sparks for me."

"And what would be acceptable to M. D. Pont?"

Her big brown eyes glanced at me, a wicked light twinkling with desire. She leaned close, her breath tickling my lips before she placed them softly atop mine.

I kissed her back, gently, allowing the taste of her to coat my tongue. And when she fell into me, I fell into her.

As much as I wanted this, craved it – needed it, I had to ask. I had to know if this was right. "Are you kissing me to distract yourself, Astra?" I pulled back slightly.

She swallowed, lacing her fingers behind my neck. "You were never a distraction, Noah."

"Never?"

"If anything," she kissed my forehead, "I've been distracting myself from falling for you."

"And have you?" I swallowed, my heart rattling against my chest. "Fallen for me?"

I could feel her tense, then soften. "You make me feel safe."

It wasn't an answer, but it was. Within its own merit, to me, it was all the response I needed.

I scooped her into my arms, kissing her nose, then her neck, and her lips. "Come with me."

She chuckled, huddling into the human arm cage I built around her. "I don't have a choice."

I stopped before the water, setting her down onto the lake-kissed grass. "You always have a choice, Astra."

Her features softened, and she took my hand, brushing a kiss over my fingers.

I took a moment to admire her, everything that she was, thanking the stars above that she was mine.

Without saying it, I knew.

And she knew.

And there was no better fate I could've chosen for us.

I crouched down and scooped a palm of pebbles into my hand, holding them out to Astra.

"Thank you?" she laughed. "What's this for?"

I grabbed her elbow and steered her towards the lakeshore. "When I was a kid, my mom told me

Meeting Dr. Praigale   *Marie-France Leger*

that if the world was ever too much for me, I'd let it go."

    I took a pebble from my palm, turning towards the water. "I let go of the outcome of my father's clinic." And I tossed the stone into the water, watching the slight ripple dissipate into the abyss.

    She took her place beside me, glancing from my palm to my face. "So you just say what you want to release, and throw the rock into the water?"

    "Is that too Nicholas Sparks for you, Miss DuPont?" I teased.

    Surprisingly, she turned to me with a look of fatigued gratitude, grabbing hold of some pebbles. "Thank you, Noah."

    I took a step back, nodding at her to go on.

    I watched her pick her first pebble, exhaling a jagged breath. "I let go of my father, the lack of him and his presence, and release."

    She tossed it into the water.

    "I let go of my mother, her parenting and the selfish choices she made… I release."

    Another stone bit the lake.

    She was quieter this time. "I let go of Liam, the way he handled me with disrespect and perversion. I release it all."

    My stomach coiled as the stone hit the surface.

    "I let go of Ruby's decision to hide her knowledge from me, I let go. I let it go."

As she whispered more and more truths, releasing them into the wind, I could see her stand straighter, her voice sounded stronger, her being... Her being just... *Better.*

"And lastly," she signalled me over. I stood by her side.

She took my hand, holding on to one last pebble. "Lastly, I let go of Malcom. Everything he did to break me, everything he thought he made me. I'm..." She squeezed my fingers, and I watched as a crystalline tear fell onto her cheek.

"I deserve to be loved."

And in one motion, she threw the pebble into the lake, and watched the final stone sink into the deep.

There were so many things I wanted to say. So many things I wanted to do.

The pride that swelled in my chest, the admiration and adoration I felt for her filling every part of my body.

And it wasn't when the sun touched her skin, but when the moon kissed her scars that I realized...

Astra Meredith DuPont was the reason why it never worked out with anyone else.

Chapter Thirty-Four
Noah

We drove back to Cloud hand in hand.

Two silent hearts beating as one.
The past behind us.
The present within us.
The future made for us.
I carried her back into her loft, afraid to let her go. Her arms were caged around me so tightly it could potentially cause suffocation.

But the thought alone made me laugh.

If I weren't here, with her, I don't know where I'd be.

If I were Astra...

I couldn't even think about *what* I'd be.

A wreck? A ruin? A ship waiting to sink?

The life she had, not to mention the *night* she had... To uncover something like that, to have lived through lies and deceit and abandonment for so long...

Pain, constant, unyielding pain that wrapped around her day in day out...

This girl needed someone from day one.

And no one came.

Even if I hadn't known her for eons, even if she wasn't a veterinarian like my father wanted, or had ghosts in her past that trailed in her wake - I knew I'd stand by her side.

Meeting Dr. Praigale   *Marie-France Leger*

She'd never be alone again.

I vowed that. Silently, I promised her everything.

She peeled her arms away from me, resting her forehead against mine. "Stay the night," she said, clutching the back of my neck.

"Whatever you want," I responded, bending to put her down, but she gripped onto my shirt.

"Hold me." The plea in her voice made my knees weak.

I kissed her forehead, "Okay, love."

She stirred. "Can we go to bed now?"

"I thought you'd never ask."

Whether it was the comment or the sheer exhaustion, I couldn't tell. She began to laugh. And then she laughed harder. And before I knew it, she was full blown cackling.

"Oh, I'm going crazy," she sputtered.

I nudged open her door with my foot. "Trust me Stargirl, I'm right there with you."

It felt like a dream, as if we'd lived one year in one night. I don't know what I was expecting when I entered her room, but it was exactly what I pictured. She had a bookshelf in the living area, but not in here. Encased in these walls, stacks and stacks of paperbacks and hardcovers littered the perimeter, placed on top of each other like building blocks.

A messy desk was pushed in the corner, notebooks and pens covering the surface. And her laptop was half-open, plastered with sticky notes.

Meeting Dr. Praigale — *Marie-France Leger*

"This is truly a writer's room if I've ever seen one." I glanced around in awe. "Am I smart enough to stand in here?"

She chuckled. "Why don't we consult your graduate degree in veterinary medicine?"

"It won't talk to you," I shrugged. "It's got a superiority complex."

She flicked my shoulder and leaned into me. "You've got a way with words, Doctor."

"I know" – I laid her down on the bed – "I'm surprised I haven't won a Pulitzer Prize yet."

"They're too busy considering me. Sorry."

"Well, I can't beat out M.D. Pont, can I?" I paused to look at her precious face, laying atop a fuzzy throw, pushing back a loose strand of hair from her forehead. "Sweet dreams, Stargirl."

As I made a move to rise, she grabbed my hand. "Where are you going?"

"The couch," I pointed, forcing the words out. It wasn't easy.

She shifted out of bed, toeing tentatively towards me. "Stay with me."

"Astra," I swallowed, glancing down at her lips. "I don't know if that's a good idea."

"Noah," she swallowed, "it's the only idea."

"Why do you say that?"

"Because my writer's brain has powered down," she grabbed the front of shirt, pulling me closer, "and I'm done thinking for the night."

Her fingers trailed over my neck, dancing across my biceps, curling around my fingers.

"If this were a book, I'd write you just like this," she whispered, tugging me gently towards the bed. "A true gentleman."

She switched off the lamp, allowing the moonlight to cascade through the windowpane, illuminating our bodies in the darkness.

Her stare was palpable, everywhere, honing in on me.

Just me.

I'd never felt... *desired* like this, wanted like this, under the heat of Astra's gaze.

And I could say with certainty I'd never want to feel it from anyone else again.

"You would tell me it's okay to work through my pain. That you'd be by my side, right next door. That's what you'd say."

My whole body surged into motion. "That's... That's what I'd say," I repeated, fighting the urge to take her face in my hands and kiss her senseless.

"And I'd let you. The me, in my books..." She settled on the bed, unbuttoning her blouse with ease, "I'd let you do exactly what we both know you're hesitating to do."

I remained paralyzed, watching as she flung the fabric over her head, revealing a black lace bra and the shimmer of her glorious skin.

A surge of heat rose through my core, blazing my skin with need.

This wasn't the right time.

This couldn't be the right time.

And yet, I found myself asking, "What is it that I want to do, Astra?"

She sat up on the bed, pulling me by my belt loops until I was atop the mattress with her. She was so close, I could smell the lilac and roses of her shampoo.

"You don't want to leave, Noah," she kissed me, so featherlight I could barely feel it. "And I don't want you to leave. And I'm sick and tired" - she trailed my neck with kisses - "of denying my feelings, of feeling so damn sad all the time because I've prevented myself from being happy.

"But you... Noah Praigale," she cupped my face, "no one's ever made me feel quite like this."

I inhaled a sharp breath, my fingers hovering gently over her skin. "Like what, Stargirl?"

She pulled me on top of her, our bodies colliding into one, her breath on my breath, her heart against mine, and she whispered, "Loved."

Chapter Thirty-Five
Astra

We were bound.

>Heart. Mind. Body. Soul.
>Fused.
>Connected.
>One.
>He peeled my clothes off, layer by layer, caressing every inch of my skin with his mouth – his fingers – his *all*.
>I was cherished.
>I was desired.
>I was *important*.
>When his teeth grazed my breast, I thought it would hurt. I was prepared for the pain, the possession of Liam or Malcom's shadows to pull me out of this elation.
>But I found only bliss.
>A heaven that caressed me in serenity.
>I was safe.
>I was complete.
>*I was home.*

Meeting Dr. Praigale *Marie-France Leger*

Chapter Thirty-Six
Noah

My skin was alight.

She traced every contour, every ridge on my body with eager tenderness.

No matter how much I wanted her, I would let her guide me – let her tell me what she was okay with, what made her feel good.

She was in charge of this.

She was in charge of me.

And if I lived the rest of my life living by that philosophy, I'd stand by it proudly.

My hand hovered above the parting between her thighs. "Astra..."

"I want this," she whispered against my mouth. "I want you."

I cupped her backside, planting a gentle kiss on her forehead before sliding a finger inside of her, worshipping the moan she released against my lips.

"More," she pleaded, begged. "I'm okay, Noah. I promise."

And with that, I slid another careful finger in, pulsing up and down, using my thumb to massage her pleasure point.

I captured all her desire in my mouth, inhaling the taste of her moans and pants, relishing in this dream forever.

Meeting Dr. Praigale　　　　　　*Marie-France Leger*

      That's what it felt like. That's what *she* felt like.

      A dream.

      When she guided my hips on top of her, stroking the length of me fully, I rested at her entrance, and met her beautiful, brown eyes.

      "We don't need to do this, Astra," I swore, taking in all that was perfection in front of me. "I'm yours either way."

      But she swerved her hips, pushing my waist down to where I sank gently inside of her in one motion – the explosion of complete and utter ecstasy pumping through my blood.

      "I want us," she promised. "I want us always."

      And as I moved inside of her, I rewrote the history of my life. Every misfortune, every curse – it was worth it because this path led me to her.

      My Stargirl.

      My yellow car.

      My Astra.

Chapter Thirty-Seven
Astra

Last Edit - 6:05am:
When Stars Collide - by: Astra Meredith DuPont
She held his hand, looked deep into his eyes and knew. Sometimes two souls found each other at the wrong time – twin flames, perhaps, a karmic connection. But then there was Taylan and Josh. And in whatever life, she knew that she'd find him anywhere. Despite the woes of her past, the pain that would continue to follow her, she was no longer alone. And when Josh woke to see her smiling face, kissing the beads of sweat that coated her lip, she leaned in and spoke the truest words she's ever spoken: You're it for me, too.

"I'm not seeing anything in my inbox, Astra." Teresa chided, pausing and unpausing the FaceTime screen.

"It's there, just give it some time." I couldn't sheathe the beam on my face. The excitement I felt to have finally finished off my manuscript at the ass crack of dawn, careful not to wake Noah.

Noah.

God, his name on my lips was sacred.

What we'd done, what he *did* to me...

I'd never felt so alive. So cherished.

So absolute.

Meeting Dr. Praigale *Marie-France Leger*

After we released together, the only thing that made sense was to write.

It was odd and eager, but it was what I needed to do. I tried to sleep, but the buzz of inspiration kept me up, gnawing at my brain to write -

Write.
Finish the book.
One more chapter.
So that's what I did.

I escaped my bedroom with my laptop cradled in my arm, taking one last admiring glance at the man who inspired this book, and concluded the story one hour before Teresa called.

Taylan Nichols and Josh Kahill got their happy ending.

And peering over to my bedroom door, feeling the unity and love that I'd never felt before, I started to think that maybe Astra and Noah could have their happy ending, too.

"Ah! Received. Huge file, holy." Teresa lit up. "I'll send this over to Parker right now and we'll be in touch within the next few days. Good work, Astra. I can feel this best-selling title in my bones."

"Thank you, Teresa. For everything." I smiled.

"Oh no problem, you're the talent, you know, and - wait," she squinted, "*by Astra Meredith DuPont?* You're..." her eyes went wide, "you're not writing under your alias anymore?"

Meeting Dr. Praigale   *Marie-France Leger*

I swallowed, shaking my head with unflinching confidence. For the first time in my life, I found my voice. The real voice that's been begging to come out for years.

"I think it's time to let Astra shine, don't you think?" The dormant butterflies in my stomach began to stir.

Teresa grinned from ear to ear. "Pleasure to finally meet you, Miss Astra Meredith DuPont."

And then the screen went black, leaving me with a feeling like no other. I basked in the morning glow seeping through the curtains, surrendering myself to the sun.

I leaned back, breathing in through my nose and exhaled.

Twenty-three years was all it took to fall from grace.

Two months was all it took to rise.

Even still, there were so many things I needed to do. So many people I had to speak with. The book was finally out of the way, but I had a world of conflict ahead of me.

Ruby. My mother. Telling Eva.

Settling into the realization that all those things were interconnected scared me.

But I was no longer alone.

And before I headed downstairs to the café, ready to handle one final feat by myself, I glimpsed into the room to see the bundle of sheets covering the reason I felt this newfound freedom.

Meeting Dr. Praigale *Marie-France Leger*

"The best thing that's happened to me, was meeting you, Dr. Praigale," I whispered to myself, and descended the stairwell to reconcile with my new found family.

***

Ruby was in the kitchen beating a pound of dough, unaware of my presence.

"Hey," I knocked.

And she tipped over.

"Oh my God, *Ruby!*" I ran to help her up, but she quickly burst into a fit of laughter.

"Just checkin' to see if I pissed you off enough that you wouldn't help an old woman up."

My heart settled back into rhythm, loose flour particles now decaling my black tee. "Goddamn, I fucking hate you sometimes."

"You smell like..." she sniffed. "You smell like –"

"Don't you dare finish that."

She took a step back, placing the rolling pin to the side and crossed her arms. "Listen, I owe you an apology, Starburst. For everything. Keepin' shit from you, the lot of it."

I sighed, labouring my breaths. It was time to talk. "I would've... I would've understood."

"Would you have?"

"With time, maybe. Yeah." I thought to myself. "Yes."

"I don't know, kid." She shook her head. "Life's a mess sometimes and I never promised to be a good person. I got thrown into this mess and that's how I handled it."

"Did my mom swear you into silence or something?"

"To tell you the truth, she left that up to me." Her crystal blue eyes met mine. "I meant what I said last night, Astra. I wanted you to create somethin' new, completely separate from the hand you were dealt."

I took a step forward, squeezing her fingers. "I understand, it's just... a lot."

"Do you forgive me, though?" She gave me her pouty eyes.

I couldn't help but smile. "I forgive you. Rubes."

Her crusty, dirty hand slapped mine. "Thank God 'cause you're the only help I've got!"

I chuckled, feeling the push of tears leak from my eyes. "You've been more of a mother to me than my own mother ever has, you know."

"And Starburst, I've been more of a mother to Susan than my own sister." She squeezed my fingers. "It's okay to need people, Astra. We're not meant to make it out of life alone."

I took in her words, realizing the truth in them, allowing the grief and relief to wash over me. "I'm going to have to talk to my mom."

"I know."

"And Eva. And definitely Beth."

"I know that, too."

Meeting Dr. Praigale   *Marie-France Leger*

"But you'll..." I swallowed, "you'll be here when I come back, won't you?" My silent plea no longer felt like desperation. And that was a comforting, foreign feeling.

She smiled. "I'll be right there with you, Starburst."

"And so will I." Noah's voice came as a startle from behind me. "So will I, Stargirl."

He was wearing my robe.

My *baby pink* robe.

I burst into hysterical laughter, tears coating my cheeks. "You've never looked better."

"It's no dancing dog bandana, but this'll do for now." He kissed my forehead, pulling me in for a hug.

I could only look up at him in appreciation, my beginning and end, blanketing me in all his safety.

Then we were pushed by what felt like a bomb, and I tumbled over.

Ruby, who never hugs, said a firm "*fuck it!*" before jumping into our bodies, stapling herself onto my back.

More tears dripped down my face.

More laughter rose from my throat.

But I was no longer in pain.

I was...

I was free.

If I could capture this moment, hold it close to my heart and never let it go, I would. Because in sixty years when I turn old and grey, and the weight

Meeting Dr. Praigale *Marie-France Leger*

of the world clamours my skin with scrapes and bruises, my heart would beat with a passion so strong that nothing could dent it.

I knew that now.

There would always be wounds, but there's strength in our scars - a story behind the bonds that tie us together. Even if it's only one second longer -

You refuse to bleed.

And holding onto Ruby and Noah, I felt the force of both their love crash into me.

The peace.

The rest, at last.

And now I knew, that just because life hurts, doesn't mean you hurt it back - hurt yourself in the process.

After all, stars were the most beautiful before the explosion of supernovas.

And no star has ever burned as bright shining by themselves.

The End

Meeting Dr. Praigale   *Marie-France Leger*

Acknowledgements

Imagine writing a romance book without using the phrase 'I love you.' Just for a second, imagine that. Because if you would've told me before I started writing *Meeting Dr. Praigale* that I wouldn't have used the most popular saying in the world of romance, I would've laughed. Hard.

Thing is, this book is meant to show in all the right ways, how to love someone. And I mean, truly love someone. My love language has always been acts of service, and I wanted to express that through Noah's actions alone.

So many events in this book happened to me, and for that I had to re-write it three times. Not because it was bad the first or second time, but because it was tough. Really freaking tough.

I wanted to depict a soulmate connection. No third-act breakups, nothing like that. If you're an avid reader of my books, you'd know I don't necessarily write fairytales, and this most certainly proves that. But just because your romance isn't some grand enemies to lovers, or a whirlwind of passion, doesn't mean there is a lack of love.

Sometimes people meet, they connect, and they fall for each other. And sometimes, my dear readers, that's all it takes for forever.

Now that that's out of the way, let's move on to my appreciations.

Meeting Dr. Praigale *Marie-France Leger*

Truthfully, I started writing this book in honour of my dog, Snowball, who passed away in early 2022. I love you B, I hope they feed you all your favourites across the rainbow bridge.

To my new dog Miko, I love you. Thank you for being another light in my life.

I'd like to thank the real life Dr. Noah Praigale, for inspiring Noah's character. You are truly one of the most genuine human beings I've ever encountered.

Next, thank you to my family and friends for supporting me with all your hearts. You've never made me feel alone. No matter how difficult I can be sometimes.

To my Grand Pa Bill. You will always be alive in my heart forever.

And lastly, to my readers.

You've been so patient with me over the last year and I can't thank you enough for all that you do, and all that you are.

You illuminate my sky every night, you lovely, lovely humans.

I pray that you find the love that you dream about. Never forget to shine.

- Mar

Meeting Dr. Praigale   *Marie-France Leger*

Domestic Abuse Resources:
Sheltersafe.ca
For Youth and Young Adults

Kids Help Phone: Call 1-800-668-6868 (toll-free) or text CONNECT to 686868. Available 24 hours a day to anyone in Canada aged 5 to 29 who wants confidential and anonymous care from trained responders.

For Indigenous People:
Hope for Wellness 24/7 Help Line: Call 1-855-242-3310 (toll-free) or connect to the online Hope for Wellness chat.

For Older Adults
Canadian Network for the Prevention of Elder Abuse (CNPEA): CNPEA's web site features information and links to resources to get help if you or someone you know is experiencing abuse or neglect as an older adult.

Please do not be afraid to reach out and get the help you need. I promise it is not too late.

Meeting Dr. Praigale *Marie-France Leger*

Printed in Great Britain
by Amazon